Acclaim for *Sea Whisperer*:

"This story of Samantha, her life, the loss of her mother, and coming to accept and use her wonderful empathic gift, is a total treasure. I love this girl. I have no idea why the internet isn't on fire, talking about this wonderful story." -- J.L.

"This book was a fantastic, fun read! It was well written, had a great pace and kept me interested throughout the entire book ... can't wait for the second book." -- B.

"Exciting, inspiring, full of adventure and emotion ... Perfect." -- C.A.T.

A coming of age adventure novel with plenty of girl power for teens and young-at-heart-adults.

Upcoming novels by Nickolai Vasilieff
Presidential Bear
Alpha She Wolf

For Janet

&

For Brant and Nikole,

without whose summer vacations in the San Juan Islands this book
would not have been possible

Join Sammy's Team

Register for advance information on Sammy's Kindle, audio,
and hard copy books and new stories from the Empath
series. Receive special opportunities to read and review
prerelease publications. Register at:

www.empathteen.com

SEA WHISPERER

A Novel

Nickolai Vasilieff

Chapter One

For days that seem like forever, I wake each morning before the world opens an eye. I sit straight up like an L, stare into the face of darkness, stretch my eyes, and expect to see my Mom. When I don't, I tell myself, if I strain enough, search enough, imagine enough, she might appear.

First, absolute blackness, empty as a hole. With my blanket wrapped tight around my shoulders, I wait. A red sliver of light soon crawls across the horizon and sneaks through my window. At the earliest hint of red, my dresser appears, painted flowers around white pull knobs just visible. The morning glow turns orange and brightens the blossoms, each different of course, Mom never painted two the same. She gave me the dresser for my twelfth birthday and it is my favorite thing in the room. As the horizon turns a fiery yellow, the morning crawls its way to my closet, a cave with a low angle ceiling and a bar on one side. I wanted to hang a beaded curtain, one with a spider in the middle, for a door. Mom called it tacky, so the closet stares at me, like a gargoyle with pants and blouses for teeth. Until this week, I never woke before sunrise. Now the sunrise is my BFF and it is my last day in the old house.

I slip out of bed, step into my jeans and tank, pull up the covers, hoist my backpack and make a final inspection. Bags of junk everywhere make the room seem small. Uncle Teddy told me, "Bring whatever you want, Sammy, as long as it fits in your two duffels and backpack."

Carefully, I sorted through my dresser and closet one item at a time. Worried I'd miss something important, an old stuffed animal, special earrings, boxes of things I'd created at school, or maybe a few pictures, I tried to stay focused. But by the time I got half way through the closet the weight of memories was too much. I tossed everything else in the trash--I didn't want all that junk anyway.

Dust floats through spears of light as I do a slow spin. A glimmer reaches out to me from under the rubble. I check my neck, pat my shirt and choke back tears. The necklace, where is it? My knees slip across the brown shag rug. I push bags aside as my fingers comb the carpet and scoop up the silver locket. I pull it to my chest.

"Geez Mom, how stupid. I'm such a cretin. I almost lost my only connection to you." The muscles in my jaw contract, teeth clench. No, I won't cry again; that's all I've done for days.

Every time I see something of hers, I cry. I want to be done with this.

I clasp the necklace around my neck and turn on my heel. My reflection in the window stares at me, wavy and warped, like I feel. Long brown hair falls to my shoulders. God, what I wouldn't give for curls. I push it behind my ears, and wipe my sleeve across my cheek. I've grown six inches, to five eight, in the past year. Skinny, legs like a giraffe. I shake my head; I'm almost fifteen and only have bumps for

boobs. My shoulders slump. Whatever.

"Well, old room," I say, then I notice the hole in the wall, "sorry about that." One final look, the dresser winks back, and I step into the hall. Heading to the stairs, the door to her room calls me and I can't help myself. My fingers brush the wall and trace a patchwork of torn edges and bubbles around a pattern of faded roses.

When I was four or five I remember sitting on the floor outside my parent's room. The door was closed, so I waited, working my fingers under an edge of wall paper, I tore bits and pieces off around a flower petal. I was so proud I'd left the flower. When they found me, Dad was angry and he slapped my hands, but Mom, she just held me. Later we sat on the floor and glued the edges back to the wall.

My fingers bump over the line of that glue as I walk to her room. Inside, dead cold silence greets me. A cavern of four walls, bags of folded clothes in the corner, her bed empty except for the worn comforter where she'd slept. I close my eyes and try to feel her--no incense, no flowers, no her. I lean on the cold doorframe and slide to the floor. Here it comes. My head jerks and the chokes and sobs begin again.

Chapter Two

Three months earlier Mom called Loren and me to her bed. Loren, my seven-year-old brother, was in his room--a large closet Dad reworked into a small bedroom. Loren called it his wonder-cave. No window. A single light--a Cyclops that stared through a small clip-on shade. The bed, pushed to the end. When he lifted his head, he could see the parade of painted zebra, lions and elephants that circled the walls, and a dresser (white with flowers of course) at his feet. With the door open, enough room for a seven-year-old to slide in and plop down on the bed. It served my purpose too; it got the little dork out of my room.

Like a rabbit, he raced down the hall toward Mom's bedroom. I sensed what might be coming and hesitated. We climbed on her bed, kittens eager for her attention. Arms wrapped around us; her breath was the only sound I remember. Shadows, from candles on her dresser, danced with the curtains. A string of smoke spiraled up through sunbeams and filled the room with her favorite jasmine incense. I leaned into her and prayed with all my might, please be good news.

"I met with a doctor yesterday," Mom said.

I tensed and squeezed my eyes shut. Please be good.

Her voice cracked and she paused, "I told you that I'm sick and was waiting for test results."

Loren slid his blond curls into her lap and I pushed my head into her breast.

"I didn't want to worry you, but now I have the results." She went on, "I wanted to tell you myself because I love you and you need to know the truth."

Mom paused, as if she searched for the right words or an answer. She closed her eyes, "I have cancer."

My body jerked and a dark fear crept in.

"It's an aggressive form of cancer," she continued, "but there's hope. The doctor said I could have a few months or years."

"Months?" I whispered.

"They don't know, my dear." She gently touched my cheek. "I believe years."

I gasped and shook my head. Should I scream, run, or stay like a scared puppy for protection? I stayed, snuggled under her arm and held her tighter.

"As of today, I want both of you around me as much as possible," she said. "You get me as often as you want: to talk, to sit, to play. No matter what happens, if you want to be with me, I'm here."

I don't know if Loren understood what was happening. He stayed for a while, silent, then slipped off the bed and wandered back to his room, zooming an x-doll like a plane. I stayed in her lap. An ocean of fear washed through me. I felt panicked, confused, like I should do or say something, but I didn't know what.

Mom stroked my hair and wound it around her finger. "Hush little baby," she sang. My body rocked with hers. Tears washed down my face and her blouse. Incense filtered across the ceiling and mixed with her scent. She reached behind her neck and removed a necklace.

"Here, I want you to have this." She opened the tiny locket, a thumbnail picture of her head next to mine smiled at me. I'd seen the necklace many times, but had never looked inside. Her face brightened. "I've always loved how the light in this picture catches your beautiful green eyes," she said. I leaned forward. She reached around my neck and reunited the clasp. The warm locket rested near my heart.

"Now you carry me with you forever." She kissed my forehead and wrapped me in her arms. Nothing to say; the locket cradled in my palm. At any other time I would have been happy, but right then all it meant was I was losing her.

The room began to spin. I pushed back. Her surprised pale-blue eyes widened. My whole body vibrated; my brain whirled like a top. The next thing I remember, I ran to my room, slammed the door, and bent over in pain ready to throw-up.

"I hate you, I hate you," I screamed at the bed. My hands gripped the covers, and with one hard pull, stuffed animals flew everywhere. The painted flowers next. I pulled out the drawers, emptied the dresser, and with a complete spin, like an Olympian, threw a drawer across the room. I pretty much wrecked a lamp and knocked that hole in the wall. Then I collapsed on the floor. Mom came in and sat with me. I pressed into her. "Mommy."

After that, I'd sneak into Mom's room almost every morning so as not to wake Loren. I wanted as much of her as I could get and that gave me an hour or so with her alone. We talked about her childhood and my grandparents, who I never knew. I asked about Dad once, but she fell silent and said we'd talk about it later--we never did.

A few weeks after she gave me her necklace her skin turned pale and she spent most of the time in her room. Only a few weeks more and she couldn't get out of bed without my help. I took care of her just fine, but Uncle Teddy hired an old beak-nosed hospice nurse. She came in and everything changed. They put Mom on meds. I still sat with her, but she only woke for a few minutes at a time. The last two weeks, she hardly knew me.

The morning she died, I held her hand so tight I was afraid I'd squeeze the blood out. Her breath was so shallow, when she stopped I couldn't tell. Beak-nose stood by me. She checked Mom's pulse, then tucked her in like she was going to sleep for the night. Three days later we scattered Mom's ashes from an outcrop of rocks high above the Columbia River named Angel's Rest--I liked that. Loren and I held the box up over his head. I slipped the lid open; the wind captured her and carried her into the mountains, like she had asked.

Chapter Three

It's funny, I remember almost everything about those three months, but I can't remember what my Mom looked like before she got sick. I close my eyes and her image is like a moving target I can't quite catch.

As I lean against her doorframe now, I search for her, but can't see her anywhere. I wait to leave until the tears stop, and swipe my shirtsleeve across my face. It's already covered with snot, and I'm not even downstairs. I want to feel the carpet one last time, so I slip off my sandals. The rug digs between my toes as I tiptoe to the steps. As I descend the stairs, pictures on the wall pass like a documentary. Starting with one-day-old me sandwiched between Mom and Dad at the hospital, and ending with my seventh-grade picture, with me smiling like an ad for green and purple rubber-banded orthodontics. Loren's pictures are mixed-in toward the bottom, and finally, a picture of Mom and Loren and me taken six months ago. She looks so young and healthy. I stare for a moment, then lift it off the wall and tuck it into my pack. Now I'll remember.

I stop at the kitchen doorway. My dad sits at the table, his head on his arm next to a pizza box. Three half eaten slices lie rejected on his plate next to an empty bottle. The light in the room is cloudy and the smell of stale whisky and pizza suffocates me. I want to speak, but I don't know what to say, so I stand there, waiting.

He and Mom split up a year ago. No announcement or anything, he just stopped coming home. Mom tried to make it seem normal, but it wasn't. "An experiment," she said, "just for a while." I've only seen him a few times since then, when he came to pick Loren up for play-dates, and the last two nights, when he stayed at the house. I wondered how he could walk out and leave us alone, but I never asked and he never explained. Part of me misses him terribly, and part of me hates him

I watch for several minutes. When I bend down to put on my sandals, my backpack slips off and hits the floor like a slap in the face. He raises his head off the table and looks at me. I hope he is about to say something, like he doesn't want me to leave, or how worried he is, or that he loves me, but he only stares. His face droops like someone pulled a cheek and it stretched, eyes watery and bloodshot, breath heavy. Then, in slow motion, like when air escapes from a balloon, he collapses back down on his arm. I stare a moment longer.

"I'll be at the dock," I say, and walk out.

Chapter Four

A cool morning mist floats over the road behind our house. I follow it for a mile or so, then take a shortcut through a dew-dampened field to the dock on the Willamette River where Uncle Teddy will meet us. He agreed to fly his float plane to Portland and deliver us to Loon Song Harbor, where Loren and I will live with him for a while. He said he'd arrive around ten.

The field, a wash of yellow grass, is cut by a path that winds through blackberry bushes at the far end. I approach the bushes and brake into a jog. Three steps and the tickle of a thick spider web spreads across my eyes. I brush my face and hold out my hand, "C'mon little guy."

Most people are afraid of spiders, but I like them. She flexes her eight delicate legs on my palm. Gold with bright green spots on her back, she is beautiful. We inspect each other for a moment, then I reach out and let her walk to a leaf. "There you go. You've lost your home like me. Now you have a new one."

The fresh smell of water and the earthy scent of mud lets me know I'm near the river. Ducks and geese feed under the ramp that bounces as I walk to the dock. My toes are wet from the dew and a chill rushes up my legs and shimmies my shoulders. I didn't sleep much last night and now that I'm finally out of the house, I relax. My whole body feels heavy, so I kick off my sandals and slump to the deck. With my pack for a pillow, I tuck my feet up under my coat and lie down, just for a moment.

I must have slept for at least two hours. Rough wood planks scrape against my skin as the dock rocks from waves of a nearby motorboat. A ball of bright yellow pierces the slits of my eyes and the heat of the morning produces sweat that stings as I struggle to look around. Along the bank, cattails mixed with green and gold grass, rustle in the breeze. Ducks and geese honk, quack and bob their heads around the stalks. I lock eyes with one goose, and jerk when she spreads her wings and lifts onto the dock. Staring me down with one eye, her plump body waddles in my direction.

Something soft and warm washes over me. I glance up the ramp. Even though I'm alone, I am self-conscious about my ability to sense what animals feel. Mom called it my special sensitivity. I don't like to talk about it. It's kind of freaky and makes me feel ... well, different. Still, in this moment, my special sensitivity is kind of nice. The goose cocks its head and her happiness washes through me so strongly I giggle out loud. Weird, moments ago I felt depressed and here I am giggling with a goose. I shake my head. Get a grip, Sammy.

Still, she must know I'm not going to hurt her, because she shuffles over. I lie back down and let her peck around my hands and make mother-like murmuring sounds that feel good. Mom creeps into my thoughts, how she used to rock me and make her own sort of cooing sounds. I hold very still, like if I move I'll break the spell, and for a moment Mom's sweet energy surrounds me. Then, as I begin to relax, the goose waddles past my face and takes a dump right in front of me.

"You nasty turd-bag," I say, pushing up and stepping toward the ramp. "I didn't feel that coming."

Above me, clouds reach out. I stretch up. An eagle circles, probably looking for food. "Hurry up Uncle Teddy," I say to the sky, "I'm ready. Really, really ready."

Chapter Five

One-hundred-fifty miles north, at the Fish and Wildlife Service near Seattle Washington, plans are in the works. An officer sits at her desk surrounded by pale green walls; her red fingernails drum on a slick plastic desk-top.

"Harold, where's my coffee?" she calls to an empty office. The coffee pot is thirty feet down the hall, but somehow Harold, the newest Officer, always takes twenty minutes to pour two cups of coffee. The sign on her desk reads, Lt. Gretchen Hanson. Her special assignment to the San Juan Region of the Washington State Sheriff's office means she visits her Seattle Fish and Wildlife office only twice a month. She spends the rest of her time in the San Juan Islands. A meticulous woman, she demands prompt accurate responses to all activities--the most important being her morning coffee. As she prepares to yell for Harold again, an email catches her attention from Animal Crime Scene Investigation.

Gretchen,

I hope this finds you well. It's been some time since we've talked, but I am in need of your assistance. One of our investigations includes poaching of sea lions and seals in the Northern Pacific region. The Coast Guard brought several animals to us for necropsy. One was alive. With the help of local veterinarians, we nursed her back to health. Now I need to make arrangements for transportation to her natural home in the San Juan Islands. Since you are assigned to the San Juan Sheriff's office, I thought you might have some contacts that could help. Any assistance is appreciated. Let me know ASAP, this female lion is roaring.

Best Regards

Dr. Kristy Singh

Assistant Director, Criminalistics

Animal Crime Scene Investigation (ACSI)

Gretchen smiles. She met Kristy a few years back when she investigated a case of whale killings. Kristy was the lead forensic pathologist on that case. Images of bottles filled with animal brains and bones that sat on Kristy's desk still float in Gretchen's mind. She scans the email and punches in the phone number.

A high-pitched voice responds, "Kristy Singh."

"Kristy. Gretchen Hanson. I received your email. It sounds interesting."

"Straight to business," Kristy says with a laugh. "How are you, Gretchen?"

"I'm fine. Sorry, I haven't had my coffee yet. What's up?"

"As you know, ACSI is responsible for doing forensic examinations on animals found dead under suspicious circumstances."

"Sure," Gretchen responds, "I remember the whale case. But what's that got to do with transporting a sea lion?"

Gretchen glances around for Harold, who hasn't yet brought her coffee. Through the phone she hears a bone saw running somewhere behind Kristy's crystal-clear laugh.

"It's an unusual case," Kristy says. "We had four Steller Sea Lions and three Harbor Seals delivered to our ACSI laboratory in Ashland a week ago for necropsy. They are both protected species and were found in your district. Some were shot, and two appear to have been beaten to death. It was a brutal crime."

The phone line crackles and there is a loud metallic bang.

"Sorry, let me step out of the room," Christy says.

"No problem," Gretchen says, as she imagines seal and sea lion carcasses cut open on slick aluminum tables. "I noticed an email alert about the killings last week," Gretchen says. "I haven't read anything since."

"We're still performing necropsy and research on most of them," Kristy continues, "but a Steller Sea Lion was one of the animals shot and presumed dead. She was on the necropsy table, and as I was about to make my first cut I detected an unusual warmth around her snout. I was startled because her body felt cold, lifeless, essentially dead. On further examination, I discovered a faint heartbeat. We immediately treated her. Over the past few days she's been kept in a special pool with water modified with thirty-five grams of salt per liter to emulate sea salt and ...

"Enough with the technical talk already," Gretchen interrupts. "What about the sea lion?"

Kristy chuckles at Gretchen's impatience. "Our sea lion is doing well, but we can't keep her here any longer. I need your help to get her back home. I'm preparing to head to Portland and hoping we can move her from there."

"Got it. Let me see what I can do and I'll get back to you," Gretchen says and leans back, stretches her long legs, and shakes her red curly hair down her back. She envisions trying to transport a six-hundred-pound sea lion. A smile creeps across her lips. Teddy Crenshaw, she says to herself, The San Juan Express, just the man for the job.

Her fingers peck the computer keys to begin an email. She changes her mind and grabs her cell phone. She knows she'll have a much better chance of convincing Teddy if she speaks with him directly. He answers on the first ring.

"San Juan Express; this is Ted."

Gretchen hears the wind whistling in the phone and the clanking of sailboat rigging.

"Ted, this is Gretchen Hanson." There is a long pause.

"Gretchen, it's been a while. Everything okay?"

To be casual, she laughs. "Yes, good as gold. How about you?"

"Good. Busy as usual. I'm about ready to fly to Portland to pick up my niece and nephew. What can I do for you?"

"I'm glad I caught you," she says. Sensing he is in a hurry she moves into business mode. "I need a volunteer for an emergency transport. Can you help me out?"

Teddy's voice drops a cautious octave. He knows Gretchen well. A couple of years ago they'd dated for a while. He remembers how she was able to talk him into almost anything. "Emergency? Volunteer? What's up?" he asks.

"It's simple Ted. A sea lion is at ACSI in Ashland, Oregon. She was rescued from poachers and they need to transport her back to the San Juan Islands. I figured, being the best float plane pilot in North America, you could help us out." Then she adds the hook. "Or, would that be TOO much for you?"

Teddy hesitates, "Okay. What's the plan?"

"Nothing fancy," Gretchen continues. "Just load a big box with a six-hundred-pound sea lion into your plane, fly her from Portland to the San Juan Islands, and let her go. Quick and easy."

"Quick and easy," Teddy repeats as he mentally does weight and balance calculations to make sure his plane will carry the load.

"You still there Ted?"

"Yes, I'm here. You're right, it might be TOO much for me."

Gretchen figures he will try to bluff her, and after a moment, agree, like the teddy-bear he is.

"What the heck," he adds, "I'll do it anyway. I could pick this 'easy bundle' up at the Vancouver Municipal Airport around two. Okay?"

"Great," she says. "They're on their way to Portland. I'll confirm with ACSI and text you."

Pleased with her morning's work, Gretchen puts both boots on her desk and pushes back. "I have to be there for this," she says to herself. Harold walks in with her steaming coffee cup in one hand and a doughnut in the other.

"Forget it," she says, as she stands and grabs the doughnut. "I'm leaving. Have to see a man about a sea lion."

Harold stares into the steam rising from her coffee cup, "See what?"

Chapter Six

Teddy Crenshaw shakes his head. "I volunteer too much," he mumbles as he shoves his cell phone inside his jacket pocket. The steel gangplank flexes and creaks with each step toward the large dock below. Wind gusts around him and black rain-clouds race overhead. A storm has been boiling all night. Reports say the pounding rain will clear by midmorning. Sheets of rain and sea spray lash his cheeks; he pulls his hood up, turns and glances down the row of boats to his right. "Rubber ducks in a tub," he comments as they bounce and sway, waves splashing over the sides. His float plane, Angie, sits to his left near a sign reading: San Juan Express - Air Transport. The familiar smell of sea brine mixed with gasoline blows past.

On mornings like this boaters usually greet him with, "Demons on the water" or "Not fit for man nor fish," and other expressions of disgust about the weather. The old guy with a limp, who lives aboard the big yacht at the other end of the dock, approaches him. Teddy smiles and squints through the rain. Old Guy raises his chin out of his rain jacket, "Crabby day," he says, then laughs at his own joke as he limps by.

"It'll blow through in an hour," Teddy yells, but Old Guy doesn't hear and the weather doesn't interest Teddy anyway. His thoughts are about his niece, Sammy, and his nephew, Loren. Sammy's words were quick and sharp when he spoke with her last night, and she hung up without saying goodbye. He knows she'll be ready, but she is angry and fragile. He is anxious, and wants to pick them up as soon as possible.

It has been a tough month for everyone. Ten days earlier, in Portland, he talked with his sister Susan and her husband Chris about what would happen after she was gone. Susan seemed very calm about the whole thing. Chris had fallen apart. It was not yet noon and he had already started drinking. It was obvious Chris could not take care for Sammy and Loren.

"Teddy, you must take the kids for a while," Susan pleaded. "I know it's a lot to ask; Chris needs time to heal, and Sammy and Loren need you right now." Susan giggled, "I promise, it's the last thing I'll ever ask of you."

He cried and shook his head, "You are so-o-o sick." They both laughed, just like when they were kids. That was the last time he saw her.

As he steps through his preflight inspection, the ailerons on the wings move smoothly and the rudder swings from side to side. He knows how to maintain his airplane and he is absolutely confident in his skill as a pilot. But, can he raise two children? Throughout the inspection he repeats to himself, "I can do this," although he has no idea how to take care of two kids. He's never had children, doesn't even have a pet. But he loves them, and he hopes that will be enough.

Being sure nothing has fallen off since his last flight, he completes his preflight inspection, and unlashes Angie from the dock. Like a wet dog, he shakes water off, removes his raincoat and slips on his old Navy bomber jacket. The brown leather shows years of wear with worn elbows and scratches around the waist, but it is his lucky charm he always wears when he flies. In the cockpit, he adjusts his headset and sets the radio frequency to the local channel. Looking to both sides, he yells, "Clear," and pushes a button on the dash. With two pops and a puff, Angie's huge engine revs into motion. The rumble and roar comfort him. He guns the engine. The long pontoons slide off the dock and he floats out of the harbor.

"Seattle Center, Charlie-1-0-9-8-8--Loon Song Harbor--taxi for takeoff." There is no air traffic control nearby, but the announcement of his takeoff alerts other airplanes in the area.

Pressure on the throttle increases his speed. The fuselage shakes and rattles. Angie hops across waves and water splashes up under her wings. After seconds of violent commotion, she lifts and soars into the air, away from the choppy waters.

He points Angie into the brightening horizon. "I love 'em. That should be enough," he repeats to himself, "that should be enough."

Chapter Seven

Five minutes after ten and I finally hear gravel crunch under tires and car doors slam. Thank goodness they're here, I think, as Dad's and Loren's voices drift down the bank. Loren appears at the top of the ramp like a caped crusader. Hands on hips, red and blue tennis shoes, goofy yellow and red superhero backpack, teddy bear (gift from Uncle Teddy) hanging like an upside-down skydiver, he hitches up his shorts, adjusts his green baseball cap, wrinkles his nose, spreads his arms and announces, "I have arrived." He's such a dork.

It's amazing, Loren doesn't seem to be affected by Mom's death at all. I'm haunted, but he continues to live in his smiley-face fantasy world while I'm more isolated and alone than ever.

Quacks and hisses come from the muddy bank below. Super-dork crouches, like he hears a gun-shot or something, grabs his roller bag and punctuates each step with a quack of his own. The dock vibrates each time his bag thumps over a skid-bar. Behind Loren's quackery, Dad wrestles a cart loaded with bags as he tries to make sure the cart doesn't crush Loren.

"Hey Duck Boy," I call, "you're gonna get your butt run over."

"Shut up," Loren yells back, scrunching his upper lip. To further irritate me, every few feet he sticks his head through the railing to talk to the ducks: "Quack, quack"--thump, thump. Near the bottom, he lets go of his roller bag. I wince as it claps down off the ramp to the dock. Right behind, Dad's feet skid. My eyes get as big as doughnuts when the heavy cart crashes down the ramp, bending the handle of the bag and barely missing Duck Boy. Never mind, he is oblivious to the whole thing as he hops toward the ducks. I snicker at the thought of Loren's bag being crushed. Dad heaves a sigh of relief, pushes the cart to one side and glances in my direction. My stomach turns.

"You okay?" he asks.

"I'm fine," I say, cheeks hot, scalp tight. His face is filled with sadness and anger. He wasn't always like that. Before he changed, we'd go camping in the summer almost every weekend. The forest was filled with the sweet smell of pitch and pinecones. I'd pick up leaves and twigs, and follow him around like a baby chick. We'd build a fire and when he tossed on pitch-covered branches, they'd explode in wild flames as big as a house. In the light, he'd make weird hand-shadows and tell ghost stories while Mom held Loren and me. I'd act scared, like I believed them. Sometimes I did. We laughed a lot, until he started drinking. After that, he got angry, and began yelling at everything. I couldn't do anything right. About a year ago he was fired from his job. The smiles that creased his cheeks and the laughter that danced in his eyes disappeared, and so did he. As far as I'm concerned, the man who stands in front of me on the dock isn't my dad. He is the man I call Dad, who left us a year ago.

Dad steps toward me. Oh God. I turn away, and shade my eyes. A chill sweeps through me. I look up. Canadian Geese, in perfect V formation, soar over, so close my ears fill with the whoosh of their wings and their energy screams a kind of wild freedom. With the tail of the last bird a large shadow sweeps across the dock.

Arm stretched out, finger pointed to the sky, Loren yells, "There he is." Behind the geese, Uncle Teddy's beautiful plane rocks its wings from side to side to greet us.

"Hi Uncle Teddy," Loren shouts, jumping up and down. My hand raises and I reach out, as if to touch him. The plane turns left. A flash of reflected sunlight splashes us as he makes a large one-eighty turn and comes back down the river. It is magical.

The plane's engine growls like a lion and makes a steep descent, as if to attack. Just as I think it's about to plunge in the river, it lifts. We all step closer to the edge of the dock. A final growl and the engine goes silent--the whir of the propeller the only sound. I am mesmerized. The plane swoops down again, as if to catch its prey. Long pontoons grab the twinkling surface, skid and splash and come to a stop. It bobs like a cork. I gasp, my breath caught in my chest. The lion roars again and Uncle Teddy points his beautiful airplane toward the dock.

Vibrations drum through my feet and we cover our ears as he comes closer. I see him through the glass, in his sunglasses and leather jacket. He looks so cool. I bounce from leg to leg like an over anxious three-year-old. All I want is to run to him. Instead, I wait as he takes forever to tie ropes to the dock. Finally, I leap forward, throw my arms around him, push my face to his jacket, and totally snivel and snort like a pig--maximum embarrassment--but I can't let go. Uncle Teddy holds me nestled against him, reaches out and pulls Loren to him.

"Hi Champ, how you doing?" he says, ruffling Loren's hair, and hugging him.

"Great, Uncle Teddy. Can I fly the plane?"

"We'll see," he says and laughs. He unwinds himself from each of us and wipes off his jacket with his arm. I stiffen when he and Dad shake hands and slap each other on the back. They step to the far side of the dock. I've seen them together so many times. They are best friends. Now I want Uncle Teddy all to myself. They lean forward and whisper to each other. Light reflects off Uncle Teddy's blond curly hair and I flash Mom. My memory of her is everywhere, it seems. He and Dad talk, shake their heads and glance my way, like people do when they talk secrets about you. They hug and Dad forces a twisted smile. Thank goodness, they're finally done.

There is a sudden clap and an echo responds from down the river, "Okay," Dad says, pressing his palms together, "let's get this show on the road."

"In the air, Dad," Loren corrects him. We all laugh and for a moment the tension releases. I hand my pack to Uncle Teddy and notice 'San Juan Express' painted in bold letters on the side of his plane, the name 'Angie' right below in fancy script.

"Nice name," I say.

"Yup, my air transport business."

"I don't mean the San Juan Express," I say, "I mean Angie. Who's Angie?" Mom use to tease him about his crush on Angelina Jolie when he was younger. "Shouldn't it be Angelina? You love Angelina, don't you?"

He doesn't even glance at me. "Who wants to ride up front?" he says.

I freeze and my chest clinches like a fist. Did I make him angry? Maybe he's upset. "I didn't mean ..." I blurt out.

Before I can finish, Loren raises his stupid hand, jumps up and down, and yells, "Me, me."

"Okay Champ, you're up front," Uncle Teddy says. His eyes move to me, he smiles, and winks, "Sammy, all right if you ride in back until Vancouver?"

With Uncle Teddy's wink the fist in my chest releases. I like to tease him. It's a game we play, but with all that has happened over the last few months, the world has lost its laughter. Now, at least, in one way, we are back to normal.

"Yeah, I guess," I say. I hate that I missed a chance to ride up front first and that I let Uncle Teddy win this round of the tease-game. But I am so grateful for his wink and smile, losing doesn't really matter. Still, in one last effort to recover, I kiss the back of my hand real smoochy-like and say, "I'd LOVE to ride in back of ANGIE!"

While I make my lame attempt to tease Uncle Teddy, Dad picks Loren up in a bear hug and spins him around. Loren wiggles and Dad whispers in his ear and tickles him. Their play reminds me of how warm and safe I felt when I was younger and he hugged me. He puts Loren down, turns and looks at me. For an instant, I want him to hold me, then a shiver creeps through me. I wave and scramble to push past the seat into the back of Angie, happy to get away from him. The bucket seat pulls me down beside a small window. I bend so Dad can't see me as I fiddle with the seatbelt and focus my eyes on the buckle, "I'm ready," I say.

Uncle Teddy adjusts Loren's seatbelt. Loren's voice drifts back, "Cool," he says, as Uncle Teddy hands him a headset.

My head feels like a bobblehead doll as Angie splashes and bounces away from the dock. Loren holds his teddy bear in a strangle hold. To maximize his dorkishness, he adjusts his headset so it covers one ear and half his mouth. I lean forward and wrap my fingers around a small handle above my head. "Kind of rough," I yell, but Uncle Teddy doesn't hear me as he guides Angie to the center of the river, talks into his microphone, gives Dad a thumbs-up, and guns the engine, sort of in that order.

Pointing down river, Angie picks up speed and a bolt of excitement shoots through me. I peek out, Dad waves and shrinks behind us. Waterfalls splash up each side and tiny rainbows form in the spray. I remember what looked like a crash landing when Uncle Teddy arrived, and my stomach turns to a knot of snakes. I've never flown in a floatplane. Half of me is totally excited, the other half--totally terrified.

A twang of sadness squeezes me. I turn to wave to Dad, but no one is there. The entire plane shakes and rattles. The noise is so loud it hurts my ears. We hopscotch across the water; waves rise up bigger and bigger on both sides. Angie accelerates and I'm pushed back in the seat. My head slams against the headrest and like a blast from a cannon, we shoot into the sky. My only thought: We're gonna die.

I blink, duck, and almost pee-my-pants when a bridge looms right in front of us. Angie stays low and flies under the massive concrete structure, close enough to take our heads off. I glance back, but can only see the headrest, then turn forward just as we are about to hit another bridge. For some reason, I try to stand up, then I'm pushed down when we swoop up over the second bridge. I put my hands over my face, scream like a Banshee, and hope no one else can hear (Okay, I also pee a little).

We turn left, cruise above the hills where one-hundred-foot fir trees reach up to wave goodbye. The city of Portland disappears behind us and a pit the size of Oregon grows in my stomach. We make a sharp turn. I swallow hard when bile rises and stings my throat. I fight back tears. I thought leaving would make it all better but, like an alien, the emptiness of my world creeps back.

I let my eyes close and lean into the side window, pressing cold glass against my forehead. The monotonous drone of the engine, the constant vibration of the window, the rhythmic rattle of sheet metal inside Angie's tiny world somehow gives my brain a rest. After weeks that seem like years, I am in Uncle Teddy's plane, leaving everything behind and flying into ... I have no idea what.

Chapter Eight

The window rat-tat-tats against my forehead and Angie's engine screams in my ears. I must have been totally out of it because in minutes I am sleeping. I wake up when Uncle Teddy says, "As soon as I get approval we'll return to Vancouver to pick up our cargo."

My head jerks, "Vancouver? Cargo? What cargo?"

"I'm doing a friend a favor," he says, "we have to pick up an injured animal and transport her back to the San Juan Islands. It should be interesting."

That's nice, I think. We'll pick up an injured dog or cat. I'll hold her in my lap when I get to sit in the front seat. My eyes follow the horizon. We fly east out of Portland, along the Columbia River, soaring over farm land that is cut by the huge iridescent-blue river and divided by roads into square patches of yellow fields. On our right is the eleven-thousand-foot-high Mt. Hood. I've seen that mountain from our home in Portland all my life, and she is an old friend. Roads wind up the mountain's steep slopes, through forests, and a snow-covered ski resort, ending at a shiny peak, like a pointy white witch's cap. The top of the cap is higher than us, and yet puffs of white clouds, like cotton, float below.

Uncle Teddy dips one of Angie's wings and we fly through the edge of a cloud, a fog bank of sudden darkness. Moments later we break out into sunshine so bright I am totally blind, even wearing my sunglasses. Below, on the river, are small piers and rows of fishing boats. Angie levels off and purrs, steady and strong.

Loren is sleeping. Uncle Teddy removes the headset and hands it to me. I slip the soft cushioned pads over my ears; most of the engine noise disappears. Now the low harmonic hum of Angie's radio, broken by streams of gibberish and bursts of muted static, fills my head. All the noise, the vibration, the steady purr of the engine, is hypnotic, a kind of sleep potion. Angie rocks like a cradle, and I snuggle down into my jacket, drifting in and out of dreams.

My stomach rises as Angie dips into a dive. I jerk up, reach out and touch Uncle Teddy's shoulder. He glances back and smiles, pulls Angie's nose up and I drop like hitting the bottom of the big-dipper on a roller coaster. He turns left. For the first time, we fly away from the river, over land, and below us is an airport runway. He makes a sweeping turn to the right. When I look out the side window I stare straight at the ground. For some reason, he's heading toward the runway. Oh my gosh, we're in a float plane. We can't land at an airport, I think, panicked by the realization he's obviously forgotten we only have pontoons. I push my hand between him and Loren and bounce in my seat, "Runway, float plane," I shout, finger pointing forward.

Uncle Teddy ignores me as we sweep over a large hill, cross the edge of the runway and numbers flash under us so fast they are a white blur. Preparing for the worst, I grab the seatbelt with one hand and the handle above my head with the other. There is a loud screech, I lurch forward and the seatbelt digs into my neck. The next thing I know, Angie is on the ground and we are rolling toward a hanger surrounded by several small planes. As I push away images of us crushed to smithereens on the runway, he glances at me, "No sweat," he says with a big smile, "we have wheels."

"Wheels? Why the heck didn't you tell me Angie has wheels?"

Near the large hanger, a tall woman stands in front of a white van with the letters ACSI on the side. Dressed in khaki colored pants and shirt, she wears a thick brown belt and matching knee-high leather boots. Angie approaches and the woman's red hair blows across her face. She quickly pulls the strands back and ties them with a band. I push my hair behind my ear. "Oh my gosh," I say, "she looks right out of Indiana Jones."

"More than you know," Uncle Teddy says, as Angie's engine coughs and pops and shuts down.

Puffs of white smoke fill the air with the smell of oil and exhaust. "Yuk," I say, pulling my shirt sleeve over my face.

"We won't be here long, but it'll take some doing to fit the sea lion in the back, so you'll both need to get out."

My lip curls. "Sea lion? We're picking up a sea lion?"

"Yes," he laughs, "it won't take long." Uncle Teddy hops out. "Sammy, stay with Loren near the front of Angie," he says walking toward the red head.

"Will do Captain." I lean forward. "Sea lions," I say in my best Halloween voice. "Sea lions are coming."

"Huh?" Loren says as he comes to life. Amazingly, Loren has slept through the entire landing.

"C'mon Punkster," I jiggle his shoulder. "We're going to watch Uncle Teddy pick up a sea lion."

"Seal-Lion?" Loren mumbles as he blinks the sleep out of his eyes and fights with his seatbelt.

Loren and I stand near the front of one of Angie's pontoons--with wheels. Loren twists and wiggles like a puppy; I grip his shoulder as Uncle Teddy talks with Red, the leather boot woman. She has a clipboard with papers that flap in the wind. Loose wisps of hair whip around her face as she points to the pages and Uncle Teddy signs them. She looks totally amazing. All the other police-type women I've seen are just normal, but she's like this athlete-woman, tall and straight as an arrow. Even from thirty feet away I can feel her strength.

A smaller woman dressed in jeans and a white lab coat, like a doctor, comes out of the hanger and picks up a hose. The energy changes immediately. She is shorter and her energy is softer. It flows like water. I remember Mom telling me that strength comes in all kinds of flavors: The strength of the huge oak tree, almost impossible to break; the strength of water, fluid, but able to dig out solid rock. Different, yet the same.

Loren pulls away. "Look," I say, pointing in front of him, hoping to catch his attention. "What do you think she's doing?"

"I don't know," he says, with less wiggle, and points to Red, "but she looks like a policeman."

"Do you think she's wears a gun?" I ask. Loren freezes as he inspects his new super-hero.

Uncle Teddy and Red walk to the van, open the back doors and slide out a large box with holes in the sides.

"This should be cool," I say. My shoulders tighten in anticipation.

As the box slides out, folding legs automatically drop down, so it stands on wheels like a hospital gurney. I flash Mom being wheeled down a corridor and the smell of medicine from one of her treatments.

Loren jerks. "Look," he says.

The white lab-coat walks around the box, spraying it with water through large holes in the sides. The energy I feel changes. There is a new energy. It is something frightened, panicked, that is much stronger. Holding Loren's shoulders, I close my eyes and the energy rushes over me. I sense I am being overwhelmed, like when I am in the cafeteria at school and I am bombarded by hundreds of people's energy and emotions. I feel myself closing down--my reflexive defense when the feelings are too much.

"The sea lion weighs almost six hundred pounds," the white lab-coat yells, "and she might move around, so be careful."

Loren looks at me, "Six hundred pounds? Move around?" All I can do is raise my shoulders and give him an, I don't know, look.

Water begins to trickle out the holes, then we hear a massive growl and the box shakes as the sea lion bangs inside.

"Geez," I say, as Loren and I both tense and he steps back into me. I wrap my arms around him and squeeze for a moment. For the first time since Mom died, I feel his pain too. Not sharp like mine, but a whirlwind of confusion. It crawls through my arms and chest; then, just as quickly, it is gone.

He realizes my arms are around him, pulls away, and gives me a dirty look. "Leave me alone," he says.

As I think about how I will pinch his scowling little face between my thumb and forefinger, we hear a deep gritty sound from inside the box. The trio (Uncle Teddy, Red, and the White Lab Coat) are pushing the box toward Angie. As they roll across the tarmac, the sea lion bangs from side to side, and we hear constant grunts and snarls. When they are only ten feet away, I feel my heart jump. I almost choke; a new pain shoots through my chest.

I must have winced because Uncle Teddy looks in our direction and yells, "It's okay, everything's fine."

I push one hand against my chest, and hold Loren with the other. The sea lion is so close; its fear ripples through me. It is like an extension cord that shoots electricity between me and the raging animal in that box.

They roll the cart around us, to the side of Angie. Uncle Teddy pushes a button and a door slides open to reveal a cargo bay, just behind the rear seats. They line the cart up and push. The box slides toward Angie, but catches on the edge of the plane and jerks back. Water sloshes out the sides. The sea lion roars and bangs. The box rocks side to side and again electricity shoots through me. It's as if I'm a lightning rod for the Sea Lions emotions.

"Be careful," I yell as my knees buckle. My weight comes down on Loren's shoulders and he responds with a particularly hard twist. Then they make a final push, the box rolls over the edge and to my amazement, slides smoothly inside the cargo compartment. The lab-coat pulls out what looks like a gun, pushes it against the sea lion's skin through one of the holes and we hear a muffled pop. The sea lion quiets, and I relax as the electric pain disappears.

Uncle Teddy jogs over, "We don't have much time, so let's get loaded," he says. I'm panting like a puppy, I bend forward with my hands on my knees when Red saunters up behind us.

"C'mon Ted, aren't you going to introduce me?" she says.

I stand and the first thing I notice is Red is as tall as Uncle Teddy and looks seriously impressive, like she could handle herself. She is kind of a cross between Indiana Jones and Laura Croft. In addition to those wicked boots, she does in fact have a gun, with several other things that hang from that wide leather belt. The tag on her shirt reads, Lt. Gretchen Hanson - National Fish and Wildlife Service. I straighten my back to be as tall as possible.

Uncle Teddy glances from Red to me, gives a short sigh, and makes the introductions. "Miss Hanson called me to help return this sea lion to the wild," he begins.

"Wow," Loren interrupts, "are you a cop?"

"Please, call me Gretchen," she says, "and yes, I am a cop, sort of. As your Uncle Ted said, I'm an officer with the Fish and Wildlife Service, but I work with the San Juan Sheriff's office to catch people who want to do bad things in the San Juan Islands. This poor girl got caught in a cross fire," she says, pointing to the sea lion. "She's lucky to be alive."

We stare at Gretchen. "Cross fire?"

As Gretchen is talking, the other woman joins us. "This is Doctor Kristy Singh," Gretchen says, stepping to one side. "She works with Animal Crime Scene Investigation."

I swear, our jaws hit the ground so hard our teeth almost splatter all over the tarmac. "CSI?" Loren and I say at the same time.

Kristy laughs, "Yes, Animal CSI. I do the lab work that helps find criminals when animals are involved. In this case, someone killed several Harbor Seals and Steller Sea Lions, and they are both endangered species."

"Do you have a gun?" Loren asks.

"Don't be stupid," I mumble, as I wonder the same thing.

Kristy laughs again. She has a high-pitched laugh that sounds like a wind chime. "It's not like the people on TV," she says. "In fact, I'm almost always in my lab where I run tests. My being here is very unusual. But, this gave me a chance to help send this sea lion home and visit with Lt. Hanson."

"Why would anyone want to kill sea lions?" I ask.

"Fish and pelts," Gretchen says. "Seals and sea lions love salmon and that decreases commercial and sport fishermen's catch. Although most countries have banned seal hunts, Russia, China and a few others still make products made from seal. So, some people make money killing them."

"That's not to say fishermen kill seals," Uncle Teddy adds. "Most people try to protect our wildlife, but there are a very few who step over the line and become illegal."

As they talk, I look at Gretchen and Kristy. I don't think I've ever met anyone like either of them, except maybe my Mom. They are so totally different, but they are the same, strong and confident. Gretchen strong like an oak, and Kristy strong like water. Each of them just naturally fills the space around them. I feel a little of my Mom in each of them and I like being near them. Gretchen looks at me, and I feel my cheeks get hot as I shrink back. "Wow, kill seals?" I say. Which makes me sound totally like an ignoramus.

"It's hard to believe that anyone would want to hurt them," Kristy says, saving me, "but it can mean big money. In the past few decades Harbor Seal and Steller Sea Lion numbers have declined by almost eighty percent, so we're here to make sure that doesn't continue."

"And," Gretchen adds, as she steps closer to Uncle Teddy and slides her hand on his shoulder, "you and your Uncle Ted are a huge help, by flying this big girl back to a good home in the San Juan Islands."

As Gretchen touches his shoulder, I notice Uncle Teddy's cheeks redden. Blushing must run in the family.

"Once she's there, we'll try to monitor her movements by using our instruments to track her beeper," continues Gretchen.

"She has a beeper?" Loren asks excitedly.

"Yup," Gretchen says. "Dr. Singh's group attached a purple tag on her tail fin that sends out an electronic signal. When she's in the water, we can follow every move she makes."

Uncle Teddy coughs and slaps the side of Angie, like he is patting a horse. "Back in the plane everyone, before our guest starts to dry out and gets upset."

As Loren climbs in the front, I redirect him. "What's the matter Chicken Little," I say, "afraid to ride in back?"

"You're the chicken," he says, as he hesitates.

"Cluck, cluck," I wave my elbows, "cluck, cluck."

I reach down to buckle my seat belt, in the front seat, and hear Kristy yell final orders.

"Remember, all you need to do is pull the rope to release the door. She won't have any problem getting out. Just go slow and stay out of her way."

Stay out of her way? Will we be in the water with her? I think.

"No problem," Uncle Teddy hollers back. He looks at Loren and me and gives us a thumbs-up. I return the gesture as the sea lion thrashes around in back. Loren holds my seat and leans as far forward as possible.

"Hands off," I say, although I lean forward as well. Uncle Teddy guns the engine and lines Angie up on the runway. Water sloshes and the sea lion shifts and bangs when we accelerate. For a moment, I think Angie won't get off the ground. Then she lunges forward, and our bodies push back in the seats. Her engine roars, the sea lion roars, and I roar. Within seconds Angie's nose rises up, and we leave the airport behind. My last thought has become familiar--We're gonna die.

Chapter Nine

We fly above the Interstate highway and play tag with trucks and the occasional slug-bug. When we gain altitude, the cars and worm-like semi-trucks become toys on a ribbon of black. We turn left and cross over a forest range with tree covered hills that push Angie even higher. Then, in an instant, we cross a rock ledge and fly out over the Pacific Ocean, so huge and empty it's frightening. Uncle Teddy makes a sweeping right turn and we follow the coastline, forests on the right side, ocean on the left, like a zipper between two different parts of the world.

Flashes of sunlight reflect off the water, like tiny LEDs winking at us. I slip in and out of dreams, until I notice the coastline has broken into small islands, patches of green on brilliant light and dark blues. They remind me of a string of beads my mother had scattered across a blue scarf, as she repaired a necklace lifetimes ago. I watch the island-beads slip beneath us; my fingers kneading the locket that hangs around my neck. Between the islands are what appear to be toy motorboats that leave long white tails in the water.

"It's beautiful." I think, but must have said it out loud.

"Yes, it's the most beautiful place on earth. I love it here." Uncle Teddy responds. He reaches over and I jerk when he pats my arm. "I'm sorry for the reasons, but I'm glad you're here, Sammy. I'm very glad you're here."

The sea lion grunts and shifts in the box causing Angie to rock and rattle. Loren wakes with a start and lunges forward out of a dream, "Mom." he yells.

Uncle Teddy gives me a look, like he's uncomfortable or something, then reaches back and brushes Loren's hair, "It's okay, Champ. They gave the sea lion a mild sedative before we left, so she'll make noise, but can't move much for another hour or so. By then we'll be on the water and have her back where she belongs."

I laugh at Loren, but also feel sorry for him. I suddenly realize I might have to be Mom for Loren. I squirm in the seat. I don't think I'm willing to take that on right now.

"That's the American San Juan Islands," Uncle Teddy says. "The two large islands next to each other are San Juan and Orcas islands. We'll land between them. They say there are over one-hundred-fifty islands up here. There is all kinds of history, from Indians to pirates to prospectors."

"Pirates?" Loren yells, shaking off his sleep, "Really?"

"Yes, really, some claim they are still in the islands. There's no doubt there are enough scalawags up here to keep things interesting."

My body presses against the side door as Angie turns. Sunlight reflects bright against the windshield and crawls across the interior. I look out the side window and stare down at Orcas Island and a small bay with tiny boats scattered in it.

"Loon Song Harbor, that's where I live," Uncle Teddy says. "We'll land just outside the tip of the island and put this big girl back where she belongs."

We circle as Uncle Teddy points Angie toward a stretch of water. Suddenly Angie drops. My stomach rises into my throat. I grab for a handle above my head. The engine noise seems to die and I catch a whiff of exhaust. I reach up to cover my nose when Angie lifts, my stomach goes through my knees, and there is a totally huge crash. We hit a wave. The plane bounces, my head jerks hard and we crash down again. Uncle Teddy guns the engine; Loren leans forward and starts to cry; the sea lion barks and bangs inside the box, and I am white-knuckled on the small handle above my head. All I can think is the plane will sink and bubbles will float up around my face while I struggled under water.

Just when I think, we're gonna ..., everything stops. Angie floats like a lazy seagull on the waves; the engine purrs and the sea lion is quiet.

"You okay?" Uncle Teddy asks.

"Yeah," Loren says quickly, as his hands brush tears from under his eyes, "I wasn't scared."

"I'm fine," I say, my heart pounding as I lean forward with my head in my hands. "What happened?"

"Sorry. I misjudged our weight and the sea lion shifted. We came down a little harder than usual. We are fine, but it was a rough ride for a few seconds. It happens, nothing to worry about."

Came down a little hard, I think as I check to see if I still have all my teeth. Loren chokes out a laugh and searches for his teddy bear while we bob in the water between the islands. Being on the water is the most magical feeling. Huge swells lift Angie up, then gently let her down, as if we are riding a wooden airplane on a merry-go-round. Boats motor and sail between the islands around us, and far off there is a big boat, a ferry I think, coming toward us.

"We're in the San Juan Channel." Uncle Teddy says as he points out the window. "Later, we'll head to the cove over there. But first we have to let our cargo go."

Oh great, here it comes, I think.

Angie's exhaust makes my stomach cramp. Uncle Teddy opens the door and unbuckles his seatbelt.

"Do we have to get in the water?" I ask.

"Just you Sammy!" He laughs, "Kidding, stay where you are. Loren, you climb up into my seat."

"Very funny," I say as I undo my seatbelt.

Loren scrambles into the front seat, Uncle Teddy climbs out onto a pontoon. He pushes a button and I hear the cargo door slide back. A wave of fear ripples through me as I wonder whether I'm feeling my fear or the sea lion's? I'm not sure.

"Now," he says, "if all goes as Kristy explained, when I pull this rope it should release the door on the box, and Miss America will jump out of the cargo hold."

"The sedative?" I ask and swallow hard to keep my guts where they belong.

"Kristy said it should be worn off, and when she hits the water she'll wake up. A sea lion can be pretty dangerous, so I'll be on the pontoon and you two stay in the plane." Then he adds, "I hope this works."

"Hope this works? Haven't you ever done this?" I ask.

"Nope," Uncle Teddy says, just as Loren, the dorkster, reaches forward.

"Can I pull?" he says.

"No, no," Uncle Teddy and I yell at the same time.

I reach out to grab Loren's hand to keep him from touching the rope, just as the sea lion grunts and shifts in the box. Its weight and a wave cause the plane to roll left and I fall on Loren. Instinctively, I reach out to catch myself and grab the rope by accident. The rope, that is, to the Sea Lion cage. I realize what I've done and jerk my hand back, expecting the worst--nothing happens. Thank goodness.

The plane rolls to the right and I hear a snap. Seriously not good. The latch releases. As if in slow motion, the plane rolls back left and the heavy door swings down and crashes against a pontoon. Uncle Teddy and I look at each other for a very long moment, then all heck breaks loose.

The sea lion pokes its head out, looks straight at Uncle Teddy, who has slipped off the pontoon and holds on to the wing above his head. He is now almost completely under water. The plane rolls back hard to the right throwing Loren and me back inside the cockpit. Uncle Teddy pops out of the water as Loren's head crashes into mine.

We roll left again; I grab Loren's shirt with one hand, and the seat-back with the other hand, as Loren is almost ejected out the door. His face splashes the surface of the water. The sea lion shifts back and forth, the plane rocks violently and we are flopping around like rag-dolls in a spinning barrel.

Uncle Teddy, holding on to the wing, flaps like a wet flag in the wind. When he goes under for a third time, the sea lion lets out a huge roar, rolls out of the box, hits the pontoon, and falls into the water. The plane rolls one more time. Uncle Teddy flies up, hits his head under the wing, and lands back under water. My hand slips and I tumble sideways.

Loren yells as together we do a summersault out the side door. My head snaps back when I hit the door frame. We both land face first in the water. I grab the pontoon with one arm and hold on to Loren's shirt with the other. We both go under again.

Water catches in my lungs. I jerk, kick and raise my head to gasp for air while I shove Loren onto the pontoon. When I push, I go down again. White bubbles float up and I am suddenly freezing. The engine hums like bees inside my ears, and a loud bang rattles through me. I feel a shooting pain in my forehead, and then silence.

I must have blacked out, because the next thing I know I am lying across the pontoon, legs in the water, with my arm around Loren. We are stunned. I pull Loren next to me, gasp and choke for more air.

"Oh no, oh no," I say as I look into Loren's face. There is blood on his forehead and blood dripping on my shirt and into the water. I reach up and stroke his eyebrow. He has no cuts, then I realize the blood is mine. "Thank you, thank you," I say to myself.

Uncle Teddy pulls up onto the pontoon next to Loren as the sea lion's freckled face pokes up behind him. Tears mixed with salt-water gush down Loren's cheeks as he rubs his forehead.

"Is everyone okay?" Uncle Teddy yells.

Scared out of my mind, I stare at him for a second. My legs kick under water. I try to think, but my lips tremble and my mouth won't work.

"You've got a cut on your head, Sammy," he adds. "Loren, are you hurt?"

Loren just sniffles.

"Yeah, I think we're okay," I say. I brush my hair back and blood flicks into the water.

"Thank goodness," Uncle Teddy says, "I don't know how the box door opened before we were ready. I'm sure I had it secured."

Cold, soaking wet, and sick from swallowing salt water, I think for a minute; Tell him Loren did it--he'll never know. Then I look at Uncle Teddy, "I think ... well, I know, I pulled the cord when I fell into Loren." My lips tremble even more and I feel tears well up in my eyes. My stomach turns a back-flip. "I'm sorry."

Uncle Teddy sighs and rubs his eyes. "It's not your fault Kiddo," he says. "I should have known better than to take a job like this with you kids on board."

Kids? I'm not a kid. I may be stupid, but I'm not a kid. While I glare at Uncle Teddy, the sea lion appears behind him. It turns its head from side-to-side, and with almost a smile looks straight at me. I feel a warm sensation trickle up my spine and wash over me, a friendly energy like with the goose this morning. I never know when it will happen, sometimes pain, sometimes pleasure. What I do know is, as I look at that sea lion free in the water, and she looks at me, I feel her happiness. Then she winks. Until this moment I don't know how I got onto that pontoon, but now I do. It is as if she is communicating with me, through her emotions. She winks again, rises up out of the water, gives me one last look and dives out of sight. The last thing I see is that purple tracking tag glistening in the sunlight.

Chapter Ten

On a fishing boat, far north in Canadian waters, the wind howls like a lonely child. A strong storm carries dark clouds and punishing sea spray across the deck as a short square-built man with a full beard stands hunched over, his back to the wind. He lifts the collar on his dirty work coat, bites down on a cigarette, and pulls a black watch cap over his ears. Every few minutes he removes the cigarette and spits, sending spittle across the deck toward two boys hunkered down near a bulkhead.

"Hey man," the smaller of the two boys yells, but the man can't or doesn't want to hear. The boy wipes his face, curses and yells. Again, he gets no response.

The taller, lankier boy holds the smaller boy's arm and shakes his head. "Freddy, don't bother," he yells, "he can't hear you."

"He a punk," Freddy yells. "They all punks. Freddy gonna kick his butt."

The taller boy laughs and turns away from the spray that pounds them. Freddy grabs for a railing and stands up, then steps forward. As the boat rocks, his tennis shoes slip on the wet deck, he stumbles and falls into the bulkhead several times before he reaches the man. They are the same height, about five-foot-four, but even in his heavy work coat, Freddy sees that the man is heavier, stockier, and stands like a weight lifter. Even though he is strong for an eighteen-year-old, Freddy is no match for the man who watches him with contempt. Since the man has his back to the wind, Freddy hunches and turns sideways to keep the full force of the sea-spray off his face. He wraps his arms around a post and tries to steady himself. He shields his eyes with his hand.

"Where the man?" Freddy yells.

"Asleep, toilet, I no know," the man yells back in broken English. "When he ready, you talk. Now go sit."

Freddy and the man stand in a staring contest for a few seconds, but the man's glare and the wind easily win. Freddy stumbles back to the protection of the bulkhead.

"Tell you Zach," he yells, "Freddy sure gonna kick that beard-punk's butt."

Zach smiles and shakes his head. His long black ponytail whips over his shoulders. In other circumstances this might have looked elegant, his black hair snaking down his back, held by an intricate beaded band. But this afternoon it seems sinister and dark, as the wind howls and the fishing boat lurches from side to side in the open sea.

Finally, a tall overweight man pushes through a doorway, his blubbery belly squeezed on each side. He leans over, talks to the shorter man with the beard, and with a sneer nods toward the boys. The beard flips his cigarette into the ocean, spreads his feet to steady himself, and walks toward the boys. Freddy's face reddens when the man grabs him under both armpits and lifts him off the ground. "Captain ready," the bearded man says. Shocked at the man's strength, Freddy tenses, but doesn't fight. His legs hang helplessly, like the tail of a kite, as the man carries him with ease and without slipping, then drops him down in front of the Captain. Zach stands to follow, but the Beard yells, "Stay," as if giving orders to a dog.

The boat rolls in the turbulent waters. A briny green foam blows up from the waves, across the deck, and covers their shoes. The Captain inspects both boys, as he puffs on an oversized cigar. He kicks his foot gently to remove the foam. They are like many young men he has hired in the Baltic Sea near Russia, before he was forced to find new fishing grounds. Strong for their age, but not fully developed, lanky, over-confident and stupid. They wear jeans, t-shirts and cheap raincoats that wouldn't keep the spit of a sailor from soaking through. They look like drowned kittens compared to real sailors. He knows they talk big, but he can break them like a twig if need be.

The Captain wears a cap with a small bill and a gold crest on the front. He has a heavy black wool coat on with a similar, but different, gold crest on the chest pocket. Zach can't decide if the Captain looks official or just officially silly, like a cartoon character. He knows, however, that the Captain looks dangerous. Zach kneels and leans forward to try and hear the conversation, hoping to keep Freddy from doing anything stupid.

"I Captain," the man with the gold crest bellows. "You want work?"

"Yeah, we want work," Freddy yells as the boat lurches and he stumbles into a post. Zach sits quickly against the bulkhead. Their inexperience on a sea going fishing boat is obvious. Freddy's face flushes and turns a darker shade of red. He regains his balance, nods toward the smaller man and yells to the Captain, "Tell that punk to keep his hands off."

The Captain smiles, leans into Freddy, blows a stream of blue-black smoke, and says, "That punk kill you if he hear you. Understand?"

Freddy inhales the putrid cigar smoke and lets out a lung-ripping cough. He can't answer. Instead he glares at the Captain, then finally chokes out, "How much?"

"Two hundred," the Captain says.

"Each?" Freddy asks, as he glances at Zach.

The Captain pauses. "Three hundred both. You take? Yes? No?"

The Captain is an experienced negotiator, so when Freddy does not respond, the Captain turns toward the door, as if he is leaving.

"Okay," Freddy yells. "Yeah, yeah, okay."

The Captain smiles. "Good." Then with a long drag on his cigar, he motions his assistant, "Victor, come."

Victor-The-Beard brings a box over and opens it. Freddy leans in to see a pile of syringes filled with milky green liquid.

"Everything you need. Two hundred doses. Inject seal, they die in one week," the Captain says. "I pay fifty now, and rest when done." Freddy starts to object. The Beard pulls the box back and Freddy realizes that to argue is pointless. He steps forward, "Okay. We're good."

"Smart boy," the Captain says. Then he adds, as he opens his coat to show a gun on his belt, "Get results, or else. Understand?"

Freddy nods. Victor-The-Beard pushes the box hard into his chest. Freddy stumbles backwards, curses, loses his balance and slides through the sea foam on one knee. Zach scoots forward and grabs Freddy just as he is about to lunge for The Beard.

"Relax," Zach yells, pulling Freddy to the bulkhead.

"Gonna kick that Beard," Freddy keeps yelling. "Gonna kick his butt."

The wind picks up and sea foam rolls across the deck in the general direction of Loon Song Harbor.

Chapter Eleven

We scramble back inside Angie, wet puppies that scatter water everywhere. Loren sniffles for a while, then finally squeaks out, "That was so cool."

I let out a nervous kind of laugh, but all I can think about is the sea lion--well, almost all I can think about. It was absolutely insane how I'd communicated with the sea lion, but then there was the rope, and my belly doing back-flips.

As Uncle Teddy guides Angie across the channel, I lean against the side window. We don't talk, I don't even look at him. I know he is mad, and I am embarrassed, super irritated, and at the same time, a little happy when I think about the sea lion.

What did Uncle Teddy expect? We'd never been in his sea plane before. We'd almost drowned. And anyway, the only thing that saved me was the sea lion--I think.

Angie motors across the water's surface, rising and falling with the huge swells. As the sea plane rises on each crest, I am able to see land. We round a point, and a small cove comes into view. The swells in the channel level off and the water smooths to an emerald green clarity. Several boats cruise past. A boy on a sailboat dumps something out of a bucket, fish scraps Uncle Teddy tells me later, and a mash of seagulls squawk and fight like crazy for them.

The dock in Portland is a single deck, but this one is two docks with boats moored on each side. Most of the boats are similar to boats I've seen in Portland, but a few are much larger, more like yachts. Behind the boats is a grassy bank that slopes up to a forest of tall fir and cedar trees. As Uncle Teddy taxies toward the end of one of the docks, I read the name Express II on the back of a boat, and on the other side of the harbor, above the dock, is a large sign:

Loon Song Harbor - Resort - Moorage - General Store - Visitors Welcome

While Uncle Teddy maneuvers Angie, we pass all kinds of boats: motor, sail, kayak, even large rubber blow-up boats. Near the dock there is a salty seaweed smell, and a large pelican inspects us from the top of a wood post. To my surprise, instead of pulling up next to the dock, Uncle Teddy taxies Angie right up a ramp onto it.

Loren breaks the silence, "You can drive on the dock?"

"Yup. This is my spot," Uncle Teddy says, with a smile back in his voice. "I built it myself. They didn't have a place for a seaplane when I came here, so, next to the boat moorage, they let me build this sea-dock with a ramp. I can taxi Angie right on it. Now it's her home."

"See Angie," I say, as my own smile returns, "he really does love you."

It doesn't take long for Uncle Teddy to hand the bags out while I load them into a cart next to Angie's parking platform. Down the dock are a string of boats parked on either side, all facing in, nose to nose, and at the end, a seriously huge yacht with a helicopter on deck. An old guy sits in a deck chair and watches us, a cap pulled over his eyes and a pipe stuck in his mouth like Popeye.

The block of ice that surrounded our mood after the sea lion incident has melted and we talk again. I'm happy about that. I can't take any more anger or isolation. I look around and take a deep breath. So, this is home.

Chapter Twelve

The cart's wheels thump up a ramp that flexes and groans under our weight, just like in Portland. A chain-link gate, thick with chipped paint, screeches when I push and we cross into a parking area filled with cars, rusty old trucks, and more carts that wait to haul things back down to the boats. We follow a path that leads through the trees. I pull my roller bag, while Loren drags his backpack and carries--drops--carries his teddy bear.

My feet sink into soft needles that cover the path leading through a grove of cedars. With each step the smell of warm, dry, sweetness, like honey, gets stronger. "How far do we have to walk?" I complain, just as we turn left and come to a small yard. The sweetness changes to the cooler freshness of sea-air. I look up and squint. In front of me is the most awesome house I've ever seen, like out of a magazine or something. It's on poles and the sun bounces off huge glass windows facing the bay. Between the glass panes are shiny silver posts and beams. The reflection is so bright I cover my eyes and peek through my fingers. It is seriously cool.

"What do you think?" Uncle Teddy says.

"Wow," Loren says, as he bends over to pick up his teddy bear for the hundredth time.

"Yeah, wow," I add, "this is awesome, beautiful. I thought you lived in an old shack somewhere?"

"I did, but last year this house came up for sale and I was lucky enough to get it. I've only been in it for about six months I still haven't unpacked everything. Maybe you can help."

"Yeah, sure," I say, "whatever."

We enter through a basement door. Uncle Teddy turns right and we follow down a hall. "There are four rooms on this floor," he says, "two bedrooms, a sort-of storage room, and a large bathroom."

He pokes his head into the first room, "There's also a bathroom in this bedroom."

I hear the word bathroom, step forward and throw my backpack through the doorway. "Dibs, I'll take this room."

"No fair," Loren whines, "I want the bathroom."

"Too late, slow poke. It's mine," I say.

"Don't worry Champ," Uncle Teddy adds, while he continues down the hall, "that means you get the other bedroom and the BIGGER bathroom all to yourself."

Loren's voice echoes from the bigger bathroom as I take a look at my new room. It's huge, like massive I mean, and bright. Very slowly I step across the threshold and do a three-sixty. Reflected light dances off one wall that is all windows. The other three walls are a medium brown wood that has the texture of warm caramel mixed with chocolate sauce. It looks yummy. On one wall is the door to the bathroom, my bathroom, and on the other wall is the bed, my bed. The room smells new and fresh like pine needles. A tall dresser, not white but light colored wood, is on one wall with another long dresser next to it. I've never seen so many drawers. A cool high-back chair, covered in purple and gold fabric, snuggles in one corner, and a small table with a rolling chair, like an office, sits next to that. This is totally awesome, I think. This is seriously, totally, brilliantly, awesome.

Sliding glass doors open to a small patio. I look out on the garden and beyond I can peek through to the harbor. I can't see the boats, but I can see their masts as they sway back and forth. The curtain slides easily when I pull it halfway shut to block the sun.

A wave of pain grips my stomach and I head for the bathroom. Where is it? I know I threw a box in. I grab my bag, toss through a few toiletries and in a crushed box find a single pad. Thank you, Mom, for buying this stuff months ago.

After changing into dry clothes, I rinse out my underwear and hang my wet things in the shower. Thank God for my own private bath. I peek into the bedroom. A white comforter with small gold feathers embroidered on it, like wisps of gold settling on snow, covers the bed. In bare feet, I slide across the carpet and stand at the foot of the bed. My hand sinks like five inches into the bed when I push down. OMG - five inches. I consider my options, then take one step back and jump--a perfect belly flop right in the middle of the bed. Poof! The cover flies up all around me. It is as soft as it looks. I roll onto my back, cross my feet, put my hands behind my head and close my eyes. This is crazy good luxury. Thank you, Uncle Teddy.

There's a knock. "Well, what do you think?" Uncle Teddy says, poking his head around the door.

I lurch up and feel my cheeks burn red; I pat the covers. "Sorry, I was just ..."

"Don't be sorry," Uncle Teddy interrupts. "This is your room and this is your home. You use it anyway you want. Well--almost--you know what I mean. This is your home now. Okay?"

"Yeah, thanks Uncle Teddy. This is awesome."

"Good, I'm glad you like it. Now come on up. I want to show you the rest of the house."

The down comforter collapses as I push my face into the covers and breath in the misty, vanilla-white flavors that surround me. I don't want to get up. I'm tired and even my bones hurt. But I force myself to roll out of bed. Turning toward the door a flash catches my eye. A red sliver of light appears across the horizon and crawls through the windows. I touch the locket around my neck. Hi Mom, we made it.

Chapter Thirteen

The room at the top of the steps is a huge open living room with more picture windows. I can see most of Loon Song Harbor, sailboat masts, and even part of Angie's wings. I realize I must be directly above my room. Beyond the harbor I can see other islands and more boats.

The kitchen is light blond wood, and sun pours in through the large glass windows that blinded me when I arrived. In the sunlight Uncle Teddy's hair turns bright yellow; his eyes, just like Mom's, are bright blue. He stands near a small counter that has three tall stools with red seats. Loren crawls up on one of them. Behind are stacks of unopened boxes around a red booth right out of one of those old-fashioned diners with a soda fountain that serves root beer floats. The sunlight gives everything a warm glow, and it is like entering a honey combed burger-bar. It is so bright, I wish I'd brought my sun glasses. All I can do is stand in the doorway and squint.

"Okay guys, we need to have a talk," Uncle Teddy says as he waves me over and hands each of us a piece of paper from a yellow pad.

A sour taste seeps through my cheeks. I'm nervous, like when you know something's coming but you don't know what it is. He is going to say something about pulling the rope--being punished, I am sure.

His lips smack once like he's going to make an important speech. He holds up the paper. "This is your house now and you get to make it your home. All I ask is that you help me take care of it. I've listed a few rules here that I want you to remember."

Rules--Remember? Cool, I can handle this.

Loren and I look at our lists and glance at each other. Loren scrunches his face in confusion and gives Uncle Teddy an, I do pictures not words, kind of look. I can't help but laugh. Loren snickers. Uncle Teddy must think we're being disrespectful because he gets a real stern look on his face. "I'm not kidding," he says, shaking the paper, "I'm going to need your help and these things are important."

"We know," I say. "We didn't mean to laugh, it was just ... well, I don't think Loren can read your writing. But we know it's serious."

He holds the paper out, squints, cocks his head, then smiles and ruffles Loren's hair, "I guess you're right, Champ; I can hardly read it myself. But it's still important."

When I look at the paper I notice the name Liz. To change the subject I ask, "Who's Liz anyway?"

Uncle Teddy clears his throat, real official like. "Liz, is a very close friend. She runs the store and her family owns the docks. I trust her with my life. She'll be your go-to person if you need help. Her phone number is on the fridge, and on notepads in your bedrooms." Then he adds, "Sammy, I included a few extra numbers on your pad."

I think for a second. "Wait. How'd you know what room was going to be mine?"

"Bath plus down-bed?" Uncle Teddy says. "Who else was going to get that bedroom?"

Loren snorts.

"Even though the bathroom is smaller than Loren's," Uncle Teddy adds.

I glance through the list: Old house--off limits; Abandon mine shafts--off limits; Stay off small islands at low tide; Do not use hot tub or sauna without Uncle Teddy.

"Hot tub and sauna?" I say, as I hold the paper out and scrunch my eyes like Uncle Teddy.

He glances up and laughs. "Yeah, the house has a hot tub and sauna right next to the weight, er, storage room. I know, I know, but they came with the house."

"Where's the pool?" I ask, trying to be sarcastic.

He thinks I'm serious and responds, "No pool, but we have a swim area just down from the docks."

"This is sweet," I say. "We might as well live in a resort."

"You are," he says. "Uncle Teddy's Loon Song Resort. And now it's Sammy and Loren's Loon Song Resort."

This just gets better and better.

I feel a slight tension and my stomach growls. I look up. "Wow," Uncle Teddy says, "sounds like the sea lion followed us home."

I giggle, but can feel the temperature rise in my cheeks. "I need to eat on a regular schedule or I go into what Mom called 'Melt-Down.' My blood-sugar level gets too low."

"Yeah," Loren chimes in. "It's not pretty."

"Can we eat now?" I ask. "Also, is there a store nearby? I need some supplies."

"Don't worry," Uncle Teddy answers as he walks to the refrigerator. "I've got everything you'll need."

Great, now how do I explain this? "Well," I say, "I need some personal things ... just for me." I raise my eyebrows-- like duh.

"Yeah," he says as he pokes his head in the refrigerator. "I think I picked up everything you like." Then he stops, hesitates, stands up and bangs his head against a shelf. "Personal items. Okay, I see," he says, his cheeks a pinkish-red. He reaches in a cabinet and turns around with an energy bar and a $20 bill in his hand.

"How about you take a walk to the general store and pick up some bread, meat, cheese, or whatever you want, and you can meet Liz. I think she can help you get what you need. Can you make it that long?"

"Sure," I say as I grab the money and energy bar. "If I'm not back in thirty minutes, send out the dogs."

"Do you have dogs?" I hear Loren ask as I walk out the back door and down the steps.

Chapter Fourteen

The Captain maneuvers the fishing vessel into a small cove on San Juan Island, just east of Orcas Island.

"Where are you taking us?" Freddy yells.

"There," the Captain says, pointing to a small dinghy where Victor waits. "He take you to dock, you take ferry home from there."

"C'mon man," Freddy protests, "it's an hour walk to the ferry from here. How 'bout a ride?"

The Captain flashes a jowly smile. "How 'bout you walk."

The boat rocks gently in the protected bay as Zach climbs down the ladder to the dinghy. He grabs Freddy's shirt,

"C'mon man, let's just get out of here." Freddy gives the Captain one last sneer, spits on the deck, and follows Zach.

Zach and Freddy sit next to each other while Victor guides the motorboat past a new concrete dock to a much older wood platform that looks like it might fall apart at any moment. Cracked and broken boards covered with slick algae stretch over ancient logs that float near a grassy bank. When Zach hops from the dinghy onto the boards, the corner sinks under water and the platform rocks like a surfboard in a storm.

While Zach tries to maintain his balance, Freddy turns to follow, then looks at Victor and raises his middle finger. The stalky man reaches for Freddy's hand, misses, trips, and falls forward. Freddy jumps onto the dock and laughs. His foot sinks under water. Freddy slips and falls forward, landing with his face in the muck. Victor revs the boat-motor, laughs loudly and yells something as he speeds off.

"What'd he say?" Freddy asks.

Zach shrugs. "What happened on the boat? How much are they paying us?"

Freddy studies Zach, then pulls out a twenty and a five. "Here," he holds the money out, "your half of the down-payment."

"Cool," Zach says as he palms the bills, "how much are they paying us?"

Freddy guesses that Zach did not hear the Captain agree to three-hundred. He pauses, "He offered two-hundred."

Zach's forehead scrunches. "But I talked him up to two-fifty," Freddy quickly adds. "We split it."

"One-twenty-five each?" Zach says.

"Yeah, man. You get one-twenty-five just for sticking a few seals. We're partners, right?"

"Yeah, partners," Zach says.

Freddy slaps Zach on the shoulder, pleased with his deception.

"One-twenty-five," Zach mumbles to himself. "I can do this."

For the next two-hours, all the way to the ferry dock and back to Orcas Island, Freddy boasts about how he will, "take care of those guys if they don't treat Freddy right." By the time the boys arrive at Orcas Island, Zach is full of Freddy's tough talk.

The front of the ferry is still three-feet from the dock when Zach leaps across the gap. "I'm out of here," Zach says, "things to do on my way home."

"Hey man," Freddy protests, "we got work to do. C'mon, let's hit the beach, there be plenty of seals down there."

Zach stares at Freddy, and wonders if he's made a good choice about partners. They've been friends a long time, as long as Zach can remember. But Freddy has changed. He's always been crazy, but lately Freddy has been involved with car theft and drugs. He is moving toward serious trouble.

The island is small, only about four hundred kids in the entire school system, and Freddy and Zach have always attended the same school complex in East Sound. As a kid, you pretty much know everyone by the time you're in the third grade, and everyone knows their own group. The geeks, jocks, barbies, nerds, preps, mean-girls and boys, punks, and the final group, the outsiders that don't fit anywhere. Zach met Freddy in the first grade, when the teacher was handing out papers. She asked if anyone had seen her red pencil.

"I have it," Freddy piped up as he raised his hand. "It's on my paper." That got a good laugh, and detention.

Freddy had been held back and was older than everyone else in his class. He pretty much spent the next ten years in detention of one sort or another. No one ever really knew, but the rumor was his father beat him, real bad. Freddy always said he fell down, but from the bruises and scars on his arms and legs, the school nurses knew it was something more, and so did almost everyone else. But Freddy wouldn't talk; he just acted out.

By the sixth grade Freddy and Zach had become best friends and were known as outsiders. Maybe it was that they both had lost their mothers, or maybe because Zach was so quiet he couldn't make other friends, no one knew. The result was Zach followed Freddy around like a puppy, and often got into trouble just for that reason.

By tenth grade, Freddy dropped out of school. Zach knew Freddy had stolen cars to take joy rides, and at times, had sold drugs near the school. Freddy had even been questioned by the police about it. Now Zach worried the trouble was escalating, and he was getting tired of Freddy's mouth.

"No," Zach calls over his shoulder as he heads down the road toward home. "I'm done for today. You go take care of them. Tell me all about it later."

Freddy watches his only friend shuffle away. He spits, partly onto the dock, partly onto his shoe, looks around, wipes his shoe on the back of his pant-leg, then starts his low-pant duck-walk toward the beach.

"No problem," he says to himself as he throws imaginary punches at Victor. "Freddy can do this, don't need you, don't need nobody. Freddy do this just fine."

Chapter Fifteen

Areusable bag reading, Loon Song Resort, hangs from my arm as I walk out the back door and munch on a yogurt and nut energy bar. I laugh at the thought of Uncle Teddy's house and my new room. Our old house was barely big enough for the four of us; this house can hold an army, and it has a hot tub and sauna. This is crazy amazing.

Memories of the old house, every memory it seems, pulls me back to Mom. I feel guilty, like I'm betraying her by thinking how cool this house is. I should feel bad, I tell myself. I shouldn't feel good. As I walk down the path, under the shade of tall trees, the sound of sails flapping and rigging clanking gives me a warm feeling. I shouldn't feel happy, I remind myself. At the parking lot, I increase my pace. But in spite of my scolding, the warm feeling inside doesn't go away. I have to admit, I like being at Loon Song Harbor.

The store waits for me as I cross the parking area. It sits on a bank with a long porch across its front. The stairway is only five steps, but their width makes them look larger. The entire building is wood shakes with solid tree trunks for porch posts. The roof is covered with moss and the edges have strings of emerald green plants that hang down. A neighbor in Portland planted window boxes hoping for the same result. Here, nature does it for free.

Closer, I notice a figure in a chair on the porch. Even closer, I can see a wrinkled old hat and jeans, a red plaid shirt, and dark-brown suspenders. The wrinkles rock to and fro in a high-backed rocking chair. I place my foot on the first step. It squeaks. My heart jumps when the hat rises up and I see an old man with a face as wrinkled as his hat. He has a long strand of grass in his mouth and his sharp, penetrating black eyes stare at me.

I stop and take a deep breath. My front teeth gnaw at my dry lower lip as I take four more steps. His eyes follow me, like a wolf watching its prey, and when he turns his head slightly, I notice black hair that falls down his back in a single braid. He has an intricate beaded band around it. I hear my stomach rumble and move my hand over; I hope he didn't hear.

Crossing the porch, I finally reach a wooden screen door and pull. The door creaks open, then slams shut behind me. I jump and am shaking.

The smell of sawdust mixed with a flowery perfume surrounds me. On the counter is a small bowl; smoke curls up from a thin stick of incense. I recognize it immediately-- Jasmine, the same incense Mom burned. A youngish woman stands behind the counter.

"May I help you?" she says.

"No," I answer, "just picking up a few things."

She wears jeans and a large flannel shirt that hangs loose around her. Blond hair, in a short pixie-cut, surrounds her smile like a golden halo. I think of Peter Pan.

"Let me know if I can help," she says, looking directly at me. "Are you off one of the boats?"

"No, I'm just visiting for a ... a while."

"Oh," the woman says. She wipes her hands on a cloth. "You wouldn't happen to be Samantha, by any chance, would you?"

"Yes. Are you Liz?"

"One and the same," she says, as she steps out from behind the wood counter and offers me her hand. She is shorter than me by a few inches, and I feel immediately like she treats me as an adult. Not like her equal, but with respect. I like her.

"Lizina Kuzminski-Smith" she says with a radiant smile. "So, your uncle is Theodore Crenshaw, heh?"

"Yes," I say, noticing she has on lace-up half-boots. Pretty stylish for an island.

"Teddy told me about your mother. I'm so sorry for your loss," she says. "I know you must be tired after the trip, so I won't keep you, but I want you to know you're welcome here. You let me know if there's anything you need."

I stiffen, stare at her for a moment, stunned that she would mention my mom. I guess I appreciate her concern, but I feel violated, like she doesn't have a right to mention her. She doesn't even know her. We lock eyes.

"I'm sorry," Liz quickly says. "I shouldn't have said anything."

Her apology releases the tension, I smile and shrug. "It's just that ... "

"I understand," she interrupts. "I've lost those close to me as well. It's a very private thing, I should have been more sensitive."

Wow, she gets it. "That's okay," I say quickly and hope she likes me. After a few seconds, I look around. "Where are the eggs?" I ask.

She points me to the back of the store. I grab some lunch fixings and start my search for the girl supplies. Checking the only four isles in the store, I find nothing. I approach the counter, not sure of what to say.

"I was wondering ... do you have any women's ... products?"

Liz looks up, stares at me for a moment. "Oh my dear, of course we do. They're right near the back." She smiles and puts her hand over her mouth. "Of course, you're living with

Ted. You poor dear, you can't talk to him about this, now can you?" I shake my head, a little surprised she is so open about it.

"Don't worry, I've got all you need. Do you know what you want?"

"Well, no. I just started."

"Okay," she says. She reaches for some boxes. "You try these and see how they work. If they're not what you want, there are plenty of products that I can get for you." She pauses. "You know how to use these?"

"Yeah, I think so. My mom showed me."

"Good." She puts her hand on my arm. "Sammy, if you have any questions at all, please talk to me. It's no big deal between us girls, okay?"

I drop the boxes on the counter with the lunch supplies and pull out the twenty-dollar bill. She puts her hand up, "I'll put this on his tab. Ted has an account, I'll just add this to it."

Cool, I get to use a tab.

"So, I get to buy whatever I want?"

She looks around. "I guess, for what it's worth. We're a boat-dock store, not a super-mart." We both laugh.

I am slow to leave the store. Pushing the screen door open, I peek out to where Wrinkles had sat. The chair rocks gently, but he isn't in it. Instead, a crow sits on the back of the rocker. I am relieved to see he's gone, but the crow is kind of creepy and at the same time, familiar. I hurry across the porch, take the steps in two leaps, and run for the house.

When I arrive, I hear Loren shouting, "four, four, four." Uncle Teddy and Loren are playing dice.

"This is so neat," Loren says. "It's a game called Farkel."

"Farkel?"

"It has a tiny seagull on one side instead of a one. Mom gave it to me before ..." Loren's voice trails off.

Usually I would have made a smart-aleck remark about him being a dork or something, but now I can't. I know he is hurting just like me. I put my arm about him.

"I know, I've been thinking about her too," I say.

Loren relaxes into me for a few seconds, then wiggles away.

"Anyway," he says, "it's a fun game if you want to play."

"Okay," I say, "but we have to eat at the same time."

Uncle Teddy rolls the dice and gets two sixes, a three and two fours. He needs three sixes.

"Third try," Loren yells, "I win." He raises his arms in his usual super-hero victory pose. We play Farkel, and Loren wins most of the games. By six thirty I can't keep my eyes open. My head jerks forward and I can't focus on the dice.

"Hey Dork," Loren says, to wake me up.

I've been up since five, and now, as I walk down the long staircase toward my new room, such a different staircase from this morning, my arms and legs ache from exhaustion. Instead of medicine and sickness, I smell fresh wood and salt air. For some reason, my stomach still aches.

It is all I can do to find my toothbrush, scrape my teeth and crawl into bed. I think about the dice Mom gave Loren, and I take off my necklace with the locket. I look at Mom's and my faces smiling back and hold it up; it spins around and light reflects off our noses. Several weeks ago, this was just a necklace, now, as I reunite the clasp around my neck, it feels like so much more. It is my memories and my new life.

Just this morning I walked out the back door in Portland and thirteen hours later I am lying in a bed, in my new home in the San Juan Islands. I've flown in a float plane, saved a sea lion, moved into Uncle Teddy's house ... my house, and met his ... my new friend Liz.

I lay my head back and feel the soft down pillow wrap around my ears. My mind drifts as I finger the locket. I know everything has changed forever and it can never be, but I still just want my mom.

Chapter Sixteen

A tapping and a whiney voice slip into my bedroom, "Sammy, Sammy."

"Go away, I'm sleeping." Hair sticks in my mouth and I roll over. A sea lion, black hat, white apron, purple tag on her flipper, carrying a tray, is outside my door.

Does she have shoes? I can't see.

"Sammy?"

"What? Leave me alone."

Pancakes, eggs, blueberries are on the tray--I call to her and she runs. I try to chase, but I am caught and I can't move. Rolling over, I'm suddenly falling, "Help, help," I yell.

"Sammy, Sammy, wake up."

I struggle to pull hair out of my mouth and push sweat-soaked sheets away from my neck as the sea lion morphs into Loren's pointy little head poking around my door.

"What?" I shout. Sweat drips off my face. "What do you want?"

"Are you awake yet?"

"Yes, I'm awake yet. What do you want?"

"I want breakfast, I'm hungry. Uncle Teddy said we could have breakfast as soon as you woke up."

"Breakfast?" I say, as I imagine the sea lion disappearing down the hall and my dream melts into reality.

"Okay, I'm awake. So, get out of my room."

"It's not your room."

"Is too--get out." My pillow slams against the door, just missing his head.

"My bathroom is bigger," he says, as his parting shot.

"You are such a pain," I scream.

We'd arrived at Loon Song Harbor only two days ago, but it already seems like another lifetime. I rub my head. I slept over fifteen hours the first night and stayed in bed most of the afternoon. Last night I fell asleep about nine and it is now midmorning--that's over thirteen hours. I don't think I've ever slept so much. My head feels like a melon and throbs. I stumble into the bathroom. The sink is full of boxes: aspirin, hair products, skin scrub, teen pads, max pads, hemp pads. Hemp pads? OMG Liz, enough. I toss everything in the corner and wash my face. I lean forward. In the mirror, my face is as big as the moon. "Okay kid," I say, "day three. Ready--set--go."

The smell of eggs, bacon, and pancakes pulls me into the kitchen. Reflected sunlight screams off the walls. I remind myself to remember my sun glasses. "Smells good," I say as I walk to the breakfast bar, shielding my eyes. This is too weird. "Are those blueberry pancakes?"

"Yup. Loren said you liked blueberries, so I thought I'd add them to the pancakes."

I make a quick scan for a sea lion with an apron, but just see Loren beaming a huge smile, and wearing sun glasses. Smart kid.

"Yeah, I do, thanks," I say.

I am famished and I'm sure I've never tasted better eggs and pancakes. While I shovel forkfuls in my mouth, Uncle Teddy says he has to fly to Alaska on a job. "I have to leave this afternoon. Sammy, you'll be in charge while I'm gone," he says. "Ah, Sammy, you have a blueberry stuck to your cheek."

In charge, I think, as I roll the berry over my lip with my tongue. "Sounds good to me," I say.

He mentions the ground rules again; no this, no that, don't go near the bad places, and most of all, stay close to Liz. Then he reminds me, "You're in charge during the day, but you both answer to Liz, keep her informed of what you're doing." He pauses. "Since I'm gone over night, Liz will spend the night at the house, so you don't have to worry about anything."

Feeling a little disappointed, yet relieved, I assure him there is no problem. "We'll be just fine. What can happen in a quiet place like this?"

Uncle Teddy drones on about his trip and some sort of engine-parts he has to deliver, while I shove the remainder of my breakfast in my mouth. My mind drifts to images of sunning in the swim area, maybe meeting someone off that huge yacht, even taking a ride in the helicopter. Then I hear Uncle Teddy say, "Anyway, I'll have to get you a new cell phone."

My head snaps up. "What? Cell phone? What's wrong with my old one?" I haven't even thought about my phone since I'd arrived.

"Oh, I haven't told you. Your dad had to cancel your cell service, but it's better, because I'll get you a phone up here. Actually, I've already called my carrier and they'll issue you a new number, but you can keep your old phone, if you want to."

"Sure," I say, "I don't care." Then I realize what I'm saying. "New phone!"

I throw my hands up, like a traffic cop. "Wait, what kind of phone can I get? Can I get a smartphone?"

Uncle Teddy looks up. "Well, I don't know ... maybe. We'll have to find out what they cost."

Cool, a new smartphone. "So, when can I get the phone?"

"How about right now," he says, checking his watch. Let's get ready and we'll drive over to the phone store and see what they can do.

Loren, who has been sitting with his eyes flashing between Uncle Teddy and me, finally figures it out. Ripping off his sunglasses, "Can I get a phone too?"

Uncle Teddy pauses.

"Guess again Punkster," I cut in.

Loren gives me a look, trying to act really irritated.

"You're seven," I add, "Mom said you could get a phone when you turn twelve."

Realizing he's lost this battle, Loren quickly adds, "Can I get an MP3 player?"

He's such a punk, but he's quick. I have to give him that.

The phone stores in Portland are massive with hundreds of phones and electronics. On Orcas Island--not. We drive about ten miles up island to the main town of East Sound. On a map, the island looks like a giant horse-shoe with the legs pointing down. Loon Song Harbor is in the lower left corner of one leg, East Sound is in the middle at the top. Around the edges of the island are forests of Fir, Maple, and a strange red tree with curly bark that Uncle Teddy calls Pacific Madrone. Driving north, we follow a twisty road over a few hills, leave the coastline and move near the center of the horse-shoe. The forest quickly turns to farm land, with stretches of wheat fields filled with sheep, cows, and horses.

Just as I'm getting used to the farms, three wooden hand-carved signs flash by announcing pottery studios. A moment later, a smaller sign announces East Sound, pop 3748. Before I know it, we are driving into a small village with lots of art galleries, coffee shops, restaurants, a food market, and a hardware store. Now that I see the biggest town on the island, I realize just how small Orcas Island really is, and how small Loon Song Harbor is. It feels kind of cute and kind of frightening at the same time. "This is it?" I say.

"Kind of small compared to Portland," Uncle Teddy says, "but we have our claims to fame, including Oprah."

"Seriously?"

"So rumor has it," he says. "We also have a pretty good hardware store."

We park under one of those curly-bark trees in front of the hardware store. The floors are wood, but otherwise it looks like a small version of the super-stores in Portland, with rows of everything from camp gear to home repair products, even a small canoe hanging in one corner. Loren immediately attaches himself to a glass case full of guns.

"C'mon Champ, those aren't for us," Uncle Teddy says, and guides him to the back of the store to what they call their electronics department, a small counter in front of a wall covered with batteries, chargers, a few tablets, and believe it or not, phones.

"Hi Marge," Uncle Teddy calls, as we parade back. "Got that order I called about?"

Surprised, I give Uncle Teddy a questioning look. He smiles as she sets out three boxes on the small counter. I really don't care how many phones they have, as long as one is a smartphone. My eyes click across the covers until I find the familiar symbol. Uncle Teddy kind of chokes when he sees the price, but with some assurance from Marge that it is, "unquestionably the best phone for the price," and with my promise that, "I'll guard it with my life," he buys it. I am so excited I literally dance around the store until they hand it to me. Uncle Teddy even buys me a purple cover. It is beautiful.

Two hours later, Loren and I stand at the big picture windows at home, look out at a silver blue sky, and watch Uncle Teddy taxi Angie away from the dock. My new phone in hand, I look at Loren. His head bounces to tunes on his new MP3 player, pre-loaded with 100 songs from kid's movies. We both have ear-buds poking out of our ears, and I rock to some seriously insane tunes.

Something feels great about being there alone. I know Liz is going to stay at the house, but Uncle Teddy trusts me to be here alone with Loren. He doesn't even question it, like I am a grown up.

A reflection flashes like an explosion off Angie's window as they taxi away from the harbor. They lift off and Uncle Teddy makes a one-eighty, and flies directly over the house waggling Angie's wings goodbye.

The engine noise shakes the windows then disappears. Loren turns to me, rubbing his hands together, "What now?" he asks, in his most conspiratorial voice.

Looking down at him, I and have the sudden urge to take his face in my hands like Mom used to do, but I know better. Loren may have let Mom kiss him, or even Dad, but I am an entirely different story. I am not sure what is happening, but I realize I'm starting to like the kid.

"How about a walk? Then we'll go swimming later this afternoon," I suggest.

"I want to swim now," he says.

"No, it's too cold. We'll swim later. Let's walk now."

"No, swim now," he insists.

My fists clinch and I seriously consider scrunching his whiny little face, then I remember what Mom used to say, "If you want someone to do something with you, make it fun."

"Well, we could swim now," I say. "But, I was thinking it might be fun to walk up around the bay and go exploring." I put my arms up like I have a sword in my hand and make a couple of lunges in his direction, "We might even find some pirates!"

"Pirates," he raises his own imaginary sword. "Okay, I'll go get my spy gear."

"Fantastic, Captain Kid, whatever you want," I say, with a satisfied smile.

Chapter Seventeen

Sandwiches sit smooshed between a box of cookies, two juice drinks and a towel. I could remake them, but they'll just get crushed on the hike. Besides, peanut butter, honey, and banana taste best all smashed together. A scraping-skid screeches up behind me. I spin around and almost choke. Loren rolls into the kitchen in a purple baseball cap, green shorts, and a camouflage t-shirt with glow in the dark letters--I'll be back. He holds his yellow super-hero backpack with, of course, his teddy bear hanging strangled from a ribbon. I swallow my laughter and check him out, head to toe. The source of the skid was like a flashing neon sign-- his high-top electric yellow skate-shoes.

"Are you sure you want to wear those?" I say. My mind scrambles for ways to talk him out of them. "We're going on a hike, not roller-derby--No sidewalks."

He gives me his, you're dumber than dirt, look, "Duh? I know where we're going. These are my most favorite shoes ever."

I take a deep breath. "Pick your battles," Mom used to say, and I sense this isn't a battle I can win.

"Whatever makes you happy, but don't wear them in the house. Uncle Teddy'll kill you if you scrape up his floors," Loren responds with a broad smile. "What's in the pack?" I ask.

Like a magician his hand sweeps to the top, he flashes open the backpack for only a second and machine-guns off a list that includes: squirt-gun, spy-glass, pencil, some essential army toys and a box of gum. "And more," he says, as he tucks the pack behind him, "A lot more."

"Great," I roll my eyes and laugh out loud, "as long as you can carry it, you can bring anything you want."

His eyebrows shoot up. "I'll be right back," he says, and is gone before I can think of what to say.

We make our way to the general store to tell Liz we we're leaving. Behind me, Loren hobbles across the garden to the trail. At the parking area, his skate-shoes scrape the dirt and small pebbles jam in the wheels. They are covered with muck by the time we reach the porch steps, but he makes it and no whining. He clomps up behind me kicking rocks out of his wheels as the screen door squeaks open. I glance sideways with some disappointment. I want to see what Loren thinks of Wrinkles, but the rocker is empty, "Good morning," Liz says through her sunbeam smile.

We'd seen Liz the night before, when she came to the house for dinner. Loren helped her make a stir-fry with vegetables and chicken. I told her I didn't like chicken (what I really meant was the thought of chicken makes me want to throw-up). She made a side dish with tofu just for me. I felt special and I loved it. This morning I notice how relaxed I feel with Liz, like I can trust her. Liz glances down at Loren's shoes as he blurts out, "We're going on a hike to find pirates."

"Pirates, eh? In that case you want to follow the road for a few blocks," Liz says, wiping her hands on the apron, "then turn left through the field."

Loren gives me the 'dumber than dirt' look again, "See, there IS a road," he says.

"Follow the footpath to the other side of the wooded area," she continues, "and you'll hit the coast trail." She glances at her watch, "Be home by four. Okay? Do you have your phone?" I nod twice.

She opens the screen door to go back inside and adds, "It'll be low tide, so stay off the rocks. They can be dangerous."

"No problem," I say, pleased she didn't say we couldn't go.

Chapter Eighteen

L oren pushes his skate-shoes from side to side making scratching sounds on the pavement as he zooms ahead toward the turn-off. "Wait up," I call as he disappears into the field. The path falls slightly from the road and is guarded by tall dew-covered grass. The wheat-like stalks shake and shimmy as the clown-colored Dorkster thrashes and stumbles in my direction.

"Yuk," he screams, running around in circles and wiping his face, "wet spider webs. You go first."

"Okay, pirate detective," I say and bend to pick up a stick to clear the way. I raise my hand and squint into the sunlight. Instead of grass and spiders, what I see is a sparkling magic kingdom. A bazillion spider webs stretched between thousands of stalks of grass. Each web has millions of dew drops on it, and each dew drop reflects the morning sun. Twinkling pinpoints of bright yellow, orange, red, mixed with green, amber and luscious brown in sparks of color that go on as far as I can see. The points of light are so beautiful it makes my head spin. I stop. Loren bumps into me from behind.

"What," he whines.

I hold his arm and pull him to me. Crouching to his height, I point ahead. "The spider webs, look how the light reflects off them like a magical fairy land."

Loren jerks his shoulder away. "So what? I hate spiders."

Even when he grabs my stick I don't respond. I am hypnotized by the work of those tiny insects.

"Come on," Loren demands, swinging the small branch, brushing away the webs. "Come on, we have pirates to find. I don't want to stand here all day. Yhaa, yhaa," he hollers, whipping his new weapon like a Ninja.

My heart drops. "Sorry spiders, here comes your worst nightmare."

The foot path through the dew-covered field joins a more wooded trail along the waterline. My shoes slip on branches and large roots while Loren magically skips over them. At times, he scrambles under downed tree trunks and I claw my way over them. I feel awkward, like the huge Alice in Wonderland following a scampering rabbit. Weird, because I was always short for my age, until about the sixth grade, when I shot up like a foot in one year. Now, I'm even taller, with gargantuan feet, and I stumble over everything. There is one advantage, I can see more--sometimes.

"What the ...? Loren, be careful, that hurt," I yell as a large branch whips across my face, stinging my cheek.

"What? I didn't do anything."

"The branches, you jerk," I say. He doesn't hear and is gone in a flash. Tears form on my lower eyelids. I scrunch my cheeks and glance up to the sun directly above us. One-twenty, my phone reads. We've been hiking for almost two hours. I hurry to catch up, slipping and stumbling onto a stretch of sand. A pounding wave crashes against large boulders and my heart races as I search for Loren. I panic for a moment thinking I might have lost him. No worries, he's already across the beach hopping his way toward a hill near the surf.

"How about some food?" I yell, as I check out the shore.

"Up there," he points. "We can search for pirates while we eat."

The hill has plenty of beach around it and lots of rocky spots with seagull poop. Grassy areas with short trees are spotted between them. "What about your skate-shoes?" I call, but he's already sprung across the shore and scampered up a steep slope. Stay off the rocks, Liz said. But this isn't a rock, it's a small mountain.

My tennis shoes suck down in the soft sand and sand-fleas hop around my ankles as I follow my brother, the rabbit. Each time I lift my foot, my shoes make a sucking-pop sound. I almost lose one shoe in the process. Slippery rocks present another problem. I have no idea how the Dorkster makes it up the hill. A root and a clump of weeds are convenient handles to pull myself up, and I scramble onto a grassy patch above a small sandy cove. Loren has already opened his backpack. Like a detective, he stares at me, holding his round magnifying glass up to his face. One eye, the size of a pomegranate, red and blurry, peers at me. His eyebrows jerk up and down, and he spins around to inspect the area.

Our sandwiches turn out to be about as thick as a DVD. The PBH&B all smooshed together. But they taste good. "Pirates?" I mumble, accidentally spitting out a hunk of banana.

"No," he says disappointedly, following my banana-spit with his spy-glass.

"Don't worry, they'll show up sooner or later," I say. "Buried treasure, they'd never leave gold behind."

His eyebrows go up again and a glob falls off his sandwich onto his magnifier. He sees the chunk as he pulls the lens toward his eye, just in time to prevent a peanut butter-to-eyeball collision. "Crap," he says.

"Hey," I say, without thinking, "watch your language." I wait for his explosive response.

"Sorry," he says.

I drop my sandwich. I can't believe it. He didn't get angry, talk back, or even defend himself. He responded like he would have to Mom. Sorry? OMG, he's never said sorry to me in his life. Now I know, things are starting to change. Like the title, Big Sister, is growing on my forehead or across my arm or something. It isn't what I'm used to, but I kind of like it.

Oblivious to my reaction, he immediately expands his search into the small cove below. For the next hour, he builds sand castles and digs for treasure. Occasionally a wave rushes in, breaks down his towers and causes him to start over. Watching him, I wonder what it was like when Indians, fur traders, and all the boats that must have sailed past this little island, were here. Maybe a pirate really did bury treasure, or a girl sat right here wondering the same things, missing her mom.

The rocks I'm sitting on remind me of the spot where we gave up Mom's ashes. True to her naturalist upbringing, Mom wanted to be cremated. "Earth to earth," she said, "means you go back where you came from." She believed that meant into the air. "Like a piece of wood burned in a fire." She told me, "I will change form, but my essence will filter into everything my ashes touch." She winked and poked me in the ribs with a giggle, like she'd told a joke or something. I thought it sounded sick.

Mom told us she wanted a short eulogy, for family only, at a spot called Angel's Rest. It's a cliff face about fifteen hundred feet above the Columbia River. "You can talk if you want to, but you don't have to," she said. "Then I want you to open the box and let my ashes spread in the wind. I'll simply float away into the Universe."

I didn't really understand, but she'd been right about the wind. A few days after she died, I carried a box, small but heavy, in my backpack. In the lead, I picked my way over boulders. Loren walked behind with Uncle Teddy; Dad followed. As we rose up the cliff face I leaned in, keeping my weight away from the edge. Cool air lashed and tore at our clothes and some gusts felt like they'd blow us over. The last one hundred feet took us up a steep rise onto a small plateau. In the distance the white caps of Mt. Rainer, Mt. Adams, Mt. St. Helens and Mt. Hood surrounded our tiny gathering, like guards honoring Mom. At their feet, the aqua-blue Columbia River snaked between gold fields and green forests, the perfect setting for a naturalist.

At the top, a crow landed nearby, squawked three times, and hopped toward us. Dad kicked at the crow and started to step forward. I quickly motioned Loren over, put my hand on his and together we unzipped the pack. The box was dark wood with a small gold clasp on the front. Holding Loren's hands, we lifted the urn onto a rock near the center. Uncle Teddy cleared his throat, I put my arm around Loren and we stood facing the cliff edge.

Wind whipped our hair and tiny grains of sand blasted our cheeks. Loren turned into me. Uncle Teddy read a few words from a piece of paper, about how beautiful Mom was and how much he loved her. Then he asked if we wanted to speak. That's when the gusher started.

I wiped tears and grime from my cheeks, "Mom, I love you."

"Me too," Loren added. The locket rested in my hand. I caressed it with my thumb. "I know your ash will rest on me forever." I gave Loren a squeeze. "Do you want to say anything else? Goodbye?" He shook his head and pushed his face into my ribs.

From behind, Dad coughed and stepped forward to touch the box. I wanted to kick him. He mumbled something and stepped back, wiping his face.

I separated from Loren, looked into his eyes, "Do you want to help?" He nodded. I opened the urn and removed a plastic bag filled with gray powder. Together we lifted the bag and I spread the top open. A stream flowed out, a ribbon wrapping itself around us, over the cliff toward the forest, river, and mountains, winding her way home. I reached out and touched my finger in the ash, opened my locket and smeared a gray streak across the picture, "Goodbye Mom." I was totally wrong, by the way. It wasn't sick at all. It was beautiful.

Lost in memories, I almost forget about Loren in the small cove below me. My back jerks straight when a huge wave crashes over his legs. I think he's squatting, but Loren is standing and water has sloshed above his waist. I slide into the cove to grab him. Rotting seaweed and foam reach up to his chest. The wave recedes and we hear a sound, a grunting bark.

Oblivious to the sea-water, Loren hops into a Ninja pose, "What is that?"

"I don't know," I say. We hear another bark. "A dog?"

"Come on," Loren yells and he leaps toward the sound.

"Loren, wait!" I grab both our packs and run after him.

Chapter Nineteen

L oren disappears around a rocky point. I leap forward and splash through swirling waves. Loren stands frozen on the other side. About ten feet from us is a seal, the size of a large dog, its body resting on one rock and its neck extended across another. It barks and lifts its head. We stand still for several minutes, my feet sinking deeper in the sand as water rushes around us. A rank smell surrounds us, like something old, dead. I look into her eyes, and feel her grief. A wave of sickness forms in my stomach. Something runs from her nose. I want, need, to touch her, comfort her. "Stay put," I say to Loren and creep forward. Loren follows. "Stay there," I whisper.

"No. I want to come," he says.

"Loren, stay!"

"I'm not your dog."

"Loren," I yell, "stay back!"

Loren winces, but holds his ground. Even though I am only a few feet from the seal, it doesn't react at all. I slosh closer; it still doesn't run. Finally, with Loren close behind, I step within a foot. The seal slowly rolls over, lifts one flipper and flops into the water, splashing both of us.

"Wow," Loren says, "did you see that? We almost touched him."

"Yeah. That didn't seem right."

"What?" Loren asks.

"The seal. She felt sick or something, and why didn't she run?"

"Maybe he liked us," Loren says.

I turn on him. "Why didn't you do what I asked?"

"You're not my boss."

I glare. Over his shoulder I spot a fishing boat off the island. Three people struggle with what looks like one or two seals or sea lions in their net. One guy holds a long stick and pokes into the net, maybe trying to get the seal out. I guess Uncle Teddy was right, fisherman do try to protect animals. It's hard to see, but near the front is a name, Anna ... something.

I turn my attention back to Loren, "Yes I am. Uncle Teddy asked me to watch out for you. I can't do that if you don't listen." As Loren rants about my stupid orders, a wave tumbles around my waist and knocks Loren down. He sputters and coughs. I pull him up next to me. "Run for the rocks," I say.

This time, Loren doesn't argue. Holding hands, we slog through the water. At the boulders above the cove, I push Loren up. Another wave hits my back and splashes over my shoulders. Scrambling up behind him, I turn and can't believe what I'm seeing. The tide is in and completely fills the cove where he was playing. Waves wash up to our feet. Now, our only way out is up.

"C'mon," I yell, "follow me."

So far Loren's skate-shoes haven't been a problem, but as we clamber up the rocky hill his wet shoes slip and slide with every step. I pull on one arm to keep him from falling. The jerk complains with every step and I clinch my jaw so as not to let him see my anger and fear. At the top I look for the crossing back to the main island, then I really get scared--it isn't there.

The beach we crossed that morning is now a river of churning waves and currents. There is no way we can cross back.

"I want to go home," Loren says, hiccupping sobs.

"I know, me too," I say. I sit next to him to think. My throat tightens. No! Not now! I think as I fight back tears. I have to concentrate. What had I learned at camp about being lost in the woods? Call immediately if possible, keep calm, stay in one place, find shelter, and signal for help.

"We can do this," I say, as much to myself as to Loren. My watch reads four-thirty-three. How has it gotten so late? It is a couple of hours before sunset. It's still warm, but the air cools quickly in the afternoon. I pull out my phone, push ON--nothing. I slap it hard against my thigh, and watch for even a flicker--still nothing.

"Darn, darn, darn. It's dead. I am so stupid." Loren watches with increasingly loud sobs.

"Okay," I say, with as much enthusiasm as I can muster, "we have to take care of ourselves until we can cross the river. This'll be fun. Let's try and build a shelter."

Loren looks at me, his lower lip vibrating like a guitar string. "I want to go home," he says.

"I know, but right now we have to find a good place where we can see the big island and watch for the tide go out. Maybe we'll see someone. This is the perfect opportunity to look for pirates."

Loren doesn't look convinced, but he follows me as my fingers scratch up the rocky slope to a grassy flat about forty feet above the waves. I can see the high-water line, a strip of greenish-white powder on the rocks about ten feet below us.

"This is good," I say. Then I remember Loren coming home from camp one year with a goofy award for Best Wood Gatherer.

"Let's see if we can find some wood to start a fire," I add. "Didn't you get the Junior Chipmunk Fire-Gatherer-Builder Award or something at camp?"

Loren mumbles something that sounds negative.

"Show me what we need to make a fire," I say.

I guess he likes the idea of showing me what to do, because he throws his pack against a tree, his bear splayed against the bark, and walks around in circles with his head bent forward. It isn't long before he's picked up an arm full of branches and twigs and holds them up, telling me which ones are best. I hold up twigs "Are these big enough?" I ask.

"Bigger," he yells with authority, as he gathers another arm full of twigs.

"You're doing great Loren," I say, my stomach empty and my throat tight. Somebody must be missing us by now. Somebody will be looking for us.

Chapter Twenty

Liz is busy all day. A large number of boats need fuel and supplies, and she has a shipment of goods from Seattle to be inventoried and stored. As she hefts a box of canned corn she glances at her watch and is surprised to see it is past four thirty and she hasn't heard from Sammy. Grunting the box to the top of a stack, she wipes her hands and blows a short puff that lifts her bangs. She taps Sammy's number on her cell phone--No answer.

"Call me as soon as you get this message," she says and sets her phone on the stack of stewed tomato cans. Each time she passes the phone she checks the time and forces herself to wait ten minutes before she calls again. Still no answer. "They're fine," she tells herself and continues to carry boxes. By five the knot in her stomach becomes too large to ignore.

If Sammy is near Loon Song Harbor, she reasons, she will have cell phone service. Even if she doesn't, she asked Sammy to be back around four and it is now past five.

"What the heck," she says as she throws her apron over the stacks of boxes and heads toward the trail. She walks with the hope of seeing their bobbing heads at any moment, but at the grassy field there is still nothing but tall stalks waving in the breeze. She knows her choices are simple: track them along the trail, which might take hours, or get help. She turns and runs hard back toward the store.

When she arrives, slightly before six, she has already developed a plan. Liz is almost out of her mind with worry, but fortunately she is a calm woman who knows how to deal with difficult situations. Out of her mind means she goes into action. There is one complicating factor, this is Ted's niece and nephew and he left her in charge. Liz doesn't want anything to go wrong.

Step One: She calls the police station, and the local deputy says he'll come to the store to talk with her. "Thanks for nothing," Liz mumbles.

Step Two: Liz knows the middle school secretary, Hanna Plinkton. She has a network of parents that have volunteered to search for any missing child. Fortunately, Hanna is home; "Give me the details," Hanna says, and while they are on the phone, she puts out a blast email and text asking for volunteers to meet at the Loon Song Harbor store at six-forty. Before they hang up, seventeen people have responded.

Step Three: Liz phones the other docks on the island to notify them of the missing children and asks if anyone can patrol the shoreline that evening. Some have already seen Hanna's email, but six additional boats volunteer to join the search.

Step Four: Get Ahanu, her nephew, and Olie to man the store. Ahanu is gone as usual, but Olie says he'll remain on the porch in case Sammy and Loren return.

The deputy arrives while Liz is printing a handout for the searchers. When he hears what Liz has already accomplished, he shuffles his feet and sputters something like, "I'll be a horse's ar..." Then thinking himself funny, pipes up, "Little lady, I need a good assistant, if you're ever available."

"Little lady?" Liz responds, raising an eyebrow. "No thanks Deputy, I've got my own posse."

"I'll keep my eyes open," he says lamely, as she heads toward the crowd of volunteers forming at the dock.

Fourteen volunteers on foot, six boats, one deputy driving around aimlessly, and me in my boat, Liz counts. Not bad in thirty-five minutes. "I hope it's good enough," she says to herself, as she approaches the crowd. The evening is getting colder, but it is clear and crisp. "I don't have pictures," she begins, a mistake she vows never to make again, "but I've printed a description of both Loren and Sammy for each of you. Hanna will hand them out. Take two if you need them." Hands reached out and people begin reading.

"These kids don't know the island, or our water. They left here about ten this morning, headed up the road and through the grass field, and should have been back by four. My guess is they're within a few miles of the Harbor, but you never know. Loren has on a camouflage t-shirt and a yellow backpack. Sammy has a red backpack and light colored shorts and top. It's good weather, but they aren't prepared to spend the night outside, so let's find them."

The deputy steps forward interrupting Liz. He clears his throat, pushes out his chest, tucks his thumbs in his belt, and pulls up his pants. Liz notices he looks at Hanna as he rests his hand on his gun holster, then he adds, "They'll be scared, probably will need food and water when they're found. Best carry some with you."

Shocked that he actually made sense, Liz adds, "Good idea. The boats will stay in contact by ship-to-shore or CB radio, everyone else please confirm your cell phone numbers with Hanna."

"What if we don't have either?" a voice from the back calls. Shocking her again, the deputy brings out five walkie-talkies.

"Here," he says, holding them out, "I thought these might come in handy."

Liz points to Hanna and asks the smiling deputy to give them to her. By seven that evening a land and sea search has begun for Sammy and Loren.

Step Five: On her skiff, Liz pulls out her cell phone. She stares at the thumbnail picture of Ted, takes a deep breath, and touches his nose. It dials. Fog rises up around her as the air begins to cool and twilight approaches. The phone starts ringing--A rich glow has formed on the horizon and she imagines the route she will take on the search. Ringing--A little more than an hour and moisture will collect in the air and it will get much colder. Ringing--By nine it will be dark, little hope of finding them. Ringing--Click, "This is Ted Crenshaw of the San Juan Express. Please leave your number and a message. I'll call back, as soon as possible."

Somewhat relieved he didn't answer, Liz leaves a short explanation, asks him to call her, and promises to keep him posted. She closes her eyes for a moment, takes a deep breath, starts the boat engine and motors out of the harbor, turning north to begin her search.

Chapter Twenty-One

It is getting colder and darker and both Loren and I are scared silly. Our side of the small island is already in shade. We have gathered a small pile of wood for a fire, but so far haven't figured out how to start it. I try rubbing two sticks together, but the only thing that happens is the bark curls off. Loren pulls out his spy kit and produces a magnifying glass and his flashlight. He holds them up, worming his eyebrows, kneels and focuses the light through the glass on a pile of pine needles. We both watch as absolutely, totally, nothing happens. Finally, I stand up and with a loud grunt threw a stick, "I hate this. All I wanted was a stupid walk and look at us. I hate this." Loren clutches his spy gear and starts to cry again.

"I'm sorry, Loren, it's not your fault." I say, sitting next to him. "We'll be all right."

"How?" he asks. "I want Mommy and Daddy. I want to go home."

"Me too," I say, reaching my arm around his shoulders. "I wish we had some matches or something to get this darn fire going."

Loren sniffles a few times, then stops crying. "What kind of matches?"

I look at him, "Any kind of matches, or anything to light a fire. How about that spy kit of yours, got any matches?" I say jokingly.

He looks at me, his eyes getting bigger. "I don't know, maybe."

Now my eyes are getting bigger, totally bigger. "What do you mean, maybe?"

"Well, I forgot until just now, but Dad threw a box away on one of our fishing trips and I put it in my spy kit. I think it might say something about matches."

I choke out a single coughing laugh. "You're kidding. Where is it?"

He scrambles to his backpack and pulls out his spy-kit, formerly known as a Spiderman lunch pail. I squat next to him, feeling like I have to go to the bathroom, but not really. He slowly, way too slowly, sets his flashlight and magnifying glass on his pack, pulls out his pencils, toy soldiers--one at a time, some string, and a box of waterproof matches. He holds it up. "Here. See."

I grab the box and shake--it rattles. My eyes lock on Loren as my finger pushes against the end of the box. It resists. I push harder and it slides out of its container. Three tiny, broken, unlit matches roll around inside. "Oh my gosh, you have matches."

Loren immediately jumps up in celebration, hits my hand and knocks the box of matches across our little camp site. "No, no," I leap up, trying to track the flight of the tiny sticks.

"Flashlight," Loren yells.

We crawl around the campsite surrounded by a blanket of darkness except for Loren's tiny spotlight. I have to admit, I never really appreciated the dork's attention to detail until the moment he shined his light on the first match. It takes us over fifteen minutes, but we eventually find the box and the other two matches.

Now it is seriously getting dark. We huddle around a small pile of leaves, pine needles and twigs Loren has stacked over a few pieces of paper towel. "Are you ready?" I ask. He wraps his hands around the pile and nods. I strike the first match on the side of the box. It sparks, but doesn't light. I strike it again and again it sparks, but doesn't light. On the third try, it does nothing. All the spark-lighter stuff is worn off. I strike it three more times, but the first match is worn to smithereens.

Loren reaches for another match. "Let me do it," he says.

"No, I'll do it." I pull the box away. He glares at me. I cup my hands around the box and strike the second match. It sparks and flares up. Quickly I hold the match under the paper and it lights. Bending down, I put my face near the flame and gently blew. Loren does the same and our combined blowing is too much. It goes out. We lock eyes. Loren makes a sad face. I nervously laugh. "Okay, here we go," I say. "No blowing until we have flames. Okay?" He nods.

I lean forward, getting ready to strike the match. A wind comes up and causes the dry pine needles to swirl up around the paper. "Wait!" Loren says. When the wind dies down, I wrap my hands around the match box. Loren leans forward and wraps his hands around the tiny teepee of kindling he built.

"Don't blow," I say. We both hold our breath, and I strike the last match--Nothing. I strike it again--Nothing.

"Crap," I whisper.

"Watch your language," Loren mumbles with a snicker.

I roll the match over until I find a thin strip of spark-lighter stuff. I position it, and strike it one last time--It flares. I hold it to the paper, and it lights. This time we don't blow on it, or even breathe near it. We just watch as the flame creeps out through the needles, then to the twigs, then the larger pieces of wood. Loren, showing why he won that Junior Chipmunk Fire Builder Award, gently places more twigs on the flames. Within minutes we have a small campfire burning. Now all we can do is keep it going ... and wait.

Chapter Twenty-Two

L iz and her team scour most of Loon Song Harbor and expand their search north. She knows the tides are strong. If Sammy and Loren have gotten onto one of the many small islands just off shore, they will be trapped, or worse, drowned. She calls Ted two more times, but receives no answer and leaves no more messages. No news is good news, she reasons. Patrolling the complete perimeter of Loon Song Harbor, she expands her search to the outer shoreline. As darkness sets in, a fog forms on the water's surface.

Within an hour she has searched two miles north of the Harbor. Other boats are searching farther north. Frustrated and discouraged she decides to try one more time by going between the smaller islands and Orcas Island. It is dark and there are strong currents that can catch a small boat like hers and throw it into the rocks; she has to be careful. The thumbnail picture of Ted watches from her phone. "I won't stop searching," she promises, as she guides her small skiff into the channel's strongest currents.

Her bow light cuts through the fog to illuminate the shoreline on her left and a small island on her right. "Come on," she repeats, hoping for good luck. Waves and currents push her dangerously close to the rocks. Ahead she notices a flicker of light high up above the waterline. Fighting her boat to the middle, Liz flashes her bow light on the black mound beside her. She sees nothing but seagull poop and decides the flicker of light must have been a reflection of her own light. "They wouldn't climb on poop anyway," she mutters to herself, sighs, pushes the throttle and speeds out of the channel away from the small island.

Flames from our fire light Loren's face and dance in his teary eyes as he slumps forward. Being Big Sister and being responsible for him scares me now. Our little camp scares me too. Outside of the firelight it is pitch black and I hear waves slapping against the rocks below us. Every once in a while, something scratches around in the brush. We jump and search, but can't see anything. The good news? Our fire continues to burn.

We feed it twigs and branches to keep the fire happy. Dry moss hangs like fingers from fir trees around us and the fire throws shadows that move with the breeze. It feels like witches dancing around us. Each time they move, Loren leans into me. It is so weird, the Punkster depending on me for safety when I am the one who got us into this mess. The truth is, without his flashlight and matches, we'd be in real trouble. I guess we are leaning on each other.

I know he would rather have Mom or Dad, but he has me and he seems to be okay with that. This is what our life will look like, I think, and a part of me feels almost okay with that--a very small part of me. Every so often I pull away from Loren and walk around our little camp to gather more wood. When an owl hoots I almost leap out of my skin. On my last walk I find a branch with dried pine needles. My fingers stick to the bark, pitch everywhere. I remember camp trips when I was little and hold up the branch. "Want to see something really cool?" I ask. He nods. "Lean back, it's going to burn really big." I toss the branch on the fire. As soon as I throw it, the branch explodes into crazy big flames. It is just how Dad did it, when I was little.

Liz wrestles the strong currents to maneuver her skiff away from the small island. With her search light, she scans the shore. The memory of the small flash of light gnaws at her. Every so often she glances over her shoulder. On one glance, from the corner of her eye, she sees a flash that sends sparks flaring high above the rocks. This time she knows it isn't a reflection of her light. It has to be a signal. She pulls on the steering wheel, turns the skiff and motors back toward the channel. On her approach, she reaches down, picks up a small boat horn and squeezes off three short blasts. She shines her light up the hill in the direction of the flash.

The huge fireball from our campfire balloons into the air. Loren rolls over backward. I step back and reach forward to grab his backpack. "You okay?" I say. A horn honks from below and we freeze. Loren jumps toward the ledge. I grab his shirt, and start waving frantically. A light flashes across us out of the fog and I'm blinded for a moment. We both start yelling our heads off. Five minutes later Liz scrambles up the hill to our camp. Loren tears from my grip and wraps his arms around her. I stay by the fire, relieved and ashamed. All I can say is, "I'm sorry."

With Loren hanging onto her, Liz walks over and gives me a hug. Tears streak down her dust covered cheeks. She doesn't say anything, just holds us. "I'm sorry," I repeat about fifteen thousand times.

Finally, Liz puts her hands around my face, palms rough with dirt, and looks me straight in the eyes, "I can't tell you this is okay, Sammy, but I can tell you that nothing matters except you are safe. Do you understand? Your safety is more important than who is to blame. I'm just happy to see you and Loren."

I let her hold me. The giant Alice in Wonderland, bending down to cry on her shoulder. It feels so good. Liz notices Loren shivering, "Get your things and let's get out of here," she says.

Making extra sure we pick up all of Loren's spy-kit gear. I look at the fire, as the pitch covered branch burns down to a small flame, and say a silent, thank you. Loren uses a stick to spread the coals and we kick dirt on the fire to make sure it is out. In front, Liz lights the way, Loren close behind with his trusty flashlight, and me holding Loren's shirt-tail, we pick and slip our way down the poopy slope to her boat.

The bow of the skiff is partially up on rocks, with the tail waving in the current. Liz holds the shore-anchor rope while

Loren and I climb in. "Sammy, take the anchor," she yells as she pushes the boat and hops on board. The engine cranks to life and she guides us into safer waters. Using the CB radio and her cell, Liz contacts everyone telling them we are safe. "Thank you for your efforts," she repeats to each person. I am horrified when she promises a big gathering at the store in a few weeks, so everyone can meet us. Her last call is to Uncle Teddy.

"They're fine, just a little cold and hungry. What?" She laughs, "No, that won't be necessary. No, I'm sure they'll be okay. I'm spending the night. Yes, me too. We'll talk in the morning."

Looking up, I notice her smile. "What'd he say?"

"He isn't mad," she says, "just relieved like me."

"What?" I ask, inspecting her grin.

"He wanted to know if I had a dog collar."

"What? You're kidding."

Seeing Loren's face, she pulls him closer, "Yes, I'm kidding. He asked if you needed to go to the hospital. I assured him you were okay. Right?"

"Right," I say, as I watch the small island disappear behind us. The night air is cold and damp. The fog lifts, and in the distance I see lights flickering from several boats that have probably been looking for us. Loren's head is in my lap; he's fallen asleep. I gently stroke his hair as I adjust a blanket around us. My shoulders shake. At the dock I see the store lights and a small trail of smoke rising from the rocker. I half carry, half guide Loren as we walk silently to the house, feet scraping dew covered grass.

"Hungry?" Liz asks as we enter. Neither Loren nor I respond. It is all I can do to reach my room. The gritty heels of my hands push into my eyes as I rub, trying to clear the single thought stuck in my head-- Uncle Teddy hates me. All he asked was for us to stay out of trouble and off the islands. Who's the dork now?

Chapter Twenty-Three

A ngie's engine roars as it powers up on the dock.

"Uncle Teddy's here," Loren yells. His footsteps padding past my door.

"Okay," I say, but I can't move. It's early Saturday afternoon. I've been in my room all day thinking about what happened and what to say. How can I explain why we were on the island and how I let us get stuck out there? I woke with an upset stomach. Liz offered me breakfast, but I couldn't. All I could do was curl up in a ball and wait. My mind is going a mile a minute, thinking of all the things he might say: Get out of my house; give me that phone young lady; your grounded for the rest of your life; or worst of all, I hate you. I'd rather be punished for a year than be hated by Uncle Teddy. I'll find out soon enough. Voices grow louder as they enter the hall and tromp upstairs. I hear Uncle Teddy laugh as they walk into the kitchen and then muffled voices. They're probably planning my banishment from the house. He doesn't even want to talk to me. He's angrier than I thought. My mind keeps spinning, until there's a knock on the door. I jerk to attention.

"It's Uncle Teddy, may I come in?"

I sit up, holding a pillow over my stomach. "Sure, I'm ready."

Uncle Teddy sticks his head around the door. "Hi," then he slowly steps into the room. "How you feeling?"

"Kind of sick," I say.

"I'll bet," he says smiling. "Big night huh?" He walks over to my bed and sits down.

"I'm really sorry," we both say, at exactly the same time. We look at each other, then Uncle Teddy laughs. I try hard not to, but I am so relieved I begin to cry. He doesn't say anything, just reaches his arm out and holds me, while I push my face into his shirt. Oh My Gosh, I keep thinking, I am so pa-thet-ic .

"I'm sorry I didn't give you better instructions," he says as he pats my back, "I should have taught you about the tides and been clear about the dangers."

I sob, "I'm so sorry I wandered off with Loren, got stuck on the island, and didn't take better care of him."

He keeps responding between my blubbering and sobbing until we run out of words. He holds me for a while longer, then puts his hand under my chin, just like my mom used to do, and looks into my eyes.

"Listen," he says, "we all have responsibilities, and one of mine was to make sure you had all the information you needed to make good decisions. I know better, I'm a pilot. But ..."

Here it comes, I think.

"But I didn't do what I should have done."

I sit stunned. He's apologizing for my mistake.

"I know that information is the most important thing you need to take care of yourself," he continues. "I should have given you that knowledge before I left. I just didn't think about it, but I will in the future."

He isn't angry at all. Seriously, nobody'd ever said anything like that to me before. When you do something wrong, most adults just try to make you feel bad, but Uncle Teddy didn't. My dad would have totally killed me. Uncle Teddy just holds me and apologizes. He continues, saying he could have done more and I begin to feel irritated, like he's trying to make me feel better by taking all the blame. That's stupid, I did something wrong and I should be responsible for it. Now it is really getting twisted; I'm angry with him for not being angry with me. He has a lot to learn about parenting. This new arrangement's going to take some getting used to.

Finally, as he yammers on, I raise my hand. He looks a little surprised then laughs, "Okay, I'll stop talking."

"Uncle Teddy, thank you," I say, "but I should have known better. You warned me and I forgot. I am mostly to blame for this, I understand that." I watch his eyes search my face, then he says something that makes so much sense, I almost agree that it is his fault.

"Okay," he says, "fair enough. You are partly to blame. Can we agree on one thing though, you still have a few things to learn?"

Duh, I think, as I nod my head.

"So, my point is," he says, "that while you think you should have known better than to get caught on an island, you couldn't have known better. I learned a very important lesson in flight school, that we all have certain capabilities based on what we know, and like it or not, we live within those capabilities. As you grow, you learn more, your capabilities increase, and so do your responsibilities. Knowing about tides, currents, and about the Islands just wasn't in your knowledge-base, until yesterday. I warned you, but I didn't educate you. I won't make that mistake again. You're only fourteen Sammy, and as you grow you'll be learning about a lot of things. As you do, trust me, I'll hold you responsible."

"Actually, I'm fifteen," I say."

"Fifteen?" He looks surprised. "In that case, you ARE in big trouble." Then he laughs. "Seriously, the way you handled yourself impressed me. Liz told me you found high ground and built a fire where she could see it. That's pretty smart."

"That was Loren."

"Yes, he told me all about the matches. But, it was you who took care of him, and you who made sure you were both safe. That's a big deal Sammy; you're a strong, smart, young woman. You've got a lot of your mom and dad in you."

"Mom actually," I say. "Dad doesn't do much."

"Really?" Uncle Teddy says as he studies me for a minute. "Listen Sammy, your dad's been though a lot. Maybe you should give him a break?"

"Maybe he should give me a break?" I say without thinking.

Boy, immediately everything changes. Uncle Teddy stiffens, gives me a hard look, and I feel myself shrink. I've never seen him look like this.

After a minute he takes a deep breath, "Do you know how I met your dad?"

"No," I say, studying my feet.

"It was when I was a freshman in high-school. Your mom was a junior; your dad was a senior. He asked her to the homecoming dance. He was the captain of the football team, a darn good baseball player, even did some gymnastics. When he came to the house to pick her up, she introduced him to me. I'd seen him at school and I idolized him. Your mom and dad kept dating and eventually both attended the University of Oregon. That's when they got married. In his senior year, he joined the Air Force, and immediately after college, he left for pilot training. He wanted to be a jet jockey, but his eyesight was too poor, so he ended up flying helicopters. Two years later he ended up in Iraq, fighting a war."

I've never heard any of this before. Iraq? war?

"I wanted to drop out of college to join too, just like your dad," Uncle Teddy continued, "but he talked me out of it. He persuaded me to finish college before I joined. Eventually, I became a pilot in the Navy, while your dad was seeing a lot of action in Iraq. He won't talk about it, but he was awarded the Silver Star for valor under fire. He's a brave man, Sammy, a hero, but he came back with problems that he is still trying to figure out. He may not be able to show it, but I know he loves you and he'd do anything for you. You have to know that."

Uncle Teddy walks to my bedroom door and looks back, "He's a hero," he says and walks out. I'm left with a million thoughts slamming around in my head: Silver Star, helicopters. I want to understand, but it doesn't make sense. If he's such a hero, why isn't he here with me? Then I feel heat rise in my face. "He gets no stars for being my dad," I yell across the room. "He's mean. How could you idolize him?" I pull the pillow off my stomach, up to my face, and scream into it, "I HATE YOU, I HATE YOU."

My pillow soaked with snot and slobber, the down comforter wet with sweat, I roll off the bed, exhausted and hungry. I haven't eaten all day, and hunger overcomes my resistance to going upstairs. I look in the mirror; my hair is a tangled mess, face blotchy, eyes blood-shot dots, and snot runs from my nose like that seal I saw on the island. I remind myself what Uncle Teddy said: Strong, smart, young woman. Straightening my back, I stand up full height. Smart young woman. Then, looking into my own eyes, I lean forward until the face in the mirror fills my vision. "Who's there? Come out, come out, whoever you are."

Chapter Twenty-Four

The smell of spaghetti and garlic bread wafts down the stairs. It's like the most incredible food I've ever smelled. I follow my nose into the kitchen. Uncle Teddy and Liz are looking at something on the counter. Loren throws noodles up and tries to catch them in his mouth. There is a small pile of his misses on the table.

"Welcome," Liz says. "Feeling better?"

"Yeah," I say, brushing my hair behind my ear. "Is that spaghetti for dinner?"

"That okay?"

"Oh my gosh yes, I'm starved." Looking out the window, I notice the sail boat masts. "Is your boat okay?" I ask Liz, remembering the rocks.

"Yes, it's fine. It's a tough skiff."

I pause for a moment, as the seal on the rock enters my thoughts. I'd forgotten all about it, snot nosed, just like me.

"I forgot to tell you something about yesterday," I say. Liz and Uncle Teddy both look up, foreheads wrinkled, prepared for the worst.

I know my talking about being able to feel animal's pain is not a good idea. I've only mentioned it to a few people, and the result is never good. Mom was the most understanding. Others usually laughed or said it was just my own feelings, so I eventually stopped talking about it. It's hard because I don't understand it either, so I really can't explain it to anyone. To be honest, I'm not sure it isn't just my own feelings. I mean, when you see a sick seal that looks green, wouldn't you get sick too? Anyway, I know this is important, so I jump right in with my story.

"I know this sounds, well, kind of weird, but while we were exploring the island we saw a seal on some rocks. It didn't look so good, like it was sick or something."

"Animals get sick up here all the time," Uncle Teddy says. "We live pretty close to wildlife and see things you don't normally see in the city. It's just the cycle of life."

"Yeah, I get that," I persist, "but this seal had something funny about it. It wasn't just old or anything, it looked kind of green." Then I pause, take a breath, and say it, "I could feel its pain."

"I didn't feel anything," Loren jumps in.

"Shut up, dork," I respond. "You wouldn't, but I did. It felt weird, there was definitely something wrong."

"Okay," Liz steps in, to prevent an argument. "It's hard to see sick animals. I'll ask around, see if anyone knows anything; but really Sammy, it's probably just the normal way of things."

I look at Liz. She's trying to be nice, but she doesn't understand. At least she isn't telling me I'm imagining things. "Thanks," I say, taking my plate from her. As she turns away, a cold shiver creeps up my spine, like what I've experienced most of my life: isolated and alone. Not the kind of alone I feel when I think about Mom. That kind of alone is sharp and piercing. This kind of alone is like ice held on your skin, a dull pain that eventually turns numb. I've learned that talking about my special sensitivity, as Mom called it, just makes me feel bad, so I normally just stay quiet. Now, trying to explain what I saw and felt to Uncle Teddy and Liz, I remember that isolation, and once again I shut my mouth. This, piled on top of talking about my dad, just pisses me off even more.

What's so normal about a green seal? Besides, what do they know about what animals feel? I don't even understand it, but I know I feel it. So I won't talk about it anymore. They're all too stupid to understand, so what's the point?

On my plate, noodles spin around my fork to the rhythm of my anger, when Liz interrupts, "Sammy, why don't you come over to the store later?"

I look up with a hunk of meatball on my fork, my rage slipping away with each drop of sauce. I shove it in my mouth, hoping I can hold on to the heat burning inside me.

"Why?"

"I have something I want to talk with you about. A surprise."

"Okay," I say, watching curiosity replace my anger. "Maybe tomorrow."

Chapter Twenty-Five

Since I arrived at Loon Song Harbor, and Uncle Teddy's house, I've felt slammed between anger and loneliness. Last night, I tried to hold on to my anger, like it could protect me. But this morning, I feel the Island taking over. My curiosity about what Liz wants to talk about gets the better of me, and I head to the store. My sandals slip through dew covered grass, cool on my soles, while a warm sun ripens my toes. On my left is a spray of wild flowers with bees busy in their buzzing. Above, a swarm of small birds chirp their morning greeting. My tongue tastes salt at the corner of my lips and I feel my heels lift with each step. As much as I try not to, I can't help it--I feel happy--I like being in the islands.

I am so caught up in my surroundings, I forget all about the old man in the rocker. He's a real weird guy, something about his eyes makes me feel like he's looking at me, even from across the parking lot. As I approach, I hunch over slightly hoping to sneak past, like he won't see me if I am real quiet and a little shorter. It doesn't work. The step groans as I approach.

"What's your name?" A voice rolls across the porch.

I almost jump out of my skin. I realize he isn't as big as I remember, but somehow he feels bigger than he is. He wears that same wrinkled black cowboy hat with a silver studded hat band and a feather in it. Pushing it back on his head, revealing his wrinkled face, he looks at me. He has a denim shirt under a black leather vest with patterns embroidered on each side. A string of beads and small feathers hang from the center of each pattern. I look at his feet, expecting to see cowboy boots, but he has flip-flops on, just like almost everyone else at the harbor.

I am so startled when he speaks that the only thing I can think of is, "I don't talk to strangers." Brilliant!

"Just did," he says laughing with a gurgling sound that is like loose marbles bouncing in his throat. Then, between coughs that shake the entire porch, he says, "Come back when you think it's okay to talk."

I watch for a second then push through the screen door as he continues half coughing and half laughing. Gross.

The door slaps behind me, I see Liz behind the counter and smell the incense and dry wood aroma of the store.

"Who is that guy?" I ask, as I make a face that clearly says, I don't like him.

Liz smiles, "That's my dad."

Her Dad? A total foot in mouth moment.

"Oh my gosh, I'm so sorry. I didn't know."

"That's okay," she says. "He's a little tough to take sometimes, but he's okay once you get to know him."

"Wow," I say, "you look so young. He's your dad?"

"Not so young, I'm in my 30s. Besides, I'm adopted."

My cheeks burn again as my face turns bright red. Hoping she won't notice, I pick up a pickle jar and pretended to read it. Liz laughs again. "It's okay Sammy. I'm not sensitive about being adopted. Besides, I like that you speak your mind. I wish more people would. It would make the world a simpler place."

I don't answer. I'm not saying another word. One foot in mouth is enough.

"You like those pickles?" she asks.

I laugh, and put them back on the shelf. "Not really."

"Tell you what," Liz says with a twinkle in her eye, "if you like putting things on the shelf, I can offer you a job."

"A job? What do you mean?"

"I mean, that's what I wanted to talk with you about. If you want to help me in the store for a few hours a week, I could use the help stocking the shelves." She points to the stack of boxes at the back of the store. "I can pay you. Not much, but enough to keep you in smoothies and yogurt for a while."

"And ice cream?" I ask, raising my eyebrows.

"That's up to you. It's your money ... and your health."

Adults.

"Yeah," I say, "I'd love to be the stock-girl. Sounds like fun. But, I'll have to ask Uncle Teddy?"

"I already asked him," she quickly adds, "and he said it was up to you. So, if you want the job, it's yours."

Wow, I have a job. "When do I start?"

"How about this afternoon?"

Chapter Twenty-Six

Sammy bursts through the screen door and bounds off of the porch, filled with excitement about her new job at the store.

Zach, who is just coming around the side of the store, notices a skinny kid run down the path. "Hi grandpa," he calls, and with two leaps clears the steps and crosses the deck. The screen door squeaks and slaps closed. "Aunt Liz?"

"I'm here Zach, in the back stacking boxes." She wipes her hands on her apron and watches her tall nephew saunter toward her. His size twelve shoes raising small clouds of dust in his wake. Making a mental note to sweep later, she reaches out to hug him, "You look like your mother in that light." Rising on her tiptoes, she says, "You must be over six foot now." He laughs as he steps around her and loads a box on the handcart.

"You make that look so easy," she comments. Looking down and wiping her hands again. "Zach, I need to talk with you about something."

Zach's breath freezes in his throat. "Okay."

"It's about what you're doing," she continues.

He adjusts his belt, wondering how she knows. He hasn't seen Freddy for several days, since they did the deal with the fisherman. How could she know?

"I noticed you've been hanging around the house the last few days."

Zach lets out a deep sigh. "Yeah," he quickly replies.

"I was wondering if you might want to put some more hours in at the store? I can't believe how much quicker everything happens when you're here. It's our family business and it's not fair to ask Olie to work."

"Of course, you're right," he says. "It's just that, ah, I've got some things I'm doing right now and I'm busy. I'll try and be here more often, I promise. Okay?"

Liz looks for a long silent minute, while Zach shifts from one leg to the other. "You mean you're busy doing things with Freddy Miller?" she says.

A cloud passes and the room darkens. "Yeah, so?" he replies, louder than he intends.

Liz takes a long breath, "Look, I know Freddy's been your friend for a long time, but he's getting into more trouble all the time. Murielle, over at Cascade Harbor, said she thought she saw him try to break into a car, and I've heard he might be doing drugs, even dealing. He's almost two years older than you, Zach, and he's trouble. Be careful. Okay?"

Zach struggles to control his anger as tension rises in his chest. He knows that Aunt Liz loves him, but he hates being told what to do, and no matter what, Freddy is still his friend, his only friend.

"Okay, I get it," he says with finality. He grabs one more box and drops it on the cart. "I'll be back later," he says and pushes past her.

"You might like being around here," she calls as he rushes out. "We have a new helper starting tomorrow."

But Zach is off the porch and gone before she finishes her sentence.

The old man watches his grandson take the porch steps in one long leap and jog away. "Be careful," he says to himself and the crow on the railing.

As Zach half runs, half walks down the path, he repeats what Aunt Liz said. "Pushing drugs. You're not that stupid, are you Freddy?" He quickens his run. "You're not that stupid."

Chapter Twenty-Seven

Later that morning, as I wolf down a snack of Wheat Puffs cereal, Uncle Teddy walks into the kitchen wearing his San Juan Express cap, sun glasses, and leather flight jacket. He really does look cool. Out of the blue, he announces he'll be leaving again for another delivery to Alaska. Oh my gosh, two days ago I'm lost on an island and today he says he's going on another delivery. My reaction is totally like dropping my spoon, trying to say OMG while swallowing, starting to choke, and milk running out my nose. How does this happen to me?

Uncle Teddy laughs. "You okay?"

"Yeah, I'm fine." I say. I know he means the milk, but I wish people would stop asking me if I'm okay. It makes me feel less okay.

"Don't you remember what happened the last time you left?" I ask.

Still laughing, he hands me a napkin, "That was then, this is now. You planning another hike or something? And besides, don't you have a new job?"

"No, I mean yes. I just didn't expect you to leave again so soon, and yes, I got the job."

He leans forward and gives me a big hug. "Congratulations. You're going to like working with Liz," he says. "She's great fun. My job, on the other hand, is flying Angie and making deliveries. I'll be gone a lot. If we can't trust each other, this won't work. So, can we trust each other?"

"Yeah, of course." I blow my nose, as the words soak in--Trust. Mom and Dad had said that to me a hundred times. We have to be able to trust you if we're going to let you do ... whatever. It was always like a test or something. If I passed I got to do something more. If I screwed up I got grounded, and I seemed to be grounded a lot. Now, I'd made the biggest screw-up of my life and Uncle Teddy is simply saying, Trust, and he means it.

"Okay." I add, "Are you leaving now?"

"No, I'm just getting Angie ready, but I'll be leaving in the morning. When Loren comes up, we'll talk over ...," he eyes my cereal snack, "lunch. No more milk though."

"Not nice," I yell, as he walks out.

As if one surprise isn't enough, during lunch he tops it by asking if either of us wants to go with him. I manage to keep my spoon in my mouth this time, but Loren jumps off his stool and is waving his hand like he has the answer to a pop-quiz.

"I do, I do," he keeps yelling. Uncle Teddy takes his hat off and pushes it over Loren's head. "You're on, Champ."

I hesitate, feeling like I have to say yes, then I remember, "My job," I say.

"Are you okay if Liz spends the night again, just so you're not alone?"

"For sure," I say. Actually, the idea of being alone in the house at night is kind of scary, so I like that idea. But being alone during the day is seriously sweet.

Immediately after lunch, Loren and Uncle Teddy head for the dock, while I send grasshoppers jumping on my way to the store. I'm not sure of exactly what I'll be doing, but it feels good heading to my first job. As it turns out, working for Liz is more like being at camp. The first thing she has me do is stack cans of beans on a shelf. She shows me how to set the price on a small pistol-like machine and how to put a price sticker on each can before I put it on the shelf. I'm a little nervous, but after labeling and stacking the first case of cans, it is easy. Just as I am thinking that I have everything under control, Liz comes running around the end of the aisle.

"EEEAAA," she yells, and shoots me right in the butt with a flurry of rubber bands. "The Loon Song Harbor Bandito strikes again," she yells, as she runs past and around the other end of the aisle. Snap! Snap!

I receive two more hits before I know what's happening. Down the aisle in the opposite direction, past the corn and beans, I run so hard my shoes skid around the end-cap of potato chips, and I begin weaving through the store to avoid any more direct hits. There are only four aisles, not many places to hide. Past the frozen food case, I leap toward the front counter and see a second rubber-band gun pre-loaded with six rubber bands. A perfect one-hand grab and the gun is at the ready; I slip behind a shelf near the door. A few seconds later, her blond hair flashes in the sunlight and she comes out to reload.

"The Stock-girl Policia strikes back," I yell, and spring out, snapping off three rubber-bands. She screams. I skip around the suntan lotion and hair products. Amidst shouts and shrieks we shoot, reload and battle ourselves to a frenzy of totally chaotic fun until, circling the islands, Liz raises her gun in the air and calls, "Truce." I've never seen an adult get so wound up about a rubber-band gun. It is totally awesome.

I creep back to the canned vegetables, with one eye over my shoulder, and settle back into pricing the beans. After that, I make sure I know where she is and keep a rubber-band gun loaded and close by. About the time I've almost forgotten the gun, something even crazier happens. A song comes on the radio and Liz goes totally nuts, "I ain't got no money, but got lots of honey," she sings as she does a crazy kind of dance, waving her arms and kicking her legs. She spins so hard her bangs splay straight out and she looks like she'll fly right out the door. I think, what a dork, but Liz grabs my hands and spins me around. It takes a turn or two, but soon my legs swing out and my feet flop around like a rag-doll. I'm yelling and dancing right along with her. On one extra hard spin I tumble into the cap and glove rack, trip, and hit the floor like a bag of jelly-beans. Liz's foot catches my leg and she lands next to me, laughing so hard she can barely breathe.

"Thanks," she chokes between breaths, "I needed that. Life gets kind of heavy sometimes. A good laugh makes it a lot easier."

You have no idea, I thought.

Then she cocks her head and raises an eyebrow, "You okay?"

I can't answer. Something about the dancing and laughing gets to me. I'm feeling ... all kinds of things I can't explain.

"That was quite a scare you had out on the rocks," she continues, "You know everyone is okay about that? But are you?"

I just nod.

"Have you talked to your dad since then?" she asks.

My dad? Where'd that come from? Now when I think of my dad, it includes the words: War, Veteran and Hero. I don't know exactly what that means, but it changes how I think about him. Is it possible to have two thoughts at once? Mine are: Maybe he does deserve a break, and he's an ass. So far, the ass is winning. I shake my head in response.

Liz reaches over and touches my knee. "You want to talk about it?"

I study my knee really hard and shake my head again.

"I'm here if you ever need anything. Okay?"

Tears form and I nod my head.

Sitting in the middle of the store, no one comes in. Beams of sunlight radiate through dust clouds kicked-up by our dance. The music stops and neither of us speak. My head dizzies somewhere between the alone place, laughing in the store, my dad the ass-hero, and my new friend--Liz. Nothing to say, we just sit. The slow rhythmic sound of the rocker creaks through the silence.

Chapter Twenty-Eight

Freddy's head pokes under the dash. "Stupid," he mumbles. "Ol' man Sanderson just a fool. Let this beautiful ride go to waste." He yanks at wires. "The Captain, he smart, pay us three hundred bucks to kill seals." Freddy joins the wires, they spark, and the broken down old Pontiac moans to life. Freddy checks to make sure there are not lights on in the house, hops in the driver's seat, and pulls out of Mr. Sanderson's driveway.

Headlights track a single dotted center line under a branched canopy of coastal pine. Freddy swerves to hit a rabbit who skitters in front of him, but misses. The heavy car, held together by rust, slides sideways around a corner and stops by a cedar shake cabin pushed back from the road. Zach runs low across the garden.

"What the ...?" Zach says, as he hops in. Freddy guns the engine; the door slams shut and Zach's head bangs against the headrest; the tires spit gravel and dust.

"Where'd you get this, man?"

"Borrow, dude. Nasty huh?"

"Rasty-nasty."

"Crazy-Rasty-Nasty." Freddy puts his hand out for a low-five.

"Did you jack this?" Zach asks, searching for a nonexistent seat belt.

"No man, borrow, I told you, Freddy got friends." He guns the engine and the car slides around a corner. A broad smile splits Freddy's face.

"How bout we take the beach today and do some business," Freddy yells.

"Yeah, okay," Zach says. "Mellow will ya. I want to live through the day."

Freddy slaps the steering wheel and pushes on the accelerator. "This be great. Let's go get rid of some seals."

The car veers from side to side as they approach the rest area near the beach. Zach's fingers clutch the arm rest, but he refuses to react. A show of fear will only encourage Freddy to do something even more moronic. They swerve into the parking area. Freddy pushes on the throttle and slams on the breaks as the front tires bump over a tire stop and land on the sand.

"Geez, you're an idiot sometimes, you know that?" Zach says. He leans his shoulder into the door and rolls out.

"Freddy know how to drive, dude," Freddy says, adjusting his jeans around his butt.

Zach shakes his head. Down the beach he sees Loon Song Harbor's swim area, but no one is near the parking lot. Straight across the beach is the old dock where seals and sea lions like to sun themselves.

Holding the wooden box Victor, The Beard, gave him, Freddy slides out of the car. "Take some skill to kill a seal," he says, "get it?"

"Yeah, I get it," Zach says, his heart pounding.

"C'mon, let's do this." Freddy says, adjusting his skull covered boxers above the belt line that hugs his rear. Zach hesitates, then drags his feet through the sand and follows.

Chapter Twenty-Nine

Uncle Teddy and Loren leave early, right after breakfast. I watch Angie lift off and circle back over the house, tipping her wings goodbye. Liz doesn't have any work for me, so I'm free for the day. My only thought is the beach. The pool, as Uncle Teddy calls it, is really a swim area marked off by orange buoys. My goal is a quiet spot on the sand. The usual exhaust from stink-pots, that's what Liz calls motorboats, fills the air as I walk past the docks. Boaters greet me with, "good morning," most warming their hands around coffee cups. I make my way to the end of the beach, pick a secluded spot, plug in my ear-buds and set in for a long day of hanging with tunes.

I wake when two kids run past kicking sand and screaming. All I want is quiet, but boatloads of people have arrived and the swim area is slammed. Down the beach I see a small dock that looks empty and quiet. I toss my things in my backpack, adjust my earbuds and head out. One problem--no tunes. I whack my phone a few times--no luck. I can't believe it. I forgot to plug it in again.

Tiny cone-shaped shells push up and the occasional sand-dollar winks at me as the warmth of the beach slips through my toes. The fishing dock isn't far, maybe ten minutes, just far enough to be alone. A kick sends a few rocks rolling. One bumps a tiny hermit crab that bounces like a ball. "I'm sorry little one," I say and gently pick her up in my palm. She doesn't respond, but after a while her legs stretch out. "Dark in there?" I ask. She disappears. She's alone too, and gets along fine, I tell myself.

A metallic clunk pulls my attention to the parking lot where an old car has leapt the curb and is parked halfway on the sand. The passenger door swings helplessly in the wind, slamming closed and then swinging open again. Hair on the back of my neck prickles when a voice cuts through the wind. Down the beach, I see two guys climbing on the dock. Plumes of sea spray rise up around them. My breath catches and my every sense is on high-alert. I'm not afraid of being alone, but something feels off, wrong. I crouch; Maybe they won't see me. Knees to chest, I stay real still.

The tall one looks around while the other, with his back to me, pounds on something. I am a statue until they finally walk back to their car. The short one does a squat-walk with his seriously stupid pants around his butt, like a wankster. The other one wipes his hands on his jeans and trails behind. They stop short of the car and appear to look right at me. I hold my breath until they crawl in the car. The tall one slams the passenger door several times before it sticks.

Refocused on the dock, I feel sick to my stomach. I pick up my pace. Someone is lying on the surface. Closer I recognize the shiny coat and flippers of a seal. I remember the incident on the island. Wow, what is it with seals around here? Distracted, I completely forget about the men on the beach, until I'm almost to the seal.

An ear-piercing whistle cuts through the sound of the surf. My attention jerks to the parked car. Both doors are open, the two guys walk toward me fast. I try to speak, but my tongue grows twice its size and sticks to the roof of my mouth. My breath freezes in my chest. I stumble closer to the seal and, like a sharp knife, a pain shoots under my ribs--the pain of an animal in trouble mixes with my own fear. I lurch forward and reach for the dock. My every impulse is to run, but I can't move.

Chapter Thirty

"What's a matter girl?" the wankster yells. "Stay away from the seal."

I glance back; she hasn't moved. "She's sick," I say.

"What? No one sick, jus' lazy." The wankster yells. "Seals good for nothin' lazy. You stay away." He waves a small box at me. "What's your name, girl? Where you from?"

Waves roll up the beach. He steps toward me, so close I gag from his rank toilet breath. My lower lip trembles. I pull my t-shirt closer around me. I figure I can outrun the wankster with his pants around his knees, but I'm not sure about the tall one. The wankster shifts from side to side inching closer.

The tall one's eyes work between his partner and me. I lean back.

"Hey, where you goin'?" The wankster's voice snakes toward me. "Come-on girl, I wanna meet you. That a hot swim suit? Show us your Bi-Ki-Ni." He takes a step.

"Don't Freddy," the tall boy says.

Freddy eyeballs him, blinks and shows his palms as if to ask a question. He glances my way and turns on me; his eyes twitch and get real wide. My throat clinches and I can barely breathe. Every muscle in my body tenses and my knees shake. Run, I think, but I glance at the seal and can't move.

"You like that seal, huh?" the one called Freddy snarls. "They stupid animals, know nothin', just lay around. Somebody need to do somethin' about them."

With a smile, he turns to the tall boy and back to me. His eyebrow raises, he smacks his lips. "I was jus' gonna stick that seal, now I jus' gonna kill it."

"Shut up, Freddy."

"You shut up, Zach." Freddy throws the box down. "I thought we was friends." He picks up a long heavy piece of driftwood with two hands. The wood rolls to his shoulder.

I stare into his eyes as he swaggers toward the seal. I want to grab the wood, but my feet are glued to the sand. He hoists it and slaps the dock. My body trembles as the sound ricochets off me; the seal and I flinch at once. Lightening shoots through my ribs.

"See. He stupid. He don't even run," Freddy says as he lifts the wood again.

"No," I yell, but I choke and the sound comes out more like a squeak.

"And if I do, what you gonna do about it, huh?" Freddy takes three steps closer to the seal, and raises the piece of wood straight up.

A strobe flashes in my head. Waves of pain and anger pour through me. The seal's pain heightens in me. I step on the dock, between Freddy and the seal and raise my arms.

"STOP!" I yell, this time with full force.

A massive wave crashes against the rocks just as I hear the whoosh of wood cutting through the air. I cringe and cover my face. I know I am totally dead.

When nothing happens, I peek between my fingers and see Zach grabbing the driftwood pole. Freddy is spinning around, legs flailing like a kite in the wind. He flips upside down, hair grazing the ground, and lands flat on his face in the sand.

"What you doin'?" Freddy screams at Zach.

Zach stands silent for a moment. He looks at me and his sadness reaches out. "Let's go, Freddy. This is crazy."

"You crazy," Freddy yells, as he scrambles up, brushes off his pants and face. "Nobody punk Freddy. Don't ever do that. Never!"

"Relax, man. I'm just saying ..."

"What?" Freddy puts his fists up and chokes to control his words. "You think you so tough because you bigger than me now?" His shoulders scrunch. He steps forward to throw a punch, but stops short. Then, like a three-year-old throwing a tantrum, he kicks the sand and swings wildly in the air.

Zach steps back and shifts the driftwood to his other hand, in front of him. Muscles in Freddy's jaw quiver as he turns toward the car. Face red, broken, lips shaking, Freddy swivels toward me, "I'll get you," he shrieks. "You be sorry bitch. I'll get you."

I shake so hard everything is a blur. The rage, the wanting, the wrenching pain that twists Freddy's face is all so familiar. I understand, I want to say, but my mouth won't work with my brain. Then it is too late.

All the way back to their car Freddy curses and yells. Zach carries the driftwood like a walking stick and Freddy crab-walks behind him. Zach turns once, stares directly at me, shakes his head, and I'm sure the corners of his lips rise slightly.

The rackety old car clunks over the curb and tires spin across the sand. A whirlwind of energy sweeps over me. My knees buckle and tears splatter my shirt. I cry for like an eternity. Waves of fear and anger rush through me; "Punks, jerks," I scream, finally, "Crack-butt Bastard." No one hears me, but I feel better.

The seal grunts. "Sorry," I say. I lock eyes with her and again the stabbing pain snakes in my gut. This time I know the pain is from the seal. She glistens in the sun, mucus runs from her nose, and her chest quietly jerks in a silent choking motion. Something's definitely wrong; nobody can tell me this is normal.

Waves sweep across the shore. Mussels and barnacles bubble and pop in the rocks. The salty ocean air fills me as my breath matches the short gasps of the seal. My fingers slip across her silky coat and her eyes follow me. "Don't worry," I say. "You're all right now," as much to myself as to the seal. "You're all right."

A seagull screeches. I straighten, stay extra still and search the shore for the car. The parking lot and the beach are empty. I am alone. A chill seeps deep in my bones.

"I'll be back, I promise," I say, and with one last stroke of her glistening fur, I run for my life.

Chapter Thirty-One

I stop and bend over to catch my breath. People sun and children play. No one notices me, even though I am sure I have a blinking red light on my head announcing what had happened. On the boat dock, the heat of the concrete rushes through my sandals and sweat drips from my eyebrows. A light breeze washes the tree tops; branches creak and leaves flutter as I approach the parking area. The air feels cool against my ears. I push strands of hair to one side, wipe my eyes and step forward. I thought I'd go to the store, but I shake all over and the hole, the emptiness, creeps back in. I would cut my arm off to have my Mom with me right now. I decide getting the necklace is a better option.

The house has an eerie feel, empty and alone. I change into my shorts and blouse and grab the necklace. "Why aren't you here?" I whisper as I do the clasp, "You should be here." The locket burns in my palm and my emotions swing between crazy anger and grief. I swallow. Get a grip Sammy. Liz said I could talk to her anytime, and it suddenly seems very important to tell her what happened.

Dry heat from dirt and gravel rise around me. The sweet smell of flowers comes from somewhere as I reach the path to the store. The old man, Wrinkles, rocks on the porch, eyes shaded by the brim of his cowboy hat. I know I don't want to talk to him. My shoulders fall and hunch.

"Come on up," he orders as I approach, "I won't hurt you."

I freeze on the first step, and watch him through my eyebrows, "I know," I say, not really sure if I do or not.

"Come on," he orders again, his voice deep and raspy, but gentle. A cross between a tramp and a kindly old grandpa, he pushes on the arms of the chair and stands up. The rocker creaks.

My feet move mechanically up the steps. I avoid his eyes and keep my arms wrapped around my waist.

"You're a brave girl."

The wind comes up again; leaves swoosh in the trees; I pause, "What?"

"Standing up to two boys takes some guts. Especially that Miller kid. He's no good."

"Miller kid?"

"Freddy Miller. He's bad blood."

The old man's words ooze into my thick pumpkin-head brain, but nothing makes sense. Only twenty minutes has passed.

"Wait! How do you know?"

"Ahanu."

I rub my forehead and clench my eyes. "Ahanu?"

"My grandson."

"How did he know?"

"He said he took the stick."

I am stunned. The tall boy, Zach, is the old man's grandson. Does that mean he's Liz's son, I wonder.

"Zach?" I ask.

"Most people call him Zach, but he's Ahanu to me."

I watch the old man, as I try to piece together the puzzle he's handing me. Zach came home, told him about meeting me and what happened on the beach. Why?

"He saved me," I say, as I pick at my finger nail and would give anything to reach the door.

"He shouldn't have been there at all," the old man says roughly. "This time I'm glad he was, not that you needed much help."

The heat rises in my cheeks. "Thanks," I say, "but I was scared."

"Scared," he laughs, "of course you were scared. Who wouldn't be? Two big boys against one ... eh ... one young woman. Fear is what makes it courageous."

"Courageous, I wasn't courageous. I was terrified."

"That's right. No fear--No courage required," he says with finality.

My dad flashes in my mind. Was he afraid? Did his fear go so deep that it never went away? Is that why he's so angry, so hurtful? And, in the time it takes for a question mark to appear in my brain, I wonder about my own anger.

"And don't worry," the old man continues, "I'll talk with the Miller boy's father. He won't bother you again, and neither will Ahanu--I promise."

"Thanks," I say, my eyes darting from him to the floor and back, hoping something, anything would interrupt our conversation.

"Thank you very much," I repeat as the screen door squeaks open.

"Well, I hear you've had another exciting day," Liz says, as she unties her apron. A wave of embarrassment rushes over me. Not able to face Liz and the disappointment she must feel for me being in trouble again, I shift pine needles around with my feet. A chipmunk hops up on the railing.

"Shoo," she says waving her apron as she steps over and wraps her arms around me. I rest my head on her shoulder.

"I don't mean to be so much trouble, Liz."

"It's not you. They are trouble makers and this time you put a stop to it. They might have hurt that seal if you hadn't stood up to them."

"Not me," I say between sobs. "It was A-A-Ahru who stopped him."

"Yes, I heard. But you stood up to Freddy Miller, and that motivated Zach to stand up to him. Otherwise, something terrible could have happened. Zach came to us because Freddy went crazy and he was scared. Zach's got some problems, but he's basically a good kid. Freddy," she says shaking her head, "Freddy's real trouble. I'm proud of you Sammy, real proud of you.

Liz steps back, "Do you mind telling me exactly what happened?"

I'm a little surprised, since Zach already told her, but I go over what happened. I end with Freddy calling me a bitch and threatening me. The old man, who is listening shakes his head. "I promise you, Sammy, I'll make sure his dad knows about that."

"Did either of them touch you?" Liz asks.

I think for a moment. "You mean touch, touch?"

"Yes. Did either Freddy or Zach touch you inappropriately?"

"No, nothing like that. It all happened so fast. Freddy came toward me, but he didn't touch me. He just threatened me."

"I can call the Sheriff," Liz says, "but from the sounds of it, there won't be much they can do. They already know that Freddy is a serious problem, but it's up to you."

I shake my head, no, and rest my cheek on her shoulder.

"I'm sorry, Sammy," Liz says. This is not what Orcas Island is like. It won't happen again."

We stand on the porch for a few minutes, no one moving. Finally, I look from Liz to the old man. My right cheek pulls up in a half smile. I wipe my eyes, sniffle, and extend a snotty hand, "I'm Samantha Carlisle."

The old man smiles, "I guess I'm not a stranger now? I'm Johnny Hania Smith." He reaches out, avoiding my hand, and shakes my wrist.

"Smith?" I say, trying to hide a bigger smile.

He laughs. "Missionary's took away our real names and gave us Christian names centuries ago. Some of us use a little of both. That's why my name is Smith. Hania is my true Indian name. Most people just call me John."

I give Liz a questioning look.

"It's okay," she says, "you can call him John, Hania, or like me, Olie for Old Man."

"Hi John, I'm pleased to meet you," I say. "I guess I've met almost the whole family now."

"Not almost, this is the whole family," Liz says. "Zach's parents, my sister and Olie's son, died several years ago. Now it's just Olie, me and Zach."

My whole head bursts into flames with embarrassment, but now I understand why Liz knows how I feel. She isn't only sympathetic, she has experienced my pain, at least some of it. A comforting warmth moves through me. She smiles and the wind whispers, "Sister," in my ear. Our eyes meet and her depth of understanding reaches into my heart. "I'm sorry," I say, "I know how hard that is."

"Yes, you do," she says, stepping over and wrapping her arms around me again.

"We get along fine," John says, in a slightly irritated, don't-leave-me-out, kind of voice. He waves his hand and turns toward his rocker, "Now why don't you two go inside and talk or cry or whatever you do, while I exercise this rocker."

As I move to turn I realize, "Wait, I forgot, there is the seal."

Chapter Thirty-Two

"Wait," I say frantically, "there is a seal down on the dock. The one Freddy threatened to kill. When Freddy tried to hit it, it didn't run or anything. As I approached, I felt the same kind of sickness I did with the other seal from the island, only worse. It was lethargic and had that green stuff coming out of its nose. You don't believe me, but I know something is wrong. Can we call someone or do something? It's probably still there."

Liz and Olie trade glances. They don't say anything, but I can tell Liz is considering it. "Okay. If the seal is still there, that could be a problem. Let's drive down and take a look. If we find it, we'll call the local humane society."

I clap my hands. Now I can show her what is wrong.

Liz drives fast, but the trip to the small dock still takes forever. We roll into the parking lot, dust billowing up around us. Between thanking Liz several times for doing this, I explain what I'd seen in more detail, the slick skin, snot coming out its nose, and how lethargic it was. We walk to the dock and I point out the stick Zach took from Freddy and the pit in the sand where Freddy fell down. My heart drops when I see the seal is gone. I bite my lip and consider my options. I decide to keep pushing.

"Isn't there something we can do?" I begin, "I know this isn't normal. Maybe we can call the police, or ask an expert, or ..."

I keep talking all the way back to Liz's truck, my pleading gaining momentum. Liz doesn't say a word, so I yammer on all the way back to the store. She pulls into her spot under a tall Douglas Fir tree, and a flock of crows rise up making all kinds of noise. She yanks the gear shift into park, sets the emergency brake, rests her arm on the steering wheel, and looks at me. I don't breathe. Birds caw in the distance and my blood pulses in my ears.

"Well, you've earned it," she finally says, "I know a marine biologist, a friend with the University of Washington Research Center on San Juan Island, Simone Dubois. She might be able to tell us if anything unusual is going on. I'll send her an email this evening."

Now I clap again and bounce up and down so hard the truck shakes. I lean over and give her a hug.

"Thanks," I keep saying. Liz laughs and shakes her head as a slow rumble rolls from my stomach. Liz's eyebrows raise up.

"I'm hungry," I say. "I haven't eaten much. Would you like to have lunch?"

"Sure, what do you have in mind?"

"Well, there's ham and cheese at the house. I can make soup and sandwiches?"

"Sounds great," Liz says, as she slides out.

My feet hardly touch the ground. My fear and trembling shifts to excitement. Trees sway against a deep blue sky, sailboat rigging clanks down at the dock, and birds are singing. Everything is perfect. She'll contact her friend, a real marine biologist, and maybe we'll get some help.

"Olie," Liz calls as we walk past the store. "Would you like to have lunch with us?"

"No thank you," he says, "I'll wait here for Ahanu. We need to have a serious conversation."

"Can I bring you a sandwich?"

"Bring a dozen," he says. "All this rocking makes me hungry."

Chapter Thirty-Three

I wake-up several times over night, always thinking about seals. The last time, I bolt upright, hearing myself say, "Marine Biologist!" My feet hit the carpet; shorts, bra, tank top, are neatly stacked on the floor and pulled on in one continuous motion. Breathless with anticipation, I lung up the stairs. Today we talk with a real Marine Biologist.

"Liz," I say, rushing into the guest room, "hear anything?" Her head bounces slightly as my butt plops down on the end of the bed.

"What?"

"Did you get an email from Simone?"

Her mouth hangs open, a drip of drool slides down her cheek. She rolls, searching the room through squinted eyes, "Time? Time?"

"Six thirty-two," I say.

"You're kidding me?" Her hand pulls the sheet and wipes her lip. She glares with one eye, and pulls a pillow over her head.

"Liz!" I protest.

"What? Go away. I'll check at nine, not before."

"But ..."

"Go away."

Liz is right, of course, her friend isn't going to email before breakfast; but it was worth checking. So, I restrain myself, eat Crispies right out of the box, watch TV for a while, pace the floor gnawing on my fingernails, listen to music, and even play a game of solitaire (which I have to make up because I don't know how to play), all to keep myself busy. Still, all I can think of is getting that darn email. Finally, I can't stand the suspense any longer. It's been over two hours, she has to have emailed by now.

I walk to the door and press my ear against its smooth surface--nothing. Placing my palm on the curved handle, I press down. The door jerks open and I stumble forward as Liz brushes past me. Her normally neat hair exploding in all directions like a punk cut gone bad. She wears white shorts, a purple top, shirt tag on the outside, and rubber flip-flops. The right flip-flop finds its way under my foot as I fall. The flop end of her flip-flop is nailed to the floor by my foot and rips off as she passes.

I haven't seen Liz in the morning, and never imagined she had an ounce of anger in her, but that changes instantly. She spins on her one still sandaled heel, eyes flashing a weird kind of blue light that drills into me. The tips of her teeth, fangs, slip between her lips. I blink.

"What the," she says, looking down at her bare foot. The fangs disappear, and her eyes reflect morning sunlight. With an apologetic shrug, I kick the torn sandal. It flips like a broken wing whipping the strap into a small question mark.

She doesn't move, just stares at the soon-to-be-trashed sandal, as if reading tea leaves. I hiccup and touch my lips to hold in laughter. Her eyes shift from steely blue to the blue of a Robin's egg, creases wrap around them and she bends forward, arms around her waist. Laughter rolls onto the floor. Between gulps and gasps, she pats my arm, tries to speak, and rolls into another series of howling giggles. Watching her, pushes me into giggles, shrieks, and more hiccups.

Bent over, she finally puts her arm around me, "Don't say anything, no problem."

I hiccup in response. She burst into snorts of laughter.

"I'm going to the store," she finally coughs up. Liz stumbles to the stairs. Curls of laughter bounce off the walls until the basement door closes and the house goes silent.

Three glasses of water later, the only thing left of my hiccups is a stomach ache. Peanut butter and jelly on toast with a fried egg helps. Crumbs dot the sink as I brush my hands, the masts on the sailboat wall clock point to nine-eleven. Simone has to have emailed by now.

The store steps groan as I bound up. Ignoring John, I push through the door. Liz is on her cell phone.

"Sure," she says, "that's great. See you then. Me too."

Please, I think, let it be Simone. She looks at me, a smile crawls up her cheeks.

"Well?" I say. My chest ready to explode.

The answer is totally awesome. Liz's friend works with the University of Washington's Roche Harbor Laboratories, one island away. She lives in Seattle, but travels to the island three times a week, and since the ferry stops at Orcas Island on its way to San Juan Island, she has agreed to spend the night with Liz, so we, WE, can talk.

"I just spoke with Ted and he's agreed to pick her up," Liz says, "so she'll be here tomorrow late morning."

"You're kidding," I scream, jumping up and down. "She'll actually be here?"

"Yes, yes," she bounces up and down in rhythm with my jumps. "She's actually coming here. It's not so rare, you know, we are friends."

"Yes, but here to talk with ME. I can't believe it." I stop. "Oh my gosh, I've got nothing to wear." I stretch my t-shirt at the waist. Morning peanut butter smeared with blackberry jam across the front. "Look at this scabby old t-shirt, and these ratty old dirt-stained jeans. I look like a street urchin, a total dork. I need something new."

"Calm down girl," Liz says laughing. "You look fine, she's very casual. Besides, she's only here for one evening."

"Not good," I say as I turn to head home. "I mean this is great, but I need clothes." I run out the door, take the porch in a single step.

"John," I yell, "I'm going to meet a marine biologist tomorrow. Can you believe it? I can't believe it. Oh my gosh!"

I glance back. The empty rocker does not respond.

That evening Angie's engine shakes the walls as she rolls onto the dock. Uncle Teddy and Loren have returned from their trip. Liz and John join us and bring a whole salmon John grilled using what he calls his secret cedar plank recipe, corn on the cob, and a yummy potato salad Liz made with gorgonzola cheese. The dorkster is a sound machine. He rattles on about their trip and how cool it was to fly over fishing boats and see whales from Angie. I stuff the tender pinkish orange fish and tangy potato salad in my pie hole watching and waiting until I can't stand it anymore.

"Stop," I say, standing up with my hand in the air. Loren sits stunned for a second, "Are we picking up Simone Dubois tomorrow?"

Blue Cheese dripping down his chin, Uncle Teddy nods.

"Proceed," I instruct. Taking a healthy chomp from an ear of corn I head for my bedroom leaving Loren's squeaky little voice behind.

Chapter Thirty-Four

Everything has to be perfect. I don't have new clothes, but rummaging through my drawers I find skinny jeans with a cool swirl design on the back-pockets, a clean tank, and my fav zip-up hoodie Mom gave me, with "Peace 4-Ever" on the back. Today, I meet the marine biologist.

I am almost ready, until I glance in the mirror. I'm so punk--skinny like a giraffe--she'll think I'm just a kid. I consider make-up, but I don't have any. I used a black marker for eyeliner once when I was a kid. It burned my eyes and ran into zebra stripes. It was so not-good. Okay, Miss Giraffe, you go au natural.

No one else is up. Not a problem, all I need is breakfast and to get over to the store. We are out of Crispies, so I taste

Loren's sugary cereal--too sweet; I try a nut cereal Uncle Teddy likes--too dry; I find a protein bar--Ahh, just right. I take the stairs down two at a time, and bound out the door.

The morning is fresh with a cool green mist. I run through the yard and grasshoppers skitter and jump around me. As I approach the store the closed sign greets me and I kick dirt. Why do people sleep so late? Dew covered moss hangs from the porch roof and the reflection of the morning light reminds me of the diamond-like spider webs I saw the other day. Trickles of water run down my back as I duck under the grandfather moss and its damp fingers tickle my ears. Boards yawn under my feet as I step on the porch. A crow squawks and lifts off, leaving the rocking chair to tip back to forth. The black wings of the crow flash silver and disappear into the trees. I rest my hand on the shoulder of the rocker. A picture of John in his brown pants, suspenders, worn old plaid shirt, and wrinkled hat comes to mind. A good place to wait, I think.

Sometimes you just know when something isn't right, like when you're about to step off a cliff, your whole body screams NO. That's kind of what happens with the chair. I steady the rocker and turn to plant my backside, but I can't. John's voice creeps through my cranium, "This is my rocker, Little One." I freak out and spin out of there fast. The steps are a much better idea.

Forever is how long I sit there. My bouncing knee makes dust bunnies dance, and my fingers tap the floor to the rhythm of bird songs. I make burping sounds in answer to a bull-frog croaking nearby. Eight o'clock comes and still no Liz. Sunbeams create dry spots on the grass and moss; I walk around in circles leaving super-long foot prints, I hop up and down the steps, bounce from one foot to the other, I even draw faces in the dirt, John in his hat and Loren in his dorky baseball cap. By nine o'clock I am ready to scream.

A whistle comes, a high-pitched warble remarkably like the Golden Crowned Sparrow Liz pointed out to me, near the store, a few days ago. To my relief, it is Liz. Birds respond to her whistles with their own songs, as if Liz is talking to them. She approaches, "Is she here?" I blurt out, even though I know better.

"My gosh, no," she says as her gaze goes from the tall trees to the faces I carved in the dirt. "How long have you been here, anyway?"

"Forever!"

She laughs, "Simone won't be here for a few hours. I think the ferry from Seattle arrives around eleven-thirty."

"That's over two hours," I whine, as she unlocks the store. I don't know why, but I am totally anxious. Inside it is cool and musty, like a fresh garden after watering; the lights flicker on when I flip the switch.

"I talked with Ted last night and we agreed we can all go to pick her up, so you won't have to wait as long as you thought. We'll leave here by ten-thirty."

She must have seen the disappointment on my face, because she quickly adds, "We can restock shelves to pass the time."

Restock shelves?

"Maybe I should go help Uncle Teddy," I say, "Yeah, I think I need to go help Uncle Teddy get ready." I back my way out the door and down the steps.

By ten I am on the dock, my butt planted squarely on the edge of Express II, Uncle Teddy's boat. The sun is high, the air calm. Boats motor in and out creating small waves, and the eternal chime of metal sail clips clank on sailboat masts; the dock creaks in response.

I spot Uncle Teddy on the gang-plank, raise my hands and shoot him a where-have-you-been look.

"What's the hurry?" he asks, as he tosses a bundle of raincoats into the boat.

I roll my eyes, "We're going to find out what's going on with the seals. Aren't you excited?"

"Can't wait," he says, "I could spend a quiet day fishing with Loren, but instead I get to drive a water-taxi."

"C'mon, this is important, and you get to spend the day with me," I say, in my most cheery voice while striking a beauty queen pose.

"Yuck," Loren says, as he approaches with Liz and pokes me in the back, "I have to spend the day with you."

"Stop it Loren."

"What? I didn't do anything."

"Just stop it," I say, as I lower my head and walk down the steps leading inside the boat. The interior is all white with wood panels and blue curtains. There is even a kitchen and a booth with a table. I push a door and find a bed and a little shower with a toilet, just like home. Footsteps thump above me and the boat's rocking seems magnified. My stomach churns and I grab the table. I haven't spent much time on boats, but I can already tell being below deck isn't for me.

"Okay, everyone ready?" Uncle Teddy says.

I swallow hard and poke my head up. "Ready Captain."

Liz hops on board and sits next to Loren on a bench-seat. Uncle Teddy stands on what he calls the flying-bridge, a small platform about five feet above the back of the boat, with a roof, a steering wheel, and a full set of controls. I eye seagulls on top of pilings as Express II glides out of the moorage. I throw my hands up to scare them but they don't pay any attention.

We pass a green buoy covered with the ever-present white poop, he guns the engine, and I immediately find out why we need raincoats. I lean out the side to see up front when a wave slaps me in the face. Loren lets out a hoot. I glance at him as another splash fills his open mouth. I let out a shriek and another spray covers me. Liz, who has moved to the middle of the boat, howls at both of us. Water sprays out either side and all over us until the boat planes. We level off and race forward, just like in Angie, but we don't fly.

The engines purr as the boat slides across the open water until we slam down hard on a wave that shakes everything.

"Wow," Loren yells, trying to stand up. "What happened?"

Liz puts her arm around him as we slam down on another wave that splashes water on all of us again.

"We're okay," she says, "just some chop."

We speed forward, hit a few more waves and the boat shakes like it might break apart. I grab the side rail, Liz holds Loren, and Uncle Teddy leans into the steering wheel up top. I am sure we are about to explode, when the waves smooth out and everyone relaxes to the low roar of the engines.

The moorage disappears behind a smaller island as we race across the bay toward the ferry dock and a small town named Orcas, the same name as the island. Why would you name a town and an island the same? I live in Orcas, Orcas-- not very creative, I'm thinking, when a black and white sheet of something surfaces and disappears near the side of the boat. I lean forward and squint into the bright reflection of the sun. It appears again, then it is gone. What the heck? Am I seeing something or not? I hold the rail, lean out and focus on one spot. The sheet appears again. I yell and point. Liz shades her eyes for a second, then she yells, "Orca! Orca!"

She quickly stands up and calls to Uncle Teddy. He lowers the throttle and spins the steering wheel so the boat turns a half circle and stops. The rail pushes against my gut. I lean so far over I almost tumble out and swells lap my cheeks.

Liz tugs my t-shirt and grabs my shoulder. "Look," she says, "Orca - Killer Whales. A group of at least two or three I think. They're fantastic. Watch."

I stare into the blue-green rhythm of the waves, trying to find anything that might be them. Loren stands up and falls into me. The black dorsal fin of a whale appears as it pushes its back out of the water, blows a spout, and rolls, showing us its white belly.

"Sit down," I push Loren away and scan the water. A huge Orca, round nose, panda-face and white belly, leaps out of the water in a perfect curve about forty feet away. As quickly as I realize what happens, a second Orca bursts out of the water. Like a marine show, but this is real.

"Wow," Loren yells as he stands up and stumbles into me again. This time I don't notice, I am so entranced with the incredible wildness of the huge animals performing in front of us. Oh my gosh, I think, this is the most beautiful thing I have ever seen.

The whales rise again, this time three. Their massive bodies pushing up, dorsal fins rising and diving. A wave of panic catches my breath as their sleek bodies shimmer under the water, getting closer and closer. I crouch and duck, sure they will hit us, but they don't. Faster than lightening, they dive directly under us. We all gasp and leap across the boat. Seconds later they rise up on the other side, exploding out of the water, and disappearing under the waves.

We stand silent until Loren yells, "That was so cool. I can't wait to tell Dad."

A quiver slips down my spine, arms tingle, and my scalp tightens as I run my fingers through my hair. Had I really seen what I thought I'd just seen?

The water glistens. I squint then glance at Liz, and up to Uncle Teddy, eyebrows raised in question. I can't speak. They are beyond beautiful.

"That ... was incredible," I finally stammer as I shake my legs and arms, trying to move the energy that pulses through me.

They both start laughing, then Loren and then me; like we've been sprinkled with some kind of happy dust we can't contain.

"They're something," Uncle Teddy says. "That's why I stay here."

"Maybe the most incredible animal in our water forest," Liz says, "I've lived here almost my entire life and it's still pure magic when I see them. They're so big, bigger than life itself."

"They are life," Uncle Teddy adds, "our life."

Our life, I think, falling back on the side bench. This is my life, isn't it? No one has said for how long, but I live here, I'll be going to school here, I even work here. My life, I keep thinking, as their wild energy slowly seeps from those Orca into me.

I don't speak for the rest of the trip. I sit and re-experience the excitement of seeing the magnificent spectacle of the Orca. When they went under the boat, it was like an electric charge shot through me. I still tingle.

This is more than just a cool place, I realize. There are animals here that bring me out of my skin and into myself. I am just beginning to understand how I know what animals feel; but today, with the Killer Whales, was a hundred times more intense than anything I've ever experienced before. I know absolutely that what I feel around animals is real, and I know now that I never want to leave.

Express II jerks, my back pushes into the railing, the engine noise increases and we shoot forward, to meet Simone.

Chapter Thirty-Five

Express II slams over wave after wave as Uncle Teddy races across the water. Sunlight sparkles off tiny droplets suspended, for a moment, in mid-air. All I think of is what Liz called, "this amazing water-forest." We reach the dock as the ferry is approaching. Like a floating hotel, massive, with what appears to be a flat bow on both ends. I get a little nervous when Uncle Teddy maneuvers Express II into a small moorage spot next to the ferry dock. The side of the ship slips past, like a giant moving sky-scraper.

"C'mon" Liz yells, she quickly wraps a rope around a cleat and runs up the ramp. A crescent-moon shaped dock with tall wood pilings covers the shore. In the center, a road twists from the interior of the island to the landing, ending exactly where the ferry will dock. A long line of exhaust puffing cars wait to board. The ship approaches and a shadow creeps over us, like a hand. An ear-piercing grind from motors and turbulent water rises up. The ferry's engines reverse in an attempt to stop before hitting the dock. I jump back as the huge ferry leans into the pilings. The dock groans and the ferry rocks back and forth, until coming to a stop, perfectly lined up with the road. "Another near-death experience," I mumble. Liz chuckles, "Don't worry. They've done this a few times."

Uncle Teddy and Loren wander down the dock pointing at boats and yakking. I shift from leg to leg as Liz and I search for Simone in the stream of people who tromp down the gang-plank. I have no idea who to look for, but I figure I'll know her when I see her. I also realize I don't know what I'll say to her. I saw a sick seal, sounds so lame, and nobody believes me anyway. Why would she? I'm a kid. I think of the seal on the beach, the pain I experienced when I touched her and the electricity of seeing the Orca. I realize, regardless of what anyone thinks, I have to tell Simone. What will I say? "Just tell the truth," my Mom used to tell me. "It's easier than making something up. You don't have to remember as much."

Cars stream from the guts of the ferry. Using my hand as a shade, I watch passengers parade down a long gangplank on the side of the ferry. Groups chat and smile, several people push bicycles, two women push baby-buggy joggers, a hoard of kids from some camp skip and jump their way through the crowd, but to me they are all pale gray--no energy at all. Finally, a shock of color appears, purple with a mane of hair like a lion. Liz steps forward; the woman waves and smiles. She carries a small overnight case and a computer bag over her shoulder. She does NOT wear jeans. She wears a stylish purple suit and white blouse. Her hair splays out in all directions in an awesome Fro. She does have tennis shoes on, thank goodness. Even before Liz waves, I recognize her. She has some serious animal loving energy.

She motions with her hand. Liz rises up on her toes and waves back, then hops-runs toward Simone, like they haven't seen each other in forever. I hesitate and follow a few feet behind. They get within ten feet and they both start talking, like at warp speed, and continue even when they hug. I hold back, a little shy and not wanting to intrude. After a minute Liz reaches back to my arm, "This is Simone Dubois, my dear friend from college. Simone, this is my newest friend, Sammy, from Portland."

Simone steps toward me. I take a gulp and, wanting to impress her, extend my hand and start to say the words I'd practiced in my head, "Hi, it's a pleasure to ..." but before I can get my words out she pulls me forward in a bear-hug.

"Any friend of Liz's is a friend of mine," she says, "pleased to meet you, honey."

I'm squashed against her massive boobs. My head pushes back, her fuzzy hair wraps around me tickling my ears and nose. "Me too," I squeak out.

In Simone's grasp I smell a wonderful perfume, and her energy is ... amazing. My body relaxes, like a weight has been lifted. She isn't holding me up; still, I know if I collapse, she'll catch me. That is the closest I've come to feeling safe since Mom died.

Mom wasn't perfect by a long shot, but somehow I always felt safe with her--like she could do anything. Until she got sick, she jogged almost every day. I'd run with her sometimes. I couldn't keep up, but it felt good. When I got tired, she'd wave, "meet you at home," and disappear down the block. Even though I felt safe then, her energy wasn't like Simone's. Mom was strong, but kind of hard. Simone is soft and gooey.

My head spins when Simone relaxes her grip and steps back to inspect me. I swim in her milky smooth vibe.

"So, you're Sammy?" she lets out a full-throated laugh. "I think we're gonna get along fine--just fine." A smile brighter than the sun spreads across her face and leaks onto mine. My nervousness drips away like shower water.

She and Liz buzz like bees. Their faces contort, smear into smiles and light up with friendship. Even right next to them I begin to feel alone, and a little jealous. I watch their mouths, and wait for a hesitation where I might jump in with my story. They pause, my words push against my teeth, eager to escape ...

"Good to see you, how are you Simone?" Uncle Teddy interrupts as he and Loren approach.

OMG, how could he do that? My shoulders droop, I kick a pebble and glare at Uncle Teddy. More introductions and blah, blah, blah, I am alone again, in a crowd of people.

The ride back is totally excruciating, sitting between Liz and Simone with them yakking non-stop like eight year olds. My head spins back and forth, trying to talk and not wanting to interrupt, Simone grabs my shoulder and they both laugh hysterically, one time so hard they cry, and finally me getting so fed up I stop listening and watch for whales. I don't see any.

We arrive at Loon Song Harbor and I am ready to run to the house when Loren pulls Simone's bag onto the dock, and insists he carry it, which only delays us more. I am about ready to scream when Uncle Teddy grabs the bag and Simone puts her arm around me.

"Come on girl, let's get up to the house," she says, "for some serious seal talk."

Chapter Thirty-Six

"How about lunch?" Uncle Teddy asks as soon as we reach the kitchen. "Let's whip up some soup and sandwiches while you talk about this seal thing."

Even though it's one more thing to do, I'm grateful because my stomach started growling before we arrived at Loon Song Harbor.

Simone consumes a stool at the counter, and as I'm trying to figure out how to start she says, "Well, Sammy, tell me about the seals. What concerns you?"

"Are you a seal doctor?" Loren butts in. Shut up Punkster, I think, keeping my mouth shut.

"No, I'm a marine biologist. I study animals, especially animals in these waters, to help protect them and protect the people living here. What you and Sammy encountered might be very important to my work." She turns to me, "Now, Sammy, tell me what happened."

I've practiced what I'm going to say for two days, and now that I am ready, my tongue is superglued to the roof of my mouth. I stammer for a few seconds. Loren starts to say something and Simone puts her hand on his shoulder to quiet him. Finally, the glue melts and I speak.

"Ahh, well, we were on a small island off the coast north of here," I begin, and as I speak a river of words flows from brain to mouth. I explain all about the seal we'd seen on the island, what it looked like, and how it felt. I immediately jump into the experience on the dock with the second seal. I leave out the part about Freddy and my swimsuit, leave in the piece about the drift wood, and I wasn't planning to, but I tell her about how I experienced animal's pain and how sharp the sensation was.

When I finish I realize Uncle Teddy has turned off the stove and almost thirty minutes has passed. The windows are open. I hear seagulls squawking and sails flapping in the wind, and the kitchen is cool, yet I am sweating. I wonder if Simone believes me, thinks I'm crazy, or that I'm just a skinny punk kid making things up.

Simone calmly takes notes. She listens to every word then sighs, "Well, there could be something, or there could be nothing."

"It's something," I interrupt.

"Okay, but I'm a scientist, so I won't know until I can do some research."

I notice her voice changes. Her diction is perfect and each word comes out slow and careful. "I know something is wrong," I say again, heat rushing to my cheeks. "I can feel it," I say.

She smiles and her energy softens. "Yes," now her silky voice picks me up in its palm and holds me, "you mentioned feeling the seal's pain. What do you mean, feel?"

I realize I've gone too far. We are into the weird stuff now and she'll never believe me. I hear a loud thumping in my head and my heart bangs against my chest. Do I stop now, or do I jump? Her eyes are soft and invite me to speak. I put my hand on the counter, take a deep breath, and jump.

"I feel things. When I'm near animals, I can feel their pain and emotions."

"Like sympathy?" Simone asks.

"No, not like I feel FOR them. I mean, I actually FEEL what they are feeling. It happens with people too. I don't talk about it much, because people don't understand. Like right now, I have to shut down a part of me, so I'm not feeling all of you." They all lean back. I laugh, "It's not so strong with people. With animals, the pain is really strong."

Except for Simone, they all look at me like they are sorry for the village idiot.

Loren laughs, "Pain? You're the pain. Ha, ha, ha."

The silence breaks and everyone shuffles around for a second, like shaking off spider webs.

"C'mon Champ," Uncle Teddy says, putting his arm around Loren, "Let's go play a game of Farkel while they talk."

I rock from side to side and stare down at my feet. Simone's and Liz's gaze burn into me.

"Crazy heh?" I say. My throat tight and dry. I feel like I might throw-up.

"You're an Empath," Simone finally says.

The word drips into my skull like honey off a spoon. Empath? She's not saying I'm crazy, imagining things or anything like that. She is calling me something I've never heard of before. I let the word roll around in my brain, into my mouth, and finally off my tongue--"Empath?"

"Yes. An Empath is someone who can sense and feel emotions and energies of people, sometimes objects, or in your case, animals. I happen to know a little about this, because I also have some empathic sensitivity."

"Oh my gosh, you too?"

"Not as strong as yours it would seem, but I know what you're talking about and I believe you."

She leans forward and whispers, "Don't tell anyone." The tension breaks and washes out of my body with laughter. My body jerks, I choke a couple of times, then Niagara Falls. Tears tumble down my cheeks. Except this time, instead of feeling stupid or useless, it feels good. Not pretty, but good. I'm snorting, convulsing, my head jerks around like a bobble-head doll, and I wipe snot on my best hoodie.

Liz comes over and holds me while I make a complete fool of myself, and Simone smiles. She's careful not to bring her purple suit anywhere near my snotty slobber. "Sammy, please know I do believe you," she says, "and I will look into this, I promise."

I look straight into her eyes. I know I can trust her.

"You feel their pain?" Liz says. "My poor baby. Does it hurt?"

I laugh. "No, not usually. Well, actually, sometimes, yes. There are times when I have to shut down, so I don't feel too much. If there are too many feelings, I get overwhelmed. It doesn't usually hurt me, really; I just know what they feel."

"You're pretty connected to animals?" Liz says.

"Yeah, I guess. I've never totally understood it. When my dad talked about animals being killed, I would experience their suffering. I always thought it was my imagination."

"Your dad is a hunter?" Simone asks.

"No, he was a game warden in Oregon, but he lost his job."

We are silent for a moment. "Well, with your sensitivity and brains," Simone says, "you're going to make a good addition to the San Juan Islands. The animals up here need all the friends they can get."

"And I need all the help I can get," Liz says, as she spreads out the sandwich fixings for lunch.

I slather mayonnaise and mustard on slices of dark rye bread before Liz and Simone add ham and cheese, and this time the laughter and banter includes me. The warmth of these two women, warmth I sometimes knew with Mom, wraps around me. This is what friendship is supposed to be like, I think, women you can be with, have fun with, talk to about anything. As the laughter and banter gently bounces around the kitchen, I let the word empath soak in. My special sensitivity almost feels normal.

Uncle Teddy and Loren join us and the conversation turns to normal girl things, like hair, clothes, and books. Finally, like out of frustration that we aren't talking about flying or fishing, Uncle Teddy interrupts and suggests we all take Simone to San Juan Island the next morning.

"We'll drop her off, and spend a couple of days on the boat," he says.

"Just like that?" I say, thinking he's kidding.

"Yup, just like that. They're our islands, and I need a few days off."

Loren and I look at each other, then stare at Uncle Teddy.

"They have a pool, and we'll do some hiking or kayaking while we're there," he quickly adds.

Sweet. Tripping around on Express II in MY ISLANDS.

"Can I bring my snorkel?" Loren asks, hopping off the stool to gather his things, "And my spy gear?"

Uncle Teddy nods his agreement.

"Maybe we'll see more whales," I say, "and ..."

"And pirates," Loren adds as he runs out of the kitchen.

"I guess that's a yes," Uncle Teddy says.

Chapter Thirty-Seven

I walk into the kitchen filled with the smells of Uncle Teddy's favorite breakfast (Liz's home-made granola, bananas and cinnamon sugar toast). Loren sits on a stool in his usual multi-colored clown outfit capped off with a swim mask, snorkel, and floppy fins. He is becoming weirder by the day. Under the swim-mask Loren's lips pucker and his eyes are all buggy. I burst out laughing so hard I drop my pack. He wobbles his head, flops his flippers, and taps a spoon into his mask--seriously goofy.

"You going to swim to the island?" I ask, as I reach for a banana and a piece of toast. He echoes something through the snorkel in response. "I think I'll walk down to the boat, if it's okay with you?" I say to Uncle Teddy.

"Sure, we'll be there shortly. Got all your stuff?" I nod, wave the banana, and half run down the stairs. A shiver crawls under the pack and across my shoulders as I step out the door into the cool early morning salt air. Liz and Simone sit on Express II. Steam rises from their coffee cups. I hesitate, then they wave. It is clear and calm, and in the distance San Juan Island floats like an apparition through the morning's mist. A sailboat idles out of the harbor with a young boy up front, his legs hanging over the bow. He smiles. The air is so crisp it almost crackles. The sway of the dock dictates the rhythm of my steps. True to his word, Uncle Teddy is close behind. He pushes a cart loaded with a cooler, two duffle bags, Loren's backpack and two bags of food. Frogman slap-slaps right behind him.

The excitement of the previous day is gone. Liz and Simone talk in quiet tones; their heads nod in mutual agreement. As I approach their energy opens and welcomes me in like an invisible hug. Their smiles greet me. I am happy. While Liz and Simone handle the cooler, I toss blankets and pillows up front and unloaded bags of food into the miniature refrigerator, stuffing cheese and lettuce on top of hamburger, sausage and some other weird purple mushy thing in a freezer bag.

"You're out for a couple of days, aren't you?" Liz asks as I step on deck.

I nod.

"I thought I might catch up with you in Victoria," she continues, "catch a ride back. What do you think?"

"That would be great," I say, wondering how she knew we were going to Victoria.

"Hey Ted," she yells up to the Flying Bridge. "Don't be surprised if you see me in Victoria. I might need a ride back."

"No problem," Uncle Teddy calls back, "you're always welcome."

"Always welcome?" I repeat, with a raised eyebrow.

Liz's cheeks flush pink. "Yes, smarty pants," she says.

When Liz steps to the dock, I grab a spot next to Simone. Express II rumbles, and within minutes we wave goodbye to Liz and are headed out of the harbor. Our exhaust mixes with mist crossing the Strait of Juan de Fuca to San Juan Island. Breeze whips my hair and flicks at my eyes. I notice Simon's hair hardly moves.

"I was wondering," she says, "what your connection with animals is like?" She has a steady gaze and isn't asking to make conversation. She really wants to understand.

I pull my hair into a ponytail, while I consider. I want to give her a serious answer. "Usually it's a sensation in my body, so natural I don't know if it's my own feeling or theirs. And at other times electricity shoots through me. A lightning bolt, like I'm plugged into them." She leans forward and waits, so I continue. "When I was younger, I'd shut down, because it was too much."

She nods, "What does Shut Down mean?"

I think for a moment, go inside myself, and try to feel. "Well, when I'm around a lot of people or animals, if I let myself, I can sense all of their emotions. Like being in a wind storm or something, everything flying around and I can't catch any of it. Mom told me, sometimes, when I was little and went shopping with her in large stores, I'd start to run around in circles, scream and cry. There was nothing she could do until she took me outside and held me. Eventually I'd fall asleep. She stopped taking me shopping."

Simone smiles, holds eye contact and nods.

"As I got older, my dad got angry. He said she coddled me. I began to believe something was wrong with me, so I went away."

"Went away?" she asked.

"Yeah, I'd turn everything off."

"Like a faucet?"

"Sort of." I close my eyes and turn my focus inside again.

"Okay," I say, "there is a ball of energy in my chest that I'm going to control. As I concentrate, I imagine the fiery ball gets smaller."

I squint through my eyelashes. Simone stares at my chest. Wiggling my body, I straighten my back and close my eyes again.

"The fire ball gets smaller and smaller. The smaller it gets, the less I feel, until there's nothing and I don't feel anything."

Simone's gaze darts between my eyes and my chest.

"Wow. You can do that?"

"Yeah. I'm not sure when I started, but now it's how I function in crowds. Otherwise I'd go nuts."

"Oh, I hear," she says. "There are plenty of times I'd like to do exactly the same thing." Her laughter fills the boat.

"My mom called my sensitivity, my Empathic Sensitivity, a gift," I say. "She always told me someday I'd understand how to use it. I never believed her, but I liked to hear her say it."

Crescents pooled on Simone's lower eyelids. "Your mother was right," she says as she wipes the corner of one eye. Her hand reaches out and points toward the horizon, "I think, honey, you may have found the reason for your gift."

The line of her finger stretches across the water. Salmon, Orca, Squid, and a thousand other forms of sea life rush under the surface. A gift--maybe this is what Mom was talking about.

Chapter Thirty-Eight

U ncle Teddy guides Express II into the horseshoe shaped Friday Harbor, around a small island and into a moorage several times larger than ours at Loon Song Harbor.

"Nice seeing you Simone," he says from the flying-bridge, "you're welcome anytime." Anytime? I've never heard him invite any men back, ANYTIME.

Simone steps to the dock. "Why don't you walk me to my office," she says to me. "I'll show you what I do."

I almost fall out of the boat when Uncle Teddy nods, "Loren and I can walk into town--get something to drink. We'll meet at the boat in an hour."

Simone is a large woman, an inch or two taller than me, and ... full bodied. I laugh when I think about what tiny part of her my swim suit would cover. She isn't fat though, just big. In fact, she's elegant. When she walks next to me she stands straight up. Her hips sway gently, a rhythm to each step. She owns the road, but not stuck-up or anything. I have to stretch out to keep up with her. She talks constantly, telling me all about herself.

"Bay St. Louis Mississippi, along the Gulf Coast, east of New Orleans," she says. "I grew up poor, lived in a two-room house along a slip of water so small the Catfish had to make reservations to swim upstream." As she relaxes I hear the music of her southern accent sneak back in.

"I never worried about being poor," she sang, "never knew what poor was. We had food, most of the time, old hand-me-down clothes, and love; Sweet-Sugar, we had love. Where I come from, all you need is music, food and love." Her deep beautiful laughter rolls out across the street and echoes off the buildings. "I guess I wasn't aware of what we didn't have, until I went to high-school, saw what having looked like."

I close my eyes to imagine what her life was like.

"In high-school I saw what other kids had," she added. "Then I decided I'd better get educated, so I could have some of that good stuff." She laughs again. "Now, I'm right back where I started, in a different place, but realizing all you really need is music, food and love." She wraps one big arm around me and pulls me into her plush bosom. "And friends, honey, nothing better than good friends." We both laugh.

Up a hill toward her office, she talks about a teacher who noticed her interest in wildlife and encouraged her to read more at a local library.

"He even brought me books at home," she says with a look of remembrance. "In high-school I took some tests, got good grades and, with the help of some other wonderful teachers, got a scholarship to the University of Florida where I studied Marine Biology. Five years later, with something no one in my family had ever even heard of, a Master's Degree, I accepted a job in what felt like another country--the State of Washington.

When I came here I hardly understood most folks," she says with a twinkle in her eye. "You don't speak my kind of English up here. Where I come from, we mix English with French to make a language dripping with Creole sauce, then we add some of our own made-up words of honey. Sweet Creole's the most beautiful thing you've ever heard."

"How do you feel?" she asks me. Before I can answer she follows with, "Vou san vou-mem byen. Now isn't that pretty? Someone asks you how you feel with those words and all you can do is smile and feel good."

Her beautiful words surround me and I do feel good, real good.

"Now, twelve years later," she continues, "I run the San Juan Research Center, and I can't imagine living anywhere else. I'm the first person in my family to be schooled beyond the tenth grade. Honey, in my world, tenth grade was considered higher education."

I picture a two-room house on the Gulf Coast of Mississippi, what it would be like to stop school at fourteen. I watch her walk, listen to her talk; she is beautiful.

She notices me staring at her, stops talking and laughs, "I do go on, don't I? Honey, if you want to say anything you have to interrupt, otherwise I'll talk the tail off a gator." Laughter bounces between us.

The office is on a side street with one large window across the front and no sign. I walk right past the door. "We've arrived," she calls, spreading her arms out. "Not much, but I don't entertain often." I peek in the door to a large table covered with maps and walls covered with charts. It feels more like a map store than an office. In one corner a stack of files spill over a small desk, and along the back wall is a computer and some instruments.

"This is my little kingdom," she says, spreading her arms. "Let me show you some of my tools, like my tracking charts."

Pointing to maps on the table, she identifies a series of pins in different colors. "These are Orca whales we are following. Even though we document their movements on our computer system, but I like to see them here." She moves her hand above the chart, like she is smoothing out sand. "I check the computer each week and move pins to identify where a few of the whales are. That way, I feel connected to them. We have three pods of Resident Whales known as J, K, and L pods. L is the largest, but I track all of them. We're not supposed to, but I name the ones I track most often." Her broad smile lights up the room, "They're my family."

"May I?" I ask. She nods. I put my hand on the map and warmth moves through my arm. "Family," I repeat. "I get that."

Her eyes track my movement and I become self-conscious. "I wish I could do what you do," I say.

"Why not?" she asks.

"I don't think I'm smart enough," I say without thinking.

She steps back, puts her hands on her ample hips and her brow wrinkles, "You stupid or something?"

"What? No, I just ... I don't think I could ever ..."

Her laughter takes off again, fluttering the maps. "You think you're not smart enough? Let me tell you a little story, girl. When I was your age, I thought I needed to understand everything, without ever being taught. I hated when people told me what to do. Partly because I was an upstart, partly because I thought I was stupid and I didn't want anyone to know."

I squirm and my body wriggles as her story matches how I feel.

"I always thought I had to be better than everyone else," she continues. "When I started ninth grade, I figured out I didn't need to know everything. That's why I was going to school. More importantly, I didn't need to be better than everyone else, there was always going to be someone smarter than me. I only needed to be better than myself."

I cock my head to one side, "Better than yourself?"

"I decided I'd learn one new thing every day. Sometimes I learned a lot more, of course, but always at least one, no matter how small. That way, I always moved forward. I competed with myself and I won." She took my hand and laid it palm down on the map. "If you want to have knowledge about animals in the ocean, you'll learn. You're very smart, Sammy, don't let anyone tell you different--especially yourself."

I smile, gulp down a choke in my throat and reach out to turn a few map corners. "I guess I've always felt stupid," I say.

"Sure you have," she says. "We all feel stupid sometimes. Why I'll bet some of those animals you make contact with are feeling stupid too." She lets out a whoop and a laugh, "Don't you pay any attention to them or yourself. You hear?" She looks out the window. "I guess it's time to go. If you'd like, you can come over any time. Maybe you and Liz can come over, spend the night sometime. There is an extra room and I could show you some of the tricks-of-the-trade."

I am so excited by her offer, I can't speak. She must have gotten the idea, because she adds, "Good, let's make a point of doing that, soon."

I take one final scan of the maps while she puts her briefcase behind the desk.

"We brought a sea lion up here a few days ago with a tracking tag on its tail," I say, mostly to myself. I feel her watch me and my lips curl into a smile. Simone stands by her desk, hands on her hips again. "Sure did," she responds, "I guess you've got more friends up here than you realize."

The few blocks back to the harbor are magical. We talk about the history of Friday Harbor and how sea life is teaching us how to live with nature in the San Juan Islands. I comment about the ferry docks being everywhere.

"Sure are," she says. "For most of the islands, ferries are the only transportation available. If we didn't have them, I wouldn't be able to have an office on this island; unless I rode with your Uncle Teddy all the time."

"That wouldn't be so bad, would it?" I ask.

"Well aren't you full of spunk," she says with a chuckle and changes the subject, "I could learn a lot from you. The spare room is empty, so you're welcome any time."

My whole body smiles as I float down the sidewalk in her sweet Creole energy-- welcome anytime.

Chapter Thirty-Nine

Earlier that morning, when we motored out of Loon Song Harbor, Liz stood at the top of the dock ramp, her arm raised waving goodbye. Simone had visited almost every month for the past couple of years, but this time had been different. Simone lit up when she talked with Sammy about being an Empath, and Sammy's excitement brought Liz and Simone together in a new way. Liz smiled at the sight of Simone's shock of black hair next to Sammy's hoody, haloing her face against the morning air. Tucked inside Simone's arm, they appeared like two heads under one bouquet of black curly hair. Two mugs Liz already loved as much as her own family.

"I'll see you soon Sammy, in Victoria," she says to herself and makes a mental note to visit Simone soon. She loves how excited Sammy is to meet Simone, and she understands how important it is for Sammy to have friends who listen and believe in her. "She's a good kid," she whispers to the wind, "but she's going to need a lot of love." As she approaches the store, Zach comes down the porch steps, "Speaking of kids needing my love," Liz whispers.

"Zach," she calls, within shouting distance, but he doesn't hear or is ignoring her. Hands pushed in pockets, head cocked forward, he kicks dirt up with each step.

He has already been at the cabin. When he didn't find his Aunt Liz he went to the store. He tried the latch, but the door was locked. He tried the coded key-box at the back but he couldn't remember the combination. With each try he felt the burn of anger rise in his neck. "I hate this thing," he yelled at the door. "Put a key under the mat or something." His anger boiled over. "Where the heck is everybody? I'm your family, not San Juan Ted and those kids." He kicked the door, "I have rights too." Bounding off the porch he yelled, "She doesn't respect me. Freddy's acting crazy. Everyone's against me. I'll just take my money from the job and get out of here. I'll go to Seattle." he confirmed to himself. "I'll go to Seattle. That'll show them."

Hearing Aunt Liz call his name, Zach drops his head and quickens his step. "I don't need anyone else," he says to himself. "I can take care of myself. I'm sixteen. I'll get a job, a real job, live on my own. Screw them. Screw you!"

Walking the center of the road, rocks and the occasional can clanks off the toe of Zach's shoe and bounces in front of him. After ten minutes, he takes a short cut across a field and turns onto the beach where Freddy is supposed to be injecting poison into seals. "Freddy," he hollers with each step, until he hears laughter. A head with a black skull cap pokes up from a pile of driftwood. Freddy holds the box in his hand and waves.

Zach's pace slows. He told Olie and Aunt Liz about the encounter with the girl on the beach. Freddy has a bad temper, and if he finds out Zach talked with them, Freddy could go ballistic. Zach has to be ready for anything and approaches carefully.

When Zach arrives, Freddy is sneaking up on a group of small Harbor Seals with gray and white patches, like Pinto horses. The seals bark and snarl as Freddy moves in. It is dangerous, and Freddy circles around the larger seals. The ones that sleep or lay quiet are his targets. Freddy laughs and jokes, taunting a smaller seal before jabbing the needle in and jumping back. A second seal lunges, catches his arm, and rips a short gash in his bicep. Freddy hoots even louder.

"Yo Dude," Zach yells.

"Dude. Sup?" Freddy says.

"Sup." Zach says back. They bump fists. Both boys stand staring at their feet, pushing sand with their heels, not knowing what to say.

"Hey man, about the ...," Zach finally says.

"Forget it. I don't wanna talk bout it." Freddy interrupts, smiles and spins around in the sand.

"See, our work is easy. All we got'a do is stick these seals, call it good."

The tension in Zach's shoulders washes through his feet. He is grateful Freddy has forgiven him so easily, but he also senses something is wrong.

Zach squints at Freddy, "What do you mean?"

"We inject these seals. Throw the rest of the needles away," Freddy says.

"We can't lie to those guys. They're not playing around, Freddy," Zach says. "They'll hunt us down, mess us up if we don't do the whole job."

Freddy laughs. "How they know? C'mon dude, stick with Freddy."

"Yeah, I'm sticking with Freddy," Zach says, laughing at their joke.

"Look, I heard Aunt Liz tell Olie she was going to leave for a night or two. She wants to meet San Juan Ted, with those jerk kids, in Victoria. We can finish the job while she's gone. No need to short change anybody."

Freddy's eyebrows rise, "That girl? The girl on the beach?"

"Yeah. Why?"

"She going to another island?"

Zach hesitates.

"Dude," Freddy cajoles, "Freddy interested, that's all. Where she going?" The blacks of Freddy's eyes slip side to side behind narrow slits. His lips wrinkle.

"Leave her alone," Zach says.

"Yeah, yeah, Freddy not doin nothin. I be here with you. What's the matter? You love her or somethin?"

"No," Zach responds too fast. "I don't love anyone."

Freddy kicks his heel in the sand. "This easy," he says as he inspects his bleeding arm. "We do them all, if you want."

"Right, okay," Zach says, "we'll finish the job, like we promised." His stomach turns just saying it.

"So they be gone, heh?" Freddy says, trying to sound uninterested.

Without thinking Zach responds, "They're going to Roche Harbor for a night, then to meet Aunt Liz in Victoria. They'll be back in a couple of days."

Freddy's lips crinkle in a nasty smile, "Plenty of time to stick more seals," he says, as he pats Zach on the shoulder. "But now Freddy got things to do." He tosses the box to Zach. "I be back in a few. K?"

Zach watches Freddy jog to a broken-down car that Zach has never seen before. He reaches into the box with shaky fingers and pulls out a syringe. Three seals lay in front of Zach. He sits and lets sand run through his fingers to build small pyramids by his hip. His neck tenses. "Fine," he says defiantly, "I'll take care of this myself."

Chapter Forty

Freddy slams the door. "I hate that girl," he says to the broken-down car, "Hate that girl. Gonna teach her a lesson." He turns the key on the old clunker and the engine groans several times before starting. He jambs it into drive and screeches out of the parking lot, tires spinning. As soon as he rounds a corner and is out of Zach's sight, he pulls out his cell phone and punches the keys. A grunt greets him.

"Captain, this Freddy. Got some information for you."

The Captain sucks on a stale unlit cigar. "What you want?"

"We was stickin' seals," Freddy says, his voice rising, "like we promised. This girl walks up and makes us."

"Make you?" The Captain throws the cigar onto the deck. "What 'make you' mean?"

"She saw us. We don't talk about you, but she knows Zach and me."

"That your problem," the Captain says.

"Yeah, I know, but I thought ... maybe ... you could help."

"Help how?"

"Look, she's going to be in Roche Harbor with her Uncle Ted of San Juan Express," Freddy says. "His boat's name is Express II. She be real trouble. Maybe you need to take care of her. Help us all out."

"Why?"

"Because she saw the needles, she knows what we was doin'," Freddy takes a deep breath and gambles the Captain believes him. "Besides, if she talks and they start snoopin' around, your name might come up."

"You threaten me?" the Captain says, dark and slow.

"No, no. I'm just sayin'. I won't talk, but Zach, his Aunt's with San Juan Ted. I can't say what he'd do. It could lead back to you. That's all I mean."

"Yes, I know exactly what you mean," the Captain says. He puts the heel of his boot on the cigar, twists and crushes it. Freddy's phone goes dead.

Chapter Forty-One

One final smother-hug and Simone sways up the ramp toward town. In her arms, I feel safe and protected. I would give anything to spend another day with her. Instead, I wave. She stops half way up, shades her eyes and sweeps one hand in front of her like a queen.

"It's only about ten miles by car, across San Juan Island to Roche Harbor," Uncle Teddy yells as we depart, "but we'll be about an hour circling the island by boat." Wind whips sails of passing sailboats and fumes catch my throat as stinkpots motor past. Express II powers into the strong currents of the San Juan Channel. My shoulders bounce as the bow slaps against small waves. Beneath the water I imagine Orca whales and sea lions with tracking tags sending out invisible signals. Uncle Teddy lets Loren steer the boat from the Flying Bridge while he explains about Express II, "... a 28-foot cruiser ... twin diesel engines ... bilge pump that automatically siphons excess water out ... best boat ever ..."

Uncle Teddy drones on, and I am lulled into dreamland by the rhythmic vibration and the steady grumble of the engine. We motor past Jones and Spieden Islands, round a large tree covered crest and, in what seems like only a few minutes, pass between two rocky points. Waves rise up and I see whirlpools swirl around us. Express II bucks like a wild horse, twisting right and left, until we move into the bay and head into Roche Harbor. As we weave our way through a mass of boats I think about Simone's work with Orca whales. I imagine them jumping and playing with sea lions and seals around the boat, when suddenly Uncle Teddy guns the motor. The boat jerks and I sit up with a start, squinting into the sun's brightness. The whale's image melts into the shape of a fishing boat that passes off our port bow. Across the back is the name Annalee--something seems familiar, but I can't remember what. A man stands on the deck, arms folded, cap pulled down to his eyes. I think he might be staring at me. His hand goes up, as if to wave, then flips a cigarette or something, and turns away. My skin crawls as if an eel has slithered down my spine.

Roche Harbor is huge, many times bigger than Loon Song Harbor, filled with boats of all sizes, including some humongous yachts. Some big enough that their pointed bows are longer than Express II. Uncle Teddy slows, and maneuvers near one of the massive boats. Ducks quack in protest and scatter, wings flapping and feet jogging across the water until they lift off. A man stands on the bow of the yacht with a long pole, ready to push us away if we come too close.

"Whoa," I yell, leaning forward when a huge shadow creeps across us. Uncle Teddy laughs. "Don't worry Kiddo, I'm not going to hit anything. We're just borrowing a little space under the bow of this ship while we have lunch." He backs up and sure enough, we fit right under the pencil-point snout, like a chick under a mother's wing. My mind drifts to my Mom for a moment, and I remember being under Simone's arm, a chick under her wing. Sorry Mom.

"Sammy, grab that rope and tie us off." Uncle Teddy says, pointing to a 'T' shaped metal cleat on the dock. I wrap the back rope around the cleat and do the same near the front. He hops off the boat and undoes each rope, rewrapping them. "Nice job, but we need figure eights to keep her tied to the dock."

"Right," I say, my cheeks flushed.

"It's okay, kiddo. I can teach you."

"Learn one thing every day, no matter how small," I remember. Okay, today I can learn how to tie a square knot or whatever.

We follow Uncle Teddy along the dock. Hundreds of boats sit moored around us. Some must be over one hundred feet long. Turning left, we pass the Harbor Master's office, and walk up a ramp. A three-story white building with the name, Hotel de Haro, welcomes us. Gardens, with gobs of colorful flowers and tall trees, spread out on either side of a dining deck. Guests chat and glasses clink from tables covered with white linen and arrangements of flowers. It reminds me of a picture Mom had in our living room of several women in large hats at a tea party. I wonder what happened to that picture. Between the gardens I smell a sweet aroma circling, and hear the buzz of bees, lots of bees lifting from flower to flower.

"Would you have a table for three near the front?" Uncle Teddy asks a woman in a floral dress and white apron. She shows us to a round table that overlooks the harbor. As I sit down my fingers slide across a smooth white tablecloth to a napkin and a set of sparkling silverware, cold and bright. It is better than being in a movie.

The food is fantastic and as I eat the last of my hamburger, while protecting my fries from the Dorkster, our waitress comes over and hands Uncle Teddy a piece of paper.

"Good news," he says, "they've found us a moorage spot. Now we can spend the night and go exploring."

"They have a pool," Loren says, pointing to a brochure that stands in the center of the table next to a pamphlet with a picture of a kayak. I'd been eyeing the image of the sleek red boat and imagining my escape.

"Look," I mumble through a mouthful of burger while I ignore Loren sneaking yet another fry, "can we go kayaking?"

Uncle Teddy glances at both of us. "Okay, so much for a hike." We both clap, as he shakes his head. Loren lobbies for swimming while I bat my eyelids and talk about how I'd taken kayak lessons with Mom last summer. The memory draws me to a darker mood and I am about to give up when he folds his arms and mutters, "Okay, but only as long as you stay in the harbor, near other boats." My mouth falls open dropping a fry. I jump up to hug him and knock over my water. He leaps up and topples his chair into the guests behind him.

"So sorry. Oops, my apologies," we both say while we scramble to pick up the glass and chair. Loren doesn't miss a beat. He finishes the rest of my fries.

The boat rental is located near one end of the dock. We slide-walk down a grassy bank to join a small crowd waiting to rent kayaks and row boats. I have on a tank and shorts, but it is hot, so I figure with my legs inside the kayak and wearing a life vest I'll be plenty warm. Loren begins his quacking routine as he follows two ducks along the bank, while Uncle Teddy falls into his parent routine.

"Hold the paddle like that," he lectures as he points to a family with two kids who are arranging themselves inside a kayak. A bald man with a beard waits to rent a kayak as well. One beautiful red kayak, like the picture on the flyer, speaks to me. I hope no one takes it. When the family finishes, the bald man in front waves us forward. Uncle Teddy lets me choose the red kayak, even though it has a rudder and is one level up from the beginner kayaks. I put on my life-vest, get in, and he adjusts the seat so my feet rest on the two peddles that control turns.

"Push left, go left" he instructs.

"I know," I say, and give him a kiss on the cheek. "Thanks."

He wipes his cheek and tries to act gruff, but I think he likes it.

"One hour," he says, waggling his finger as he pushes me off, "and stay in the harbor." I paddle around in a figure eight, showing him I can make turns, then wave and head out past the dock.

"One hour," he yells again. I wave, not looking back.

Chapter Forty-Two

A cruel wind blows. Sand stings Zach's arms. He's sat for almost two hours, since Freddy left. Several syringes roll between his shaking fingers. In front of him lay three seals. "I can stick you," he yells to them, "inject you with this poison." But killing doesn't come easy for Zach. Days before, on the dock, while Freddy danced and jabbed the needle, all Zach could do was pretend. A seagull cautiously walks around Zach. "Freddy thinks I'm stupid," he says to the seagull, "like I don't know what he's doing." The gull squawks in response and pecks at a shell. "Why else would he leave? He's going to try and hurt that girl." The bird lets out a screech and takes flight. Zach eyes the gull as it joins a group fighting over a dead crab near the seals. "Freddy enjoys killing, but I don't," he finally admits.

"Life is sacred," his grandpa Olie taught him, "and animals are our spirit guides. They are part of the environment that gives our people life on these islands. Killing even one animal diminishes all of us. Sometimes we must kill, to feed the village and give life; but senseless killing, killing for pleasure, is wrong."

The tide is rising. A wave tumbles, hits the beach and splashes. The seagulls lift like a cloud. The seals bark and roll and, as if sensing danger, follow the rushing surf back to the ocean. Their black heads bob and disappear beneath the foamy surf. Zach pushes his fingers deep into the sand and digs a trench near his leg. One at a time, from each of the syringes, he ejects the poison into the sand.

A blurred image of his mom and dad appears in his thoughts. He doesn't often think about them. His dad had been a fisherman. Zach was only ten when they died in a plane crash in Alaska. He hardly remembers their faces. "It doesn't matter," he says to the ocean, "I can't bring them back." As Zach watches the last of the poison seep into the sand, he knows he can't do this. He can't even pretend to kill. No matter the consequence, he has to confront Freddy and find out what he has done--right now.

The road from the beach circles through the woods. Zach walks at a quick pace to the Miller home to find Freddy. No one is there, so he returns along a narrow road across the inlet bridge. A squeal warns him. The rust-bucket comes careening around a corner, swerving and spinning part way around, and stops inches from the edge of the road.

"Yo, dude," Freddy yells through his dust caked teeth.

Zach raises his hand and jogs toward the car, forehead taut, cheeks flushed and lips pressed hard and cold.

The eyes of a crow, Freddy might be thinking as Zach's pupils condense into small black beads. Freddy recognizes the look of anger moving toward him. He's seen it many times in his father's eyes, just before he took out the belt. Freddy's reaction is normally to fight, but this is Zach, his best friend. Why would Zach be so angry?

"What did you do?" Zach blurts out from twenty feet away.

"What, man?"

"What nothing, you want to get back at the girl. Tell me what you did."

The tone of Zach's voice, the anger in his eyes, tells Freddy everything has changed between them. No need to pretend any longer. "I call the Captain, tell him where she is."

"Are you crazy? He'll hurt her."

"No, man. He just scare her."

"Those guys are killers," Zach says. "If they think she knows what they're doing, they'll hurt her bad."

Freddy doesn't flinch, doesn't move, doesn't respond.

"You don't care?"

Freddy shrugs, "Dude, that's life."

"No Freddy that's death and it's wrong, but you don't understand, do you? I'm done Freddy, I'm out," Zach says as he breaks into a run toward the store.

"Don't do nothin' stupid," Freddy shouts after him. "Don't do nothin' stupid or we all get hurt."

Chapter Forty-Three

The front porch of the store is a place of quiet contemplation where Olie spends many days listening to nature and watching the Universe unfold. A fisherman, like his father, he raised a son who also loved the sea. A son who died too early, but left a gift named Ahanu. Olie vowed to raise his precious grandson in the traditions of the island people. So far, he feels he has failed.

Face red and dripping, Zach approaches the store and finds the back door unlocked. Inside, he scribbles a short note explaining what has happened and that he is going to make things right. He sets the confession on the counter and grabs the round foam key ring that holds the boat key. Skirting the back of the store to avoid Olie, he runs toward the dock.

Aunt Liz's skiff, always fueled and ready in case of emergency, is tied to the dock. He checks the supply box: knife, fish gaff, rope, fishing gear and an old marine radio. The engine starts on the first pop. Within minutes he heads out, full speed, toward Roche Harbor.

Leaves whisper in the trees as a heavy wind pushes the sound of the skiff motor and the smell of trouble toward the quiet porch. Olie glances up to see Ahanu leaving the harbor. A crow circles and lands on the railing. "Scá'a'," the old man says, addressing the crow. "Trouble is in the wind and Ahanu needs your help. You are his spirit guide. Follow him."

The crow's head cocks to one side. One yellow eye studies the elderly fisherman. Three caws, wings spread, the crow lifts into the darkened sky and heads for the harbor.

Large swells slam against the skiff as it runs fast across the Strait of Juan de Fuca. Waves break over the bow spraying over the windshield and Zach. In this rough water, he calculates, he'll reach Roche Harbor in about two and one-half hours. Seagulls and cormorants are common on the water, but rarely does one see crows, so Zach takes notice when a large black bird keeps crossing his bow and cawing. Amused at first, by the fifth pass Zach becomes irritated. Years ago, Olie told Zach, "As with me, my grandson, the crow is your animal spirit guide. Respect and listen to them." But Zach isn't thinking about spirits. His concern is to reach San Juan Ted and Sammy before the Captain.

The irritating bird makes another pass, this time close above Zach's head, swooping forward and to the right. A wave smashes into the bow and pushes the boat to the right. Zach waves his arms, "Get away. Go home," he yells as he turns the boat to correct its direction. The bird doesn't listen. Hovering next to Zach's face, it caws three times and veers right again.

One can imagine, if crows could talk, it might be saying, "Follow me you idiot," but of course crows don't talk, at least not so Zach can hear. The crow makes one more attempt. This time from in front of the boat, dropping one wing and returning to the center of the bow before swooping again.

What triggers Zach's understanding is anyone's guess, the crow's antics, his own sensitivity, or maybe the animal spirit in his DNA. Whatever guides him, Zach finally redirects to the right and, without knowing his destination, begins heading for Queen Charlotte Island.

Chapter Forty-Four

The sleek red kayak skates through the dock area, as I weave in and out of a crush of boats. It is so cool of Uncle Teddy to rent it for me, but now I stare straight up at the hulls of yachts in the harbor. Although I fit between them, it's dark in their shadows and I worry about being squashed. I duck as I weave through them, and for safety I follow the shoreline toward the edge of the harbor. With each pull, the long kayak lunges forward like an Orca chasing salmon. The faster and harder I paddle, the stronger I feel. It is exciting to move so fast through the cold water as it sprinkles my warm skin, and a salty crust rings my lips. Before long my arms tire and I make a final pull. My back pushes against the kayak seat, I lie back, close my eyes and let the boat glide forward.

My eyes aren't closed for more than a minute, and it doesn't feel like I kayaked for very long, still, when I search for the dock, it's gone. I've been careful to follow the shore line, but I must have turned a corner or something, because I can't see the hotel and the water is no longer smooth. Ripples with currents and whirlpools swirl around me.

Even though I'm not paddling, I'm totally stunned to realize that I am moving out to sea--fast. Frantically, I turn the kayak to head back and paddle hard. The current proves stronger and pushes me backwards. C'mon girl, I think as I stroke, you can do this . It's no use, the current is winning. "Go to shore to avoid strong currents and wind," I remember my kayak instructor saying. I paddle toward the shore line, but it's too late. I'm headed into the Strait of Juan de Fuca, filled with boats and ferries hardly able to spot me, and twelve foot waves that can swamp me in a second. I can't stop it and yes, the thought occurs to me, I'm going to die.

The small chop of the inner harbor has turned into huge swells that push my tiny kayak under water one moment and throw me up on a crest the next. Rocked by the turbulent waves, I fight to keep my narrow boat from turning over. Twisting and spinning in the violent waters, my breath becomes short and my stomach tightens. Sea water splashes up to my face constantly and instead of liking the salt taste, it makes me sick. I rotate in my seat to find the harbor, but it is all water now and I am lost. A wave sweeps over the kayak and I swallow gallons of salty liquid. Between my coughs I hear three short toots of a horn. I brush my face and search; the nose of my sixteen-foot kayak needles to the top of a crest and a light, directly in front of me, flashes.

"Need help?" someone yells.

I wave frantically.

"Hold on," he yells, "be there in minute."

I try to yell as another wave washes over me. Saltwater and foam fills my mouth and my sinuses sting.

From a distance, the boat doesn't seem too big, but as it comes closer, it grows larger and larger. Thank goodness the boat stops a long way from me. Rising and falling in the swells, their engine sputters and I inhale exhaust and gag. On the back, the name Annalee rises above the waves and I recognize the man with the black beard. He's the man I'd seen at the kayak rental. I should feel good about that, but for some reason I don't. He leans over and drops a metal ladder that clanks against the hull of the large boat. "Paddle here, we get you out," he yells.

I hesitate. He climbs down the ladder and motions me over as another wave spins me around. Using every ounce of strength, I paddle hard. Waves push me alongside their huge hull. I rise up and he extends a pole with a hook that slips through the rope-loop on the front of my kayak. My tiny red boat jerks, I fall back and the next moment he grabs my life vest and pulls me next to him. A garbage-dump stench surrounds him. I reach for a rung of the ladder just as my kayak washes out from under me. For a moment my feet dangle in the wind, then he puts his hand on my butt and forces me up the ladder, like a totally uncomfortable elevator.

The next instant, my legs swing over a chain railing and my feet hit the deck. Crouching over, I hold on to a pipe and throw up as a wave washes the bile away. I see two men standing off to one side. My kayak crashes to the deck next to me and the bearded man ties it to the railing posts. The men's beady eyes track me as I begin to slip off my life vest. I kill that idea quick when I remember I only have on shorts and a tank.

"Thank you for stopping," I say, shivering. "I couldn't get back to shore and my Uncle's waiting for me at Roche Harbor. He'll be worried."

"Yes, of course. We take you," says a fat man with a captain's hat. He speaks with a heavy accent.

Remembering the boat I saw when I was on the rock island with Loren, I blurt out, "Do you help seals?" It's the only thing I can think of.

The captain's hat inspects me. "What you mean?" he asks.

"I don't mean anything. There were fishermen helping seals and I thought you might ..."

"You watch us?" The third man says, skinny and tall, his face wrinkles as he squints his eyes into tiny black slits.

"Yes. No. Not you really, just a boat named Anna," I stammer, realizing it might have been their boat near the small island with the sick seal. Like a shadow surrounding me, I know I'm not safe and pull out my cell phone to call Uncle Teddy.

"No." The beard says, reaching his hand out. "Bad for instruments. No phone."

"But I have to call my Uncle, he's waiting," I plead. My throat tightens. "Is there another phone?"

"No," the Captains Hat says quickly, "No phones. We take you home, then you be with him."

Something dark, sinister reaches out to me. I can't argue, so I put my phone away. An uncomfortable urge moves through me. Embarrassed, I ask, "Do you ... do you have a bathroom on this boat?"

The beard turns toward the Captain's Hat, "Captain?"

The Captain nods and says, "Be quick, you understand?"

The boat is all steel, painted gray. A dark hall leads to a door marked HEAD. The beard opens the metal door, puts his hand on my back side, and pushes me in. He stands, watching me.

"I need to close the door," I say.

He doesn't move, then smiles. "Hurry," he says, and slowly closes the door. I quickly rotate a metal handle to the lock position. Thinking they forgot about my cell, I pull it out, but deep in the hull of the ship there is no signal. Toilet water sloshes and a kind of evil lurks in the darkness. My stomach does back-flips. Something is terribly wrong. Crouching over my knees, I open the door slightly to listen. Waves slap the hull and the engine seems to grumble as the ship rocks. The beard is talking to someone and I pick up bits and pieces of their conversation,

"She watched ... she danger."

"No, she not ... nothing."

"She knows ... now she ... identify."

"Don't be ... she child. She ... nothing."

I lean farther out the door to hear better. I almost jump out of my skin when a hand clutches my shoulder.

"Come," the Captain says, and pulls me out on deck.

I am totally confused. "What's happening?"

"Idiots," he yells. "She listen. You are stupid. Now she know too much."

"But Captain ..." the skinny third man says.

"Shut-up." The Captain says. Half carrying me, his floppy jowls and two stomachs jiggle against me when we walk. My flesh crawls. "The boy right. She know too much. Victor," he orders the beard, "lock her in cabin below. Take cell phone. Andre, set course for ..." He glances at me. "Set course for our island and take us out of here."

"Wait," I yell, "I didn't hear anything, honest. I don't know anything. I have to get home."

The Captain looks at me, his fat cheeks turning red and jiggling as the engine idles. "You spy on us with seal, yes?"

"No, I only saw a fishing boat. Honest." The Captain pulls a cigar out of his pocket. The beard named Victor slouches.

"You were helping the seal, right?" I plead.

"Right," Victor says, laughing.

~ 229 ~

"You watch Miller with seal, yes?" the Captain says.

I blink, "What? Miller?"

"The boy, Miller," the Captain says again.

Thoughts and images race through my mind. On the beach with Freddy and Zach; Freddy spinning to the sand; Freddy's eyes drilling into me and screaming, "I get you bitch."

"Do you mean Freddy? Freddy with the other sick seal? That's right ...," I begin, and stop. "How did you hear about that?"

"We know you. Now you know us," he says. "That not good for no one." The Captain nods toward a hole in the deck.

I try to move toward my kayak, although I have no idea what I will do if I reach it. My feet slap the deck. Victor grabs me after two steps and wraps his hairy arm around my face. His skin reeks of smoke and sweat. He pushes me across the deck, and drops me down the hole.

My foot hits a ladder rung; I slip and fall. Get up, I think as his grubby fingers snake under my armpits. Twisting a handle, he opens a door and shoves. The sill catches my foot and I skid on my knees across the wet slimy floor of a small room. I push against the gunk to stand, but I feel Victor reach his big grimy hand in my shorts, tearing the pocket. My scream echoes off the walls as he pulls out my phone and throws it. Plastic parts shatter everywhere. His lips wrinkle in a nasty grin and he grabs for me again. I jump back. My head hits the wall and I am trapped. He pushes his face into mine. A gross stink reaches through his beard and his grimy fingers grip my shorts. I hold his hands, but he is too strong for me.

"Victor, where are you?" the Captain's voice rings from above.

Victor stops, his cold eyes stare at me. "You lucky this time," he says, stepping back. He scans me, head to toe, then turns to leave, slamming and bolting the door behind him.

I stand in the damp cave of a room, my eyes adjusting to the dark. A rank smell, like rotten eggs, swirls around me. As bad as the odor is, Victor's breath was worse. My skin prickles against the mucky cold steel and I can't stop my hands and legs from shaking. The boat jerks, my knees buckle and I crouch into a sloppy liquid that sloshes around my feet and in my shorts. Oh my gosh, this can't be for real. They just want to scare me. They'll let me go soon. This is stupid--totally stupid.

Chapter Forty-Five

Each time the boat rolls, the stinky liquid sloshes across the floor. My hand touches a gooey ball. I jerk back, push up, slip and go down. A wave slams into the hull and I bounce. Slime slops on my face and I almost puke. Finding a metal edge, I hold on tight until the next wave. It's like being inside a washing machine and I tumble for what seems like hours, until finally we slow down.

With my hand gripping the metal edge, I'm able to stand and check out my prison. About eight-foot square I guess, above me is a porthole covered with green slime. A single sunbeam peeks through, lighting the room. Mushy globs of yellow-brown muck and things that look like eyeballs wash around my feet. The room is filled with the heavy smell of oil mixed with the totally putrid odor of dead things. I shiver at the thought and stop looking. Across from me is a metal door, with a huge handle. I keep thinking they only want to scare me, but seeing the exit triggers something. My shoulders begin to shake, waves of fear and anger rip through me, my knees buckle, and to keep from sitting I grab the porthole. The next thing I know, I'm heaving sobs like an out of control one-year-old. The reality that they really do want to hurt me begins to sink in.

In the midst of this new reality, my finger catches the chain around my neck and the locket Mom gave me. I snap the gold oval open and hear her voice.

"You are courageous, strong and beautiful. Don't let anyone take that away from you."

The comfort of seeing my face next to hers warms me like a blanket. Eyes closed, I pull the locket to my chest, and hear her voice again, "Okay girl, get it together. There's no one here but you, so start thinking." Mom always had a way with words.

I pull myself up and shake my head. I'm alone. No one here but me. What can I do? The only way out is through the door or the porthole. I'm skinny, but no way am I going to fit through that tiny porthole. That leaves the door. Uncle Teddy has to know I'm gone by now, he must be looking for me. The problem is, he will search at Roche Harbor, and I am ... who knows where. The first thing I have to do is get out of this stinky room.

Pain in my stomach bends me over. Oh no, not now. I need to use the bathroom again. I reach up and hold on to a pipe, to steady myself, as the pain passes. My fingers grip the flanges on the wall and I half-stumble half-slide to the door. Whap! Whap! I slap the door. Nothing--they can't hear me. A bright red sign catches my attention. It reads: IN CASE OF FIRE ONLY. Above the sign hangs a fire axe with a blade on one side and a sharp pick on the other. Maybe I can bash their heads in, I think. But I settle for just bashing in the door.

The axe is held tight to the wall by clamps. I pull and its weight surprises me. The boat rocks, my hands slip and the axe lands next to my foot on the floor. Careful Sammy, you could lose a few toes. I struggle to hoist the axe to my waist. My feet spread apart to steady myself, I make a weak side-swing and hit the door, barely making a sound. I make a few more lame attempts, my swings timed to the rocking of the boat—still nothing. Finally, I hoist the axe on my shoulder, like Freddy had held the stick. I grip the handle with both hands, heave it up over my head, trying very hard not to let the pick come down on my skull, and swing with all my strength.

Kapow! comes the thunderous sound. I swing again, this time I let out a little yell. YAA! Better.

I swing again, this time letting out a larger yell. YAAEE! Even better.

As I keep swinging my anger rises and I let out screeching Tarzan like yells each time I bash the door. Rising up for one more windmill swing, I scream at the top of my lungs, the door cracks open, and Kapow! I hit the door.

"Stop, stop. You crazy?" A voice comes from the other side. "What you want?"

"I need to use the bathroom," I yell between gasps.

"No." the voice says.

Without hesitation, "YEEAA!" Kaboom!

"Okay, okay. Stop! I let you use toilet."

I hold the axe near my body. Sweat drips from every pour. The door creaks open. Victor's beard snakes around the edge.

"What you do here?" He asks, his eyes the size of tennis balls.

I raise my hands, "What?"

"You crazy. Leave axe. Come. Toilet here," he says, not getting the joke.

I pull the axe tighter to my waist, but realizing I can't win, I drop it. He waves me through.

The narrow hall leads past an entry marked Engine Room, and to the door marked Head. Victor stands so I have to squeeze past him. I face the wall and push past as quickly as possible. His creepy chuckle is in my ear. Inside, I lock the door and sit down, shaking so hard my teeth chatter. I push my shorts down, but too late, I've already peed my pants.

My jaw clinches to hold back tears. I try to think of what to do. No windows, only one door, no knife, no gun, no poison, no nothing. I run through every option. I'm blank. C'mon Mom, help me out. Bread crumbs. I remember Hansel and Gretel used bread crumbs to mark their trail. Brilliant, but I'm on a boat. How do I get bread crumbs? Besides, the ducks would eat them. I look around: a sink, a toilet, nothing else. I jump when he bangs on the door.

"Come out now!"

"I'm sick, I need a few minutes."

He doesn't respond. I imagine him using that pea-brain of his to figure out what to do next. The boat rocks violently and my head bangs against the bulkhead.

"Yes," I hear from the other side, followed by a whole bunch of foreign gibberish.

"You stay. Do not move, or I kill you," he says, then silence.

I put my head in my hands. Now they're going to kill me. I really am going to die. Tears well up again and dribble down my cheeks onto my shorts currently wrapped around my ankles. What a crappy ending.

Chapter Forty-Six

Knowing they want to kill me makes me realize I have nothing to lose. I wipe my tears, pull up my shorts, slowly unlock the door and survey the hall. The boat rocks like a crazy carnival ride. No one is around. I notice the Engine Room, and in two large steps I am inside, door locked, with no idea of what to do. "Hansel and Gretel, bread crumbs ..." I repeat to myself.

The sound from two huge engines in the center of the room smashes through my ears. The boat pitches and rolls. I find a railing along one wall and hold on tight. Searching the room, I see boxes, a pipe marked oil, an axe, another pipe marked water, a fire extinguisher ... I hesitate two beats and refocus on the pipe marked oil. Oil leaves oil slicks. It's in the news all the time. I touch the locket hanging around my neck, "Thanks Mom."

The good news is, I have oil. The bad news is, I'm inside a boat. How do I get Uncle Teddy to see it? The pipe is metal, so I can't push it out a porthole. I relax my grip on the railing and the boat lurches. I'm knocked to my knees onto a large grate covering a hole in the floor. Pain shoots through my legs as the sharp edges dig in. I roll off the grate and watch blood stream down my shins. To my surprise, the blood mixes with the oily water on the floor, forming tiny rivers of Dracula's favorite drink and dripping through the grate into the hole.

A new sound whirs to life, a small motor or pump from inside the hole. I remember Uncle Teddy telling Loren, "... bilge pump switch, automatically pumps water out ..." If this were a bilge pump that pumps water outside, there is a good chance it will pump blood and oil too. Bread crumbs. Now I know exactly what to do.

Across the room is my new BFF, a shiny red fire axe. I pull on the railing and work my way across the room. The axe slips out of the wall-bracket as soon as I touch it. My instinct is to reach out. I do and catch it by the blade. The knife-sharp edge cuts a long red slice in my palm that gushes blood. Pain shoots up my arm to my shoulder. I watch the blood cascade out of the cut. Can't stop. Can't stop, I tell myself.

I grab the axe handle, push it against the cut, and scoot toward the oil pipe.

When I stand up, lightning bolts flash through my knees and hands. Ignore the pain.

The oil pipe is my target. If I hit it once, I might cut through. Propped against the wall, I swing the heavy axe and miss. I swung again. The blade glances off the side of the pipe leaving a small hole with some oil dripping. Again and again I swing the axe, each blow cuts deeper, until the axe drops at my feet. My whole body aches. Blood splatter is everywhere from my knees and hands. My legs buckle and I drop to the floor. I can't do this.

"C'mon Sammy," Mom's voice says. "It's only you. You are strong. Don't quit now." My shoulders rise through the pain and knees straighten. With both hands, I pick up the axe. Over my shoulder, the axe is heavier than a freight train. I study the pipe, stare at the small hole that drips oil, raise the axe and swing. I hit the pipe, but nothing happens. I'm exhausted, disappointed, and ready to give up when the boat rocks again. The stress on the hull twists the pipe and it breaks. Oil gushes out, splashes on the floor, pools and runs straight to the grate. I drop the axe, trip, and my feet hit the oil. Luckily, I slide to the door. For a split second I am a surfer dude.

Oil pours out of the pipe and runs into the hole. I crack the doorway and peek out. No one is around. Two steps and I'm in the Head. I twist around and lock myself in. Seated, I let out a huge sigh. My body feels like I've been through a tornado that picked me up, slapped me around a thousand times and threw me to the ground, with a house landing on my head. My knees and arms ache. Blood drips from my hand and four or five other cuts, and my skull pounds like there is a donkey kicking from inside. I lean forward and press my forehead against the cool steel door.

A pounding slams against my forehead and I jerk up.

"Girl, girl, you come out now."

OMG. What next?

Chapter Forty-Seven

My ear presses against the steel door. There are muffled footsteps, then nothing. Unlocking the door, I peer out. Suddenly it's jerked away from me and it flies open. The jelly-belly Captain fills the hallway. Victor's silly beard peeks out between Jelly Belly's elbow and his jiggling stomach. The Captain's face flashes red and purple. His forehead bulges out from under the bill of his cap. "What you do?" he yells as he pulls me out. "Look, pipes cut, engines failing. You do this?"

My bloody, oil stained, knees and hands drip on the deck, "No, I didn't do anything," I say.

The Captain's flabby face shakes as he studies me. His hand squeezes my neck, twists my head, and he pushes me past Victor into my original cell.

"Stay," he orders, as the door slams, and the handle twists shut.

"Not if I can help it." I yell.

The boat has stopped moving. The engines run, but they pop and choke like a cat coughing up a fur-ball. Taking short breaths to keep the stink out, I carefully slide to the porthole, hold onto the ledge and pull up on my toes. There is driftwood pushed up on a beach about a hundred feet away.

Straining to hold myself up, a surge of warm energy moves through me--totally not what I felt a second before. Through the porthole I see something rolling in the swells. I pull up higher. It rolls again. I rub the slick cold glass with my palm to clear a hole. My heart jumps, and a tingle of excitement washes through me. In the water, about thirty feet from the boat, is a flipper, a slick black body, tail fins and a shiny purple tag. I can't believe my eyes. I don't know why I am so excited to see the sea lion. I don't even know if she is the same one we helped, but seeing her gives me new hope, like her finding me means Uncle Teddy will too. Stupidly, I wave and lower back to the floor.

A survey of my prison tells me my BFF, the axe, is gone. Slushy water slops in half the room with the eyeballs clumped in one corner. My phone is in pieces spread around the floor, the body here and the battery there, both out of the crud.

What the heck. I pick them up, jam them together, and press the power button. OMG, the screen lights. I hit Call and the light goes out. I push and hold Power. Lights flicker and flash in a reboot. This time, when it comes on, I don't try to call, I select TXT, pick Uncle Teddy, and type: OIL PURPLE TAG. As soon as I hit send, the door unlocks. With a flip of my wrist, the phone smashes against the wall and busts into pieces--again.

"Come. We go now," Victor's revolting voice orders. I instinctively step back and he grabs me by my shorts and the back of my neck. His tobacco breath sucks in my nostrils as he pulls me close. I strain to turn my head, and he squeezes harder. His beard scratches my cheek.

"Victor," the Captain's voice calls. Tobacco Breath pauses, his lips touch my cheek. "Next time," he says through his puke-face beard.

I stumble up the ladder into the blinding sunlight. At least now I can breathe. I never realized how good air smelled, just clean air. The other man, Andre, stands off to the side. He wears a backpack. Beyond, I can see the boat is tied to a dock on what looks like an island.

"You smart girl," the Captain says. "You break oil line to stop us. Now we take care of you." The Captain puffs on a cigar, smoke climbs up his over-ripe cheeks. Andre takes off his backpack and struggles with the zipper.

"Take care of me?" I ask.

"Yes. You be okay." The Captain says, taking a long drag off the cigar and tapping the ash onto the deck. "We give you shot, make you sleep. Someone find you. You be okay." A snaky smile slithers across his lips. He looks so satisfied he almost lights up.

Victor holds me, his arm around my neck, and pulls me against his chest. Andre, who had figured out how to open his pack, holds a syringe filled with a milky green liquid. A huge three-inch needle extends from the end.

Victor ducks when a crow sweeps over the deck, barely missing his head. I scream, push on Victor's arm and squirm.

"Sleep medicine," the Captain says, jiggling all over as he laughs. "You sleep good."

Andre holds the syringe and squeezes a shot out of the needle. It arcs like a little boy peeing into a pond. He steps toward me.

A slight breeze blows my hair. Wisps of clouds float against a pale blue sky behind the crow who circles above. Andre comes at me. I kick but miss him. He reaches toward my shoulder with the needle. The crow swoops again, grabbing at his hair. I drop my chin and bite hard into Victor's hairy arm. He yells and I feel his grip relax. I twist sideways as Andre shoves the needle into me. A sharp pain penetrates my shoulder. I break free of Victor's hold, spin around and push onto the railing. As I turn, the needle snaps and slides into Victor's arm. The last thing I hear is Victor screaming, "Get the antidote," and the Captain screaming, "Grab her," and the crow cawing three times.

After that, there is nothing but deathly cold.

Chapter Forty-Eight

Thirty minutes overdue. Uncle Teddy paces the docks and scans the shoreline at Roche Harbor. Loren runs behind, his gaze moving between the empty water and Uncle Teddy's face. Normally thirty minutes wouldn't cause worry, but a darkened sky accompanied by an increasing wind stokes Uncle Teddy's fear as high swells form outside the harbor's entrance.

"She's got to be here," Uncle Teddy keeps repeating.

"Is she lost? Why can't we find her?" Loren asks. When he doesn't get an answer he begins to yell, his voice cracking. "Sammy, Sammy," he calls through his tears.

It is a few minutes before Uncle Teddy hears Loren's fear. "I'm sorry Champ," Uncle Teddy says, bending to one knee.

He wraps his arm around Loren's shaking body. "I forgot I wasn't alone. There are two of us looking for Sammy. We'll work together and find her." He scans the harbor, "We need to search from the water. Let's tell the Harbor Master that she's overdue and we'll be on Express-Two."

By one-thirty they have begun a search of the shoreline. Whitecaps rise across the bow and a vicious wind whips their boat. Twenty-five minutes later Uncle Teddy realizes they need help and he radios the Harbor Master, "We haven't found her," Uncle Teddy says, his voice shaking. "We need a full-scale search."

The Harbor Master puts the word out amongst the guests and contacts the Coast Guard. Within an hour, seventeen boats are searching the waters. Reading the currents and winds, it is obvious that if she wasn't in the bay, she had to have been blown into the Strait of Juan de Fuca.

Uncle Teddy calls the Harbor Master. "The tide's going out. If she was anywhere near the entrance to the harbor, she was probably pulled out by the current."

The Harbor Master agrees and directs half the search boats to expand their search outside the harbor. "Sammy has experience with a kayak," Uncle Teddy explains, "but there are twenty to thirty foot swells and even the best kayaker is no match for the Strait's powerful currents and high waves. In the channel, she is in life threatening danger."

Uncle Teddy continues to scan the horizon, but feels trapped. He is a pilot at heart. "Angie," he keeps saying, "I need Angie." Thirty more minutes of churning waves and his patience breaks. He radios the Harbor Master. "We have plenty of boats in the water," he explains. "I'm heading back to Loon Song Harbor to get my float plane. I can cover a lot more territory from the sky. I have a marine radio on board and will stay in contact."

Life jackets on and Loren glued to the seat, Express II skips across waves at full speed. Teddy calls Liz to inform her of what is happening. "I have bad news," Liz says. "Zach has left a note for Olie, it reads:

'Grandpa,

I'm sorry. I've done something terrible. The other day, we weren't on the dock to hassle seals. We were there to kill them. Fishermen hired Freddy and me to kill seals to protect their salmon catch. The girl saw us. Now Freddy's gone nuts and told the fishermen that Ted and the girl are at Roche Harbor. They will try to hurt her. I'm sorry and I will make this right.

Your loving grandson,

Ahanu.'

"Olie contacted Freddy's father," Liz says. "Together, they confronted Freddy. He was belligerent, but with his father threatening to beat the life out of him, he finally confessed that he and Zach were hired by fisherman who had a commercial fishing license for a coastal area along the US-Canadian border. Seals had decreased their catch, so they decided the best way to get more salmon was to kill the seals."

"Freddy said the Captain was in charge of the operation, but Freddy insisted he didn't tell the Captain anything about

Sammy. We know he's lying through his teeth." Liz continues. "I'm afraid Zach might be right. The fishermen may try to hurt her. We could be looking for a fishing boat, not a kayak, and Sammy may be in more danger than just rough water. These fisherman sound like killers."

Bad weather and rough seas, and now the possibility of Sammy being kidnapped, triggers Uncle Teddy's military training. He gives Liz a list of supplies and asks her to take them to the dock.

"We have to expand our search. I'll be at Loon Song Harbor in less than an hour," he says. "Loren can stay with Olie. We'll leave immediately in Angie." He turns to Loren, "I need you to help me out, Champ. I need you to man the radio at the store while I do an air search."

"But I want to go with you," Loren protests.

"I know you do, but right now we need the best allocation of resources, and I need you on the radio." Uncle Teddy rests his hand on Loren's shoulder. "I'm going to try and contact your dad. If he calls, he'll want to talk with you."

"Allocation of resources," Loren repeats having no idea what that means. "Dad?"

"Yes, I'm not sure I can reach him, so he may not call. If he does, you should be there, and you're the only person I can count on to man the headquarters. Understand?"

"Man the headquarters," Loren repeats as he sits up a little straighter and adjusts his multi-colored baseball cap.

Express II sweeps full speed into Loon Song Harbor. The red and green buoys rock in their wake as Uncle Teddy cuts the power and turns into their boat slip. Liz is on the dock.

"I've loaded our gear in Angie," she yells.

"Take Loren and get him set-up at the radio with Olie. I'll be back in a minute." Teddy says. He gives Loren a hug and presses their foreheads together, "I'll find Sammy. You stay on the radio and we'll talk. Okay?"

Loren closes his eyes; his small body trembles in his Uncle's arms. "Okay, I'll be at the radio. Is Sammy okay?"

Uncle Teddy takes a deep breath wondering what to say to a seven-year-old. The truth, he decides. "I don't know, Champ. I promise I'll do whatever it takes to bring her home." He kisses Loren's forehead. "You man the headquarters. That'll be a big help."

In minutes he scales the ramp to the house. His first stop is a closet in his bedroom and a tall metal safe. He spins the round lock, right-left-right, and turns a large handle. The heavy door swings open. A number of long bags stand at attention. He selects two of them and slings them over his shoulder. He picks up two holstered pistols and three boxes of ammunition. "I hope I don't need these," he mumbles, as he straps one holster around his waist and shoulders the other. The safe door slams and clicks as he twists the knob. Minutes later, the weapons safely stowed in back, Angie chugs to life and slides into turbulent waters.

"Was Loren okay?" Teddy asks, as they skip across white caps.

"He was upset," Liz says, "I assured him Sammy would be fine. He perked up when he put the headset on to monitor our radio communications." She looks at Uncle Teddy. "Did you bring everything?"

"Yes, we've got enough fire power for a small army," Uncle Teddy says.

"Good." She puts her hand on his arm, "We're going to find her. We will get her back safe."

"I hope so," he says.

Uncle Teddy announces their take-off on the airplane radio just as his cell beeps. Thinking it is Sammy's dad, Chris, he hands the phone to Liz.

"It's a text from Sammy," she says, almost dropping the phone. "OIL PURPLE TAG. What the heck does that mean?"

"Text back - WHERE ARE YOU?" he says.

"Done," Liz says and repeats, "OIL PURPLE TAG. What does that mean?"

"She's giving us clues. OIL could mean a storage facility."

"Or an oil tanker," Liz adds.

"Yes, it could mean almost anything."

"How about PURPLE and TAG? What is she trying to tell us?"

"Purple, purple, purple tag," Teddy repeats as he guides Angie toward the search area.

"The sea lion." Uncle Teddy says. "That sea lion we hauled up last week had a purple tracking tag on its tail. Sammy's telling us she's near the sea lion. That has to be it."

Liz smiles, "Smart kid that Sammy."

Teddy makes a call to Gretchen Hanson at the San Juan Police Department and is directed to a marine radio frequency. "Lieutenant Hanson," says the voice.

"Thank God. I need your help Gretchen." He explains their situation.

"I'll set up a command post immediately," she says. "With Kristy Singh's help we should be able to locate the sea lion."

"I know a marine biologist with the University of Washington research center that," Teddy starts to say.

"Simone Dubois," Gretchen interrupts. "Great idea, she has a lab full of tracking equipment and she knows the currents. I'll alert her as well. I'm already in a patrol boat and can meet you wherever we locate her."

Liz keeps sending texts to Sammy. "Nothing," she says.

"No problem," Uncle Teddy says with determination, "this may be all we need to find her."

About fifteen minutes later, Teddy's cell phone rings.

"We've set up scans and I think we've found the sea lion," Gretchen says. "She's moving north, just west of Queen Charlotte Island. Based on her speed and the currents, our best guess is she was somewhere near the south end of the island at the time you received Sammy's text."

Teddy makes a sharp turn pointing Angie due north, and accelerates to top speed toward the island.

"I'm about seventy miles south of Queen Charlotte Island," he says. "We should arrive in about forty minutes. I'll call if I see anything." He hands Liz the phone. Angie speeds north, whipped by increasing cross winds. A series of islands dot the water's surface below, "Like pearls spread out on a blue carpet," Uncle Teddy says.

"Pearls?" Liz asks.

"Just something Sammy said. There's only one pearl I want right now," Teddy says, "the one named Sammy."

Chapter Forty-Nine

At full speed the skiff makes better time than expected. By midafternoon Zach is well north of Roche Harbor. His small craft is a tiny cork in the huge swells. At times the bow slams against waves and falls fifteen feet straight down before being lifted onto another crest. Amidst the sound and fury, the crow appears every ten minutes or so, and Zach soon finds himself using his totem, the crow, as his only guide.

With feet spread apart for balance, his arm raised as a shield against sea-spray, he hears a crackling static--like a cell phone with bad reception. He has forgotten all about the two-way radio his Aunt Liz left on the boat. "Where are you," he says, as he searches the storage compartment for the small, beaten up device. Seeing a short antenna near the seat, he grabs it. The radio drops and slides across the deck. To reach it, he must let go of the steering wheel. He reaches out and leans. "One, two, three," he says, and lunges. As soon as he lets go of the wheel, the boat twists violently in the waves. Zach stumbles to his knees and slides to the stern of the boat. Grabbing the radio, he is thrown against the side of the boat with the ocean rising toward him. He rolls, gripping the seat and the steering wheel. The boat steadies in the general direction of the crow. Gasping for air, he wraps his arm through the steering wheel for control and twists a knob on the archaic communicator. The static grows louder, then fades into Ted's voice.

"I need your help Gretchen. Sammy's lost near Roche Harbor. We aren't sure, but she may be kidnapped. I'll explain ..." The scratching returns and Ted's voice fades. Zach slams the walky-talky against his leg and adjusts the dial until the voices return.

"Thanks Gretchen. Contact me as soon as you have something." The radio goes dead. Zach immediately presses the call button, "Ted, this is Zach. Zach calling Ted, do you read?" Nothing. Zach continues for several minutes, but only hears a scratching sound, and silence.

With the volume turned up, he sets the hand-held device on a shelf and searches for the crow. "You better know what you're doing," he yells. "I'm completely lost and it sounds like the Captain's got Sammy." The bird swoops close and heads left. Zach cranks the wheel to follow. A lump forms in his throat and he swallows hard. "Please," he whispers, "Please help me."

Chapter Fifty

When I jump off the boat, I hit the water thinking I can touch bottom. Wrong. I sink like a hundred feet and realize I didn't take a breath before going under. I open my eyes and glimmering pearl like bubbles rise around me. Pushing my hand out, my fist slams into something hard. It's the boat. Still under water, I kick and rise up, banging my head into the hull. I gasp for air. "Find her, shoot her," I hear the Captain say. "She not get away."

Dropping under again, I swim beneath the hull toward the bank. Underwater, I hear a zinging sound, and see something spear in front of me. Rising to the surface, there is a gunshot and I dive. Swimming hard, I have the urge to gasp, and my lungs seem ready to explode. In my swim class I could hold my breath the longest, too long sometimes. The difference is,

I could always push off the bottom. Now I kick and there is no bottom. I thrust my head up, gasp and take in as much water as air. Two more gun shots ring out behind me and there is an excruciating pain in my left arm. My chest heaves, eyes blur, I choke and suck in more water. Come on Sammy, Mom screams in my head, but I'm choking. My chest heaves and my arms go limp. SWIM, Mom screams, SWIM, but I can't move.

Through the slits of my eyes, I register a blue-green light around me. Long strands of seaweed sway under me as I float somewhere under the surface. A shadowy, ghost like figure undulates, twists, and flows past my face like a silk scarf in the wind. It glides, rolls, and tickles my nose with its whiskers. It moves against me. When I don't move, it pushes its muzzle under my arm. I squeeze and my arm wraps around its smooth neck. Like a soft cushion against my side, the animal pushes me, first down, then fast toward the shore. A rush of water flows past my face. Bubbles snap around me, and moments later I am thrust to the surface and a blinding light.

On the muddy shore, I roll over coughing up green bile. Salt water runs from my nose. Twenty feet away a tail fin flashes purple. I blink in amazement. The sea lion blinks back. Maybe I'm dreaming, no matter. Eighty feet away, the fishing boat thumps against the dock and the three fishermen stand on deck. The Captain aims a pistol at me. A gun shot splatters in the water near me. "Get her," the Captain yells.

The muddy shore is slick like ice. I slip and slide until my feet hit sand and dry grass. Several loud bangs erupt behind me. The three men wave their guns and argue, but a glance tells me they are not yet chasing me. Moving, my arm aches, my skull is thick like a melon, and my entire body is in pain. I push up on one arm and lunge forward. My foot hits something and I go down. One of my sandals flies into the brush. Forget it. I struggle, push up again and scramble into the forest.

Minutes later I reach a clearing. Huge cedar trees sway in the wind around me. I lose my balance and my knee pushes down into the soft forest undergrowth, like my down bed. The cushion of plants and needles caress me and for a moment all I want to do is rest.

For several beats, I sit confused, until I notice a circle of nine huge Beings around me. Some as tall as fifteen feet, they look down with long faces, like aliens or something. Some have huge owl-eyes with straight pointy noses carved into them. Some smile and others have big teeth, as if wanting to eat me. I push away from the toothy one and fall into another. The rough ancient wood grinds against my skin. A musty odor chokes me. I recognize them as totem poles, like American Indians make, but I have no idea why they are here. My fingers trace the deep grooves of one and it speaks to me, like an angel or demon. "Fight," it says. I turn and another says, "Death." I hobble across to a third and it says, "Run."

"I'm tired," I say to the tall one with a crow sitting on its head.

"Run little one," the totem says, "run for your life."

My life? I suddenly remember where I am. I scan beyond the circle of totems. Tall trees let drops of light reach the ground around me. The sweet scent of pine and pitch swims in the air and I flash campfires and my dad carrying wood. Smaller trees and bushes rustle in the wind. I look up at the tall beings to thank them and take a step. A sharp rock digs deeply between my toes on my bare foot. The pain paralyzes my right leg. I scream so loud branches shake and I collapse again. A pool of black-red liquid gushes from my foot. The extreme pain clears my thoughts for a moment. A real crow lands on the top of the crow carving on the tallest totem.

"Run, run," it says to me.

"I'm trying," I yell and push up, clench my jaw, and stumble down a path.

After several steps, I remember the Captain and his men. They will follow me. I can't outrun them. My only chance of escape is to go deeper into the forest and to make them follow a different path. My teeth grind as I force myself to put weight on my right foot and stumble back to the clearing. There are six paths leading out from the totem circle, like spokes on a wheel. Bread Crumbs, I think. If I can leave bread crumbs that lead them away from me, I'll have time to get away. Eons ago, when I was a kid, I watched a Saturday morning cartoon where a girl walked backwards to leave tracks that fooled someone. I know it was a cartoon, but I'm desperate, so what the heck.

I limp about thirty feet along a trail and, without turning and with great care to step on my footprints, I return walking backwards. I do the same on two more paths. On the third trail, I throw my other sandal to one side. From the center of the totem circle, I pick up a broom like branch and, as I hobble down a forth path, sweep away my foot prints and drops of blood.

Deeper in the forest, my head pounds and my vision is fuzzy. I move from tree to tree and rest against their elephant trunks. My arm throbs. Pain fires with each step. Moss and ferns rise up between huge trees to form lush miniature gardens. Birds sing and in the distance a crow squawks. My vision spins like I'm on a carrousel. Bright greens, yellows and blues mix together and flash by in a blur. Voices push from behind as I stumble from garden to garden. I am so very tired. Maybe I should just lie down here, just for a moment. No! The voice rings in my head, and I push on.

Every step is like walking through quick sand, each breath like sucking air in outer space. I stumble over roots and logs and fall in a field of bright emerald moss, so cool and soft, the smell like fresh flowers. My hands and head sink into the spongy softness. My arms and legs are heavy, my body is too big. In front of me, a hole appears, a rabbit hole, just the right size to crawl in. I touch my necklace. "Mom, can I lie down here?" I scoot forward and darkness surrounds me. "Thanks Mom, I've found your lap and I'll just sleep for a ..."

Chapter Fifty-One

Lost in an ocean of desperation, Zach keeps the motor of the skiff on high and surrenders to the guidance of the crow. For several minutes after the radio chatter between San Juan Ted and the policewoman ends, the black bird swoops and dives in front of him. Then the bird is gone.

On the ocean, with no watch or phone, time becomes irrelevant. Five minutes feels like an hour, and hours pass in seconds. His only reference is a small boat compass that he uses to maintain a northerly direction. Zach has no idea how long he's traveled when the crow returns. Wings spread, the crow not only swoops in front of him, this time he hovers in mid-air like a humming bird, almost touching Zach's nose.

Then, as if pulling the boat on a rope, the bird flies to the front and remains there.

"Where have you been," Zach hollers, his words choked with relief as he turns to follow. The bird continues to swoop and glide leading the skiff, and for some time Zach notices the black backs of Orca and sea lions rising around him. Soon the water calms and ahead he sees an island. He has no idea where he is, but it is obvious this is his destination. He adjusts his direction and in blind trust heads for a small bay.

Chapter Fifty-Two

"**S**he get away," the Captain yells, but Andre is fumbling with the syringe stuck in Victor's arm. Moments later the Captain sees Sammy roll up on shore. To his amazement, a sea lion rises near her. He aims his pistol and shoots. The sea lion goes under and Sammy takes off running. The bullet lands harmlessly in the sand.

"Grab guns," the Captain orders as he kicks Andre's hand away from Victor and Victor slides to a seated position. His face flush, veins pulsing in his forehead, the Captain turns his gun on Victor. His finger twitches on the trigger, but he does not fire. "You worthless," the Captain says. "You stay here," and he throws the hand-gun on Victor's lap. "If she come back, shoot her."

"The antidote," Victor pleads.

"Shoot her," the Captain says as he leaves the boat. "Then you get antidote."

The Captain and Andre begin their chase thirteen minutes behind Sammy. About twenty-five feet down the trail the Captain finds her sandal. He bends down, but his huge stomach prevents him from reaching it. "Pick that up," he orders Andre. A slip of spit crawls out of the Captain's mouth as he checks his wristwatch and smiles. "We have her soon. Only twenty more minutes, then she be dead," he says with confidence.

Moving slowly and deliberately, they reach the ceremonial circle of the ancient totem-poles only minutes after Sammy departs. Each totem is cut from a large log, and the faces of animals watch them approach. It is cool and the wind dances through grandfather trees rising over one-hundred feet in the air. Others lay on the ground with ferns and moss growing out of them.

"Frightening," Andre says, his shoulders slouching away from the totems. The sound of an airplane engine rumbles through the trees. Through the branches he catches a glimpse of a wing and pontoons. "An airplane," Andre points out.

"I hear, stupid," the Captain says. "It just another sea plane. There are hundreds here." The Captain takes a swing at Andre and nicks his shoulder. "Keep looking."

Bent forward, the Captain's cheeks droop like an old bloodhound. Andre and the Captain move around the clearing, searching for clues. "What do I look for?" Andre asks.

"Idiot," the Captain bellows. "Prints. We want footprints."

"So many," Andre says. "Everything looks like footprint."

Trees creak and moan in the wind. Leaves and needles drop around them. Andre keeps peeking at the totems, worried they are watching him. He brushes the needles off his head and stares at his feet. His eyes catch a print he hasn't seen before. In the front is a reddish splotch, moist and fresh. Andre points, "Maybe this her."

"Shut up," says the Captain, seeing what he thinks is a sandal print on another path.

"This her," he orders. "Go this way."

Andre shakes his head, but not wanting to get hit again, he follows the Captain's order.

Chapter Fifty-Three

Angie flies high and slow above the water. Liz searches with high-power binoculars for oil, if there is any, and to identify a boat, if there is one. The sea lion's locator tag has given them a general location, but now they have to find the exact fishing boat and hopefully Sammy. "We'll start with a grid search," Teddy tells Liz, "covering smaller areas east to west, while working our way north. That way we won't miss anything."

The sun leaves bright reflections on the ocean surface that follow them as they crisscross the blue and white spray. They are in an area where smaller islands disappear when the tide rises. Larger islands are a solid mass of dark green from the air, covered with trees. On a right turn they speed above the tip of one of the larger islands and Liz yells, "Below."

Uncle Teddy dips one wing and inspects the shoreline. A vessel sits at a dock on the isolated island.

"That's not a private craft," Uncle Teddy says. "It's a commercial fishing trawler."

Liz searches the charts. "This is SGang Gwaay (Skung Gwhy) Island. Many Native American tribes consider this sacred ground, and it's a World Heritage site. You can't fish here."

"This could be it," Uncle Teddy says.

"Look," Liz says, pointing down to a rainbow of color **from an oil** slick leaking from the stern of the fishing boat.

"OIL PURPLE TAG," Liz says. "That could be the oil she was referring to. We may have found her."

Uncle Teddy continues straight over the island. "One man is on deck. He's sitting down, hurt or sleeping," he says. "I'm taking us down. We'll approach from the opposite side so as not to attract attention." He guides Angie away from the island, and makes a hard one-hundred-eighty-degree turn.

"I see another boat approaching the island," Liz says. She scrunches her eyes and adjusts the binoculars. "That looks like ... Oh my gosh, that's my skiff." Her face goes white. "That must be Zach and he'll be on the island soon."

Uncle Teddy guides Angie to the north side of the island, cuts the engine, and goes into a steep dive. Liz grabs the hand-hold above her head. They approach the water at a high speed, but in silence. At the last second, he pulls the nose up and makes a perfect landing just out of sight of the trawler. Hitting the water, he shuts the engine down and guides Angie onto the bank. They stop immediately. He clicks on the radio.

"Gretchen, this is Teddy. We've found a trawler on the west side of SGang Gwaay Island."

"We're on our way," Gretchen's voice rings. "You're in Canada, you know that?"

"We'll deal with that later," Teddy says. "No time for formalities now. We're going in to get Sammy, but we have one more complication. Liz's nephew, Zach, may be on the island too. I think he's trying to help Sammy, but keep an eye out for him. We're armed and loaded and I'll have my cell on silent. Get here as soon as you can."

"10-4," says Gretchen, "I'm on my way with four deputies. We'll be there in thirty minutes."

"Uncle Teddy, Uncle Teddy," a voice chirps in.

"Darn it, I forgot about Loren," Teddy whispers. "Hey Champ."

"Is she okay?" Loren's voice is pitched with excitement.

"We don't know yet Champ, but I'll keep you posted. You man the headquarters. We'll talk later. Out."

"Which ones do you want," Liz asks. She holds the two rifles and has a pistol at her feet. Uncle Teddy points to one rifle. "I already have a pistol," he says. As soon as they stop, Liz hops out, opens the cargo hold and pulls a folded raft out while holding on to a rope. The tight bundle slides across a pontoon, the rope pulls, and a dim pop comes from an air canister. The raft expands like an eagle's wings.

"Take the raft around that point," Teddy says, "Approach from the water. I'll come in from shore."

Liz straps on the pistol and slings a rifle over her shoulder, "If Zach's here," she says, "he could be anywhere, on the island, or the boat, or even captured like Sammy. And that guy on the deck, he's probably armed, so be careful."

Teddy glances back and reaches out to her. He touches her hand for two heart beats and nods, "You too," he says.

As Liz launches the small life raft, Uncle Teddy runs to the woods. He stops and kneels on one knee, checking the pistol around his waist, and the rifle hung over his shoulder. He was trained as a pilot in the Navy, but he also had survival and firearms training. He doesn't like guns, but knows exactly how to use them.

The forest is dense, filled with broken branches and downed logs. He steps with great care, but still makes more noise than he likes. Halfway to the fishing boat a deer jumps across his path. His hand moves toward the pistol, then he pauses. Adrenaline pumps through his veins, his temples throb. "Calm down Teddy," he says to himself. "You need your wits about you. Don't get over anxious, don't move too fast." A crow caws in the distance and he notices something strange, unfamiliar--an energy surrounding him. He shakes to clear his head and moves forward.

Small waves lap against the shoreline. A few feet back, Uncle Teddy crouches behind a tree. The man on the boat seems to be alone and is sitting. The boat rocks and his head lops to one side. Assured that the man on the boat is not aware of him, Uncle Teddy moves forward. As silent as a cat sneaking over wet grass, he creeps onto the dock. Rotting wood planks creak and moan with each step, but Victor doesn't move. The sides of the boat rise about four feet above the dock, so Uncle Teddy is able to crouch low and stay out of sight. A ladder hangs down from a chain railing. The boat rocks, banging against pilings as strong waves wash in. Teddy scurries to the ladder and cautiously peeks in across the deck. Victor sits holding a pistol. His chin rests on his chest, eyes shut; he snores. Beyond, Teddy sees Sammy's kayak lashed to the side rails. Like a ghost, he slips to the ladder, rests his rifle on the deck at shoulder height, and takes aim.

"Hey, Sleeping Beauty," he calls. "Wake up and don't move,"

Victor snorts, jerks and points his gun in several directions before focusing on Uncle Teddy. He stares for a moment, mouth open, drip of drool slipping over his lower lip. He shakes his shoulders, sits upright, and smiles, "Is what you call a stand-off, heh?"

"From where I stand, it looks more like two against one." Liz says from the other side of the boat. She stands with the barrel of her rifle resting on the railing. All Victor can see is the top of her blond head, her eyes, and the large hole in the end of the barrel. Victor sweeps his eyes from Liz to Teddy and back, then carefully sets his gun on the deck and raises his hands. Teddy keeps his weapon pointed at Victor while Liz climbs up the far side. She kicks Victor's gun across the deck, and bends to pick it up. Ted hurries across the deck to the cabin door. Gun ready, he kicks the steel door open. "Empty," he says. He walks to the ladder leading below deck. "Is anyone below?"

Victor shakes his head, "No."

"What's this?" Liz says, pointing to the syringe and the backpack. "This doesn't look good Ted."

Uncle Teddy opens the backpack and holds up another box. He glances at Victor, "What is this stuff?" When Victor does not answer, Teddy raises his pistol. "Tell me what this is, now!"

Victor tries to spit, but coughs and spits up on his shirt. "Help me, I help you," he finally says. Teddy kneels in front of him and pushes the muzzle of his gun into Victor's forehead. "Is this really worth dying for?"

Victor squirms, then says, "Poison."

Teddy looks at Liz, "Poison." He holds up another box. "And this?"

"Antidote."

"Is she infected?" Uncle Teddy says grabbing Victor by the shirt collar.

Victor winces, "Yes. And me."

"Is she on the island?"

Victor nods.

"And the antidote, did she get it?"

Victor's chin falls to his chest as his head moves side to side.

"How much time?" Teddy yells, feeling his sense of urgency rise as the questions take forever.

"Fifteen, twenty minutes." Victor answers. "And me?"

Teddy pushes the box of antidote into his coat.

"You watch him, I'm going after her," he says, taking a step.

He stops, and points his gun at Victor again.

"Is anyone after her?"

Victor holds up two fingers. "Please, me."

"Teddy," Liz says, keeping her gun on Victor, "wait for Gretchen. Please."

"No time," he answers. He opens the box, pulls out a syringe, and rolls it to Liz. As he jumps off the boat, he says, "I think this is what he's asking for."

"The antidote," Victor says and points to the syringe on the deck.

Liz realizes he is asking her to save his life. As the syringe rolls toward the edge of the boat, she struggles with indecision, but she can't murder anyone, even a man who has harmed someone she loves.

She grabs the rolling object as it is about to roll off the boat. "You don't deserve this," she says, "but I'm not like you." She holds the needle like a knife, steps next to him and with one strong thrust, stabs the needle into his chest. "You better hope she is okay," she says.

Chapter Fifty-Four

On the opposite side of the island, waves rush over the bow of Zach's skiff. He approaches a small cove, slows and shuts the engine down as the hull grinds over clam shells, rocks and mud, coming to rest between driftwood tree trunks. Zach bends to pick from his tools as a sea plane passes in the distance. The crow circles above. Zach chooses the fishing knife. "This might come in handy," he says to the crow and loops the sheath over his belt. He lifts the rope over his head. "You never know," he says and loops it over his head, so it crosses his chest. He adjusts both to make sure they are secure in case he needs to run. His final choice is the fish gaff with a large sharp hook on the end. "Fly fast and I'll follow," he says, waving the hook. The crow caws and hovers in mid-air, flapping its wings. Holding the fish gaff like a walking stick, he inspects the bottom of the boat. Water sloshes around the fishing gear and the old marine radio that is at his feet. He picks up the radio and tests it. There is no sound, so he tosses it back. "Ready," he says, and climbs out of the boat. Looping the bow-rope to a small tree, he begins a slow jog following the crow who is cawing and speeding toward the center of the island.

Unaware that Ted and Liz have arrived at the north end of the island, Zach moves cautiously. The crow flies ahead and every few minutes circles back over him before jetting off through the branches again. Leaving the cove, he edges along a path overgrown with low bushes and ferns. A gust of wind shakes branches and he hears something like a scream. Zach freezes, remains silent, but hears nothing else. "Sammy?" he says to the trees and steps forward.

At a split in the trail, the whoosh of broad wings and several squawks pulls Zach toward the center of the island. He soon loses sight of the black wings of the crow and quickens his pace. Impatient, he breaks into a run until he catches sight of movement through the brush and drops to his hands and knees. He slows his breath and gently pulls back a branch. Across an opening he spots the familiar gold emblem on the Captain's hat. Even at a distance he smells the scent of stale cigar. Behind, he recognized Andre, who drags his feet and mumbles to himself. The Captain says something and points.

Zach's heart pounds as he crouches and strains to track the gold patch through openings in the brush. The crow hovers beyond. It seems he wants Zach to pass where the men stand. With the wave of his hand, Zach hopes to make the crow move to one side or the other. The large black bird does not. "Stupid bird," Zach hisses.

In order to pass, Zach's only hope is to lure the Captain and Andre toward him and circle around the two men. With rabbit like speed, Zach scurries to his left. His fingers scratch the dirt and scoop up three stones the size of golf balls. Several feet closer, he rises up and lobs a stone to the far side of the clearing. It thuds on the forest floor. The Captain slaps Andre and points down the trail. "You hear that?" he says. Andre shakes his head. "Come," the Captain orders and as if walking on nails, tip-toes in the direction of the dull thump. Zach watches Andre kick dirt and amble away behind the Captain. Satisfied they are gone, he circles around the clearing and, checking frequently over his shoulder, follows the crow.

Chapter Fifty-Five

U ncle Teddy runs fast and quiet. Head down, he scans front and side for any movement. His impulse is to call out to Sammy, but he knows that would alert the fishermen. All he can do is move forward and track the footprints on the trail. What appears to be sandal prints in the dirt becomes one sandal. "She's barefoot," he says and quickens his pace.

Minutes after the Captain and Andre leave the clearing, Uncle Teddy arrives at the circle of poles. Kneeling behind the largest one, he inspects the area. His fingers knead the surface of the pole, and he realizes he is tracing the intricate pattern of a carved face. "Totems," he says. Knowing he would be exposed if he moved into the clearing, he decides to use them as shields. There are no signs of activity, so he quickly steps behind the next totem to his right while searching for prints.

"Okay," he says, talking to the carved images. "I need your help. Have you seen anyone lately?" He kneels and sees many animal prints. Deer, badger, possibly bear have been in the area. He also finds human footprints. Several people have passed recently, some with heavy boots, and one with a smaller shoe and a bare foot. He touches the bare footprint. "It's okay, Sammy. I'll find you soon," he whispers. Every couple of feet he spots another impression of her bare foot, narrow and delicate. Circling the totems, he starts to follow one trail, but is confused when he finds Sammy's foot print at another trail, and eventually four paths leading away from the clearing. Uncle Teddy inspects each trail again. Bending close, he rubs his thumb in each heel print. At three of the trails her prints are deeper and misshaped, like she was heavier, or had stepped on them more than once. He looks at a totem. "I see what she did," he says. "Smart girl." At the last trail, he slings his rifle over his shoulder, reaches down and touches his finger to a reddish-black glob. It is the faint red of blood. "You're hurt," he says. "I'm coming."

Chapter Fifty-Six

The Captain and Andre continue in the direction of the thump, while the Captain lectures Andre on how smart he was to bring the poison, "No one ever know she was poisoned. It seem like illness or something," he says. "Only five minutes and it be over."

Andre follows behind loathing the Captain more with each step. Andre notices that the footprints have changed to boot and animal prints, but he doesn't say anything. He doesn't like the Captain and is afraid of him. "If I'm so stupid," he mumbles to himself, "why are we walking down the wrong trail?"

It isn't long before the Captain bends forward, looks over his stomach, and realizes the girl's footprints are gone.

Throwing his hat at Andre, he curses and pushes and slaps him. "Stupid, she not here," he yells. "Turn around. Stupid."

Andre flinches and mumbles his apologies, afraid to remind the Captain that he, not Andre, made the choice. With his belly jiggling like jelly and Andre's skinny legs stumbling behind, they hurry back toward the clearing. Near the totem circle the Captain pulls Andre behind a tree. "Do not speak," he whispers, and points to the clearing. Facing away from them stands a man wearing a leather flight jacket, with a pistol on his hip and a rifle slung over his shoulder. He is studying the ground, inspecting something in the dirt.

"Someone here to save her," the Captain whispers to Andre. "Time we finish this." He sucks his floppy belly in and pulls a pistol from his pants. With great care, he leans against the tree, supports the barrel of the gun on a branch and aims at the man's back.

The man looks up and appears to speak to the totems.

"Squeeze gently," the Captain says to himself.

Chapter Fifty-Seven

Following the crow, Zach planned to circle back to the path, but the fishermen have returned. The Captain is upset; he waves his hands and, as usual, hits Andre who stumbles over roots and into branches. Zach holds back, and then follows them along the trail. Approaching a clearing, they stop and the Captain pulls out a gun. He sneaks to a tree, and with one eye scrunched, he takes aim. Following the line of the barrel, Zach recognizes San Juan Ted crouching near a totem. Sometimes, there is no time for thought, just action. Zach picks up a rock, takes position and throws.

He doesn't play sports, but he tried out for the baseball team as a freshman. In pitching practice Zach threw the ball seventy-eight miles per hour. The coach went wild, but Freddy teased and Zach never went back. Now his natural ability takes over. In less than a second the stone reaches its mark. In that second the Captain's finger gently squeezes the trigger. Before the bullet reaches the end of the barrel, the rock strikes the

Captain's temple, his head crashes against the tree trunk, and his hand jerks. The bullet is diverted a fraction of an inch, just enough to make it hit Uncle Teddy in the shoulder and not the heart.

Zach picks up the gaff and runs. Andre spins around to face the sound that approaches him; Uncle Teddy falls forward from the impact of the bullet. A pain the size of an ocean shoots through his back. The bullet passes through and hits no organs. He stumbles to his feet, raises his rifle, and aims at who shot him. In his sight, he sees Zach hurdle two bushes and land with both feet on Andre's chest. A shriek emerges from the pinned-down Andre as the point of the gaff rests on his neck.

"Don't move," Zach says. "Don't even breath."

"No worry, no worry," Andre pleads, "I surrender."

The Captain moans and rolls over from where he fell next to the tree. "What?" he says, looking into the barrel of Uncle Teddy's rifle.

"Where is she?"

"I no know," the Captain sneers and smiles at the sight of blood pulsing from Teddy's shoulder. "I got you," he adds.

With no time to waste, Teddy knows his best action is to track Sammy. "You know how to use these?" he asks as he hands Zach his rifle and the pistol the Captain dropped.

"My Grandpa taught me," Zach says.

"Good. Shoot them if they move. I've got to find Sammy."

Chapter Fifty-Eight

Forgetting about his shoulder, Uncle Teddy runs, full speed now, crashing through the forest like a bull elk. As the deadline approaches he yells, "Sammy, Sammy, where are you? Sammy!"

A cavernous hole grows in his stomach. Too much time has passed. His toe clips a raised root and he drops to his knees.

"Sammy," Uncle Teddy says. Tears form beneath his eyes, then a sound, something faint, as tiny as a pearl, reaches out to him.

"Mom, Mommy ..." the voice says.

"Sammy, Sammy," Uncle Teddy yells, scrambling back toward the voice. Light filters through the forest canopy, small animals skitter away in the underbrush and Uncle Teddy lumbers on, breaking branches, and falling in the moss.

"Mommy," he hears again, the words only feet away. He pushes his face to the earth. Under a fallen tree, in the moss and undergrowth, he sees a small opening. In the darkness, he barely recognizes the shape of a delicate foot. His fingers scratch through the ferns and moss as he crawls on his belly.

"Sammy," he repeats, "Sammy, I'm here." Able to reach her, he pulls out the small box of antidote. His hands shake and the box sticks. He howls in frustration until the catch releases. Pulling her into his arms, she falls across his lap, limp and lifeless. His hands shake as he fumbles to pick a syringe and he drops it. He quickly grabs another, steadies it against his knee and slips off the cap, exposing a three-inch needle. He pricks the point against her neck and pushes. Yellow liquid drains from the syringe. It has been twenty-seven minutes since he left the boat. He bows his head and holds her, "Sammy," he whispers as he rocks back and forth.

Chapter Fifty-Nine

Stunned from the blow to his head, the Captain sits in the dirt, his wide belly and butt spread out like a jellyfish. He squirms in an expanding puddle as his fingers search for balance. It doesn't matter; he now stares into the business end of a rifle. Andre's hands are bound with the rope and he is tied to a tree. The Captain's face turns red and blotchy; sweat drips off his cheeks; his pants are soaked with urine. "You think you know how to kill?" The Captain says, trying to distract and humiliate Zach. "You can't even kill a seal."

"You're right," Zach says. "I don't kill seals, or any other animal. We're all connected, even though I don't understand how garbage like you fits into this whole mess. But just for the record, I'll shoot you anyway if you move."

"No need," comes a voice from the grove. "Put your weapons down on the ground in front of you, very slowly." A group of police officers with a tall red-head in the lead, walks toward them, guns drawn. "You're Zach Smith. Is that right?"

Zach nods as he gently lays the rifle and pistol in front of him on the dirt. "Step back please," Gretchen says, "I think we can handle these guys from here. I'm Lieutenant Gretchen Hanson, San Juan Police Department. Have you seen Ted Crenshaw or Sammy?" she asks.

"Yes, Ted ran that way searching for Sammy," Zach says, pointing through the grove. "This man shot him, so Ted will need help."

"You've got this situation," Gretchen says to an officer, "I'm going after Crenshaw."

"May I come," Zach asks.

Gretchen hesitates, studies his face a moment, "No. You stay here."

Zach steps forward, "But it's my fault."

The officers step forward as one. Gretchen pushes her hand up, "Stay here. I don't have time to argue."

As if something breaks, Zach's face twists, his hands rise up to his cheeks and he sits heavily on the ground. His head flops forward and his shoulders jerk. Maybe he feels relief, or maybe he realizes that he is, along with the fishermen, a prisoner.

Gretchen takes three long strides and her cell phone rings. "Teddy?" she says.

"I'm in a small cave on a trail just north of the totem circle. Sammy's alive, but in pretty bad shape. We need an air ambulance and a medic ASAP."

"Will do." Gretchen says. She immediately calls for a Medical Evacuation Team. Assured they are on their way, she follows the trail of footprints north of the clearing.

"Teddy ... Sammy," Gretchen calls. She is fifteen feet passed the small cave when she hears Teddy. "Over here. We're over here."

Moments later she peers into the darkness. Sammy lays in Teddy's lap, her head propped back. Sammy's chest rises and falls every few seconds as Teddy breaths into her mouth, administering CPR.

"Is Medevac on the way?" he asks between breaths.

"They'll be here any minute," she says, and places her hand on Sammy's neck.

"Ted, I don't feel a pulse."

Chapter Sixty

Shivering, cold, like an icicle between refrigerator sheets, I pull the covers up and a fire bolt shoots from my arm though my shoulder. My fingers tingle. Thick, I try to wet my lips, but it's like licking a frozen pipe; my tongue sticks to them. My eyes are closed because my eyelids are stuck together too, like someone ran superglue over them. I turn over. Everything goes dark.

I wake, push my hands out trying to sit up and moan. What the heck is happening?

"Sammy. Can you hear me?"

"Yes, of course I can hear you. Yes," I say, but nothing comes out. I try again, this time my lips move, but there's no sound. Geez, mouth dry, tongue stuck to the roof of my mouth, teeth huge as boulders, whale lips

"How's she doing?" a woman's voice asks.

"I think she's waking up."

"Mr. Crenshaw, your CPR may have saved her life. She had respiration when she was brought in, but barely. We had a hard time detecting a pulse."

I try to speak again, this time something comes out. It sounds kind of like, "arrghhettha." I have no idea what is going on, but I am in no position to argue. The pain is too great, so I lie back and hear myself groan.

"I brought gelatin and some liquids for her. Try giving her some when she wakes up. They'll help with her dry mouth. As the medications wear off, she'll come around. She'll be fine."

Medications? What medications? I'll be coming around. Around what? Is that good?

I crack open my eyes to an almost dark room. I rub them. Crusty ridges scrape my fingers, like scratching barnacles off of a sea lion.

Sea lions. A flash of purple races through my mind. I feel cold, so I reach for my down comforter and hit something hard, metallic. I remember putting my foot up on a railing.

Above me blinks tiny green, blue and yellow lights. A slow, low beep-beep-beep fills the room. The smell of disinfectant swims around me and Uncle Teddy sits in a chair next to my bed. I shiver and a wave of terror sweeps through me. I'm not in my bed. I'm in a hospital. I must have moaned because Uncle Teddy wakes up. He leans forward and takes my hand.

"Sammy, you're okay. I'm right here. It's okay," he says, over and over.

"Uncle Teddy. Where am I?"

"We're at the Island Hospital in Anacortes. Medevac flew us here after I found you."

"Medevac?"

"Yes, but don't worry. You're safe. I'm with you." He turns to the wall. "Loren and Liz are here too."

Liz sleeps on the couch with Loren lying in her lap. I shiver again and reach for a blanket. Uncle Teddy pulls something over me--soft, warm and heated. It feels so-o-o good.

As I sink into the warmth, images appear in my mind: The Captain's face--his fat jowls wiggling as he laughs; the man with a beard holding me, the boat, oil, the island. On a metal table next to me sits a covered tray and a bowl of shiny pink gelatin. I touch the cart and the pink jiggles.

"Oh my gosh!" I yell at Uncle Teddy. "There are men on an island. They have guns."

"It's okay, Sammy, we caught them," Uncle Teddy says. "Gretchen came with the police. They've been arrested. You're safe."

"Gretchen? Indiana Jones Gretchen?"

Uncle Teddy laughs. "That's a pretty good description."

His laughter causes him to wince and he touches his chest. My eyes focus and I realize he has a bandage wrapped under his shirt. "What happened?" I ask, my voice cracking.

"It's nothing, just a wound from chasing the fishermen," he says as he pats my hand.

His comment triggers more memories and everything begins to flood back. I feel pain in my knees and my stomach. I remember them shooting at me.

On the cart by my bed I see the barrel of a syringe. "What's that for? Is that for me?" I ask, feeling a shooting pain in my shoulder.

"Just for pain," Uncle Teddy says as he grabs the plastic tube and tosses it into a trash bin. "You were right about the seals. They had been poisoned. Those fishermen were crazy, Sammy. So crazy they thought catching a few more salmon was worth killing seals and you."

"Killing me?" I ask.

Liz, who just woke up, steps around Uncle Teddy, her golden smile lighting our space. "Yes, they tried," she says, "but we got to you in time."

A small face peeks around Liz. Loren steps to the bed and puts his head next to mine. "Hi Sammy."

"Hi Punkster."

"I'm glad you're home," he says.

That's when I lose it. I choke, gasp, tears stream down my face. I grab Loren's head, kiss him over and over, holding him in a head-lock. "I love you," I say. "Are you okay. I hope you're okay."

"I'm okay," he says. "Geez, let go will ya. I'm fine. I'm okay." Then he yells, "Oh Yukkk!" as I lurch over and puke.

Chapter Sixty-One

The room explodes with light when I wake. Sun streams in, making everything a yellowish white. A covered plate on a cart gives off a gravy smell and two glasses sit nearby, one clear, one orange. Across one wall flowers line up like a florist shop. I snuggle down in the covers and watch. Uncle Teddy sleeps in a chair next to me. I remember Liz and Loren are here from earlier, but they aren't in the room now. The thickness in my mind remains, but not like before. My whale lips have returned to near normal. I can open my eyes and I begin to see things more clearly. I remember Uncle Teddy saying we are at a hospital and I am safe, but I worry.

A few days ago I'd just begun to feel happy, now I'm in a hospital. I couldn't have screwed up any more if I'd tried. He'll probably send me home, is my first thought, then I remember I don't have a home. My home is gone and so is my mom. Like a baby, I pull my knees against my chest. The emptiness of totally being lost aches in my bones and my only thought is, Why?

I try to picture her, but something is wrong--she won't appear. Fragments of moments come into view, like still images frozen in time; a puzzle with most of the pieces lost. I close my eyes, concentrate, and imagine. Her eyes stare deeply into mine. I smile, and the next moment my dad appears. My dad, the ass-hero.

I don't try to remember him at all. I shake my head, hoping he'll fall out my ears. He doesn't. He just stands there, totally sad. For the first time, I feel something about him, something painful. Not my anger, but his anger, his pain, like he is locked inside some kind of dream, or nightmare. I experience his emotions, watch him, imagine reaching out to him--he disappears like he always does.

I look at Uncle Teddy, as if continuing my vision. I reach out and touch his hand. He jerks, and smiles, "Hi Kiddo."

"Hi Uncle Teddy."

We are silent for a moment, he gets that big dumb Uncle Teddy grin on his face that makes me laugh no matter what, and I do.

"Where is everyone?" I ask.

"Liz and Loren went down to get some breakfast," he says.

Without thinking, I ask, "Is my dad here?"

Uncle Teddy's grin fades, he studies his knees. A cloud passes and the room darkens. I become aware of the monotone beeps from the machines. "Listen Kiddo," Uncle Teddy begins, "he wanted to be here, but he couldn't ..." His voice trails off. He struggles with his words for a few moments, then continues, "Oh, what the heck. Listen Sammy, I can't lie to you. Your Dad's in trouble, not with the law or anything, but emotional trouble. I told you about his service in the Iraq War. Nineteen ninety, he flew a helicopter in Operation Desert Storm. For a lot of people the war was a cake-walk, but plenty of service men and women went through hell. We won, but we also paid a price."

He takes a deep breath, "Your father became a hero during the war. He transported troops in and out of active fire zones, where people shot at him. A small platoon of soldiers was cut off from their company. He flew in several times to pick those soldiers up and carry them out. On his last flight he was shot down, captured, and ..."

"What? Please tell me."

"He was tortured, Sammy, for several weeks before our troops found him and got him out. They sent him to Germany first and eventually he came home. About three months later, after being deemed physically fit, he was sent back to the Middle East to complete his tour of duty. He didn't have to go, but he volunteered. When he finally came home, he received the Silver Star for his valor. We thought the war was over for him."

I rub my forehead and try to understand what I am being told. "But it wasn't, was it?" I say.

Uncle Teddy surveys the room, and continues, "What we weren't aware of then was trauma can cause what's called Post Traumatic Stress Disorder. PTSD is the lingering result of trauma affecting many returning Veterans. The military's getting better at identifying the symptoms and helping service people, but no one spotted it in your dad and no one did anything--not the military, not me."

"So, what's that mean?"

"It means he's got serious emotional problems: short temper, anger, depression, alcohol abuse. People with PTSD withdraw from others, even those they love most. Whatever you think your dad is, Sammy, I don't think he's at fault."

I feel a nervous energy giving me the jimmy-leg. I pull a pillow over my tummy and knead the sheets with my thumb. A cold sweat breaks out on my forehead. Part of me screams, "Excuses, excuses, all I hear are excuses." But another part of me registers, "PTSD. He's sick. He needs my help, I've been an ass." Finally, Uncle Teddy comes into focus, I lock on his face.

"Where is he?" I ask.

"I don't know. I spoke with him after we reached the hospital. He said he'd try to get here, but he sounded shaky. I suspect he's been drinking." Uncle Teddy scratches his head. "I'm telling you this because you need to know the truth about your dad, both good and bad. I know the bank took possession of the house and he's moved out. I'm concerned he might be, well, he might be on the streets."

My brain spins. "Dad worked with the Forest Service before he got fired," I said. "How could he be on the streets?"

"With his PTSD, and your mom's death, he's pretty messed up. I don't know where he is, but I'm searching for him. I'll find him, I promise." He reaches out and touches my arm. "I haven't said a word to Loren about any of this. We should keep this between you and me. Okay?"

"Yeah, sure." I say. What a family. Mom's gone, Dad's a mess, I'm a mess. My emotions rise up and in that moment, I want to put Loren in another head-lock and hug him.

The door opens and Liz walks in carrying a stack of folded clothes. Loren steps from behind her wearing a surgical mask, rubber gloves, and a light green surgeon's cap. He pushes his fingers together in the oversized gloves like a spider on a mirror. "I'm sorry to tell you," he says in his best Dracula voice, "we have to operate, ha, ha, ha." I reach for him, but he's too quick and steps back.

"Good news," Liz says, "you get to go home tomorrow, as soon as the doctor does his rounds. And look," she adds, holding up a copy of the Seattle Times. "You are a celebrity."

I don't recognize the face under the headline - LOCAL GIRL CAPTURES SEAL KILLERS. My eyes focus on the image. "My eighth-grade picture," I say to the face smiling back at me. "I'm the Local Girl? What? Why am I in the paper?"

"Word got out about the rogue fishermen and the seal killings. Someone found out about your kidnapping, how you escaped, and the news was published today." Liz explains. "Apparently the story went online last night. I'm told it went viral, whatever viral means. The nurses tell me they saw reports on the news and some morning shows are even talking about you. People have been calling the store and the San Juan Express lines all day. You're a star."

"I'm a star? No, I'm not. I almost died. This is crazy, really seriously stupid."

As I try to make sense of all that has happened, Uncle Teddy's phone rings. Liz answers. "No," she says, "not now. Who is this?" She stops talking, listens for a minute, and looks at me with eyes the size of sand dollars. We all stare at her as she shakes her head, reaches out and hands the phone to Uncle Teddy. "I think you should take this Ted."

"Theodore Crenshaw," he answers in his most, 'I'm the man,' voice. "You're serious? How do I know?" He goes silent, straightens his back and stands a little taller. "Yes sir," he says. "It's for you Sammy," and he hands me the phone.

I hesitate and rub dribble from my cheek with the sheet, "Hello," I say, expecting my dad. "Who? Wait a minute, who is this? You are totally kidding!"

Chapter Sixty-Two

I'm so startled, I fumble the phone. It hits my cheek and the line goes dead. I push a few buttons and the voice reappears. "Hello, hello, he says."

"Is this a joke?" I say.

"No, I'm really the President."

I put my hand over the speaker, "Oh my gosh, this is the President of the United States," I say, pointing to the phone.

"I'm calling, Sammy ..." He pauses, "May I call you Sammy?"

I nod my head.

After several seconds of silence, he continues. "I'm calling to congratulate you and tell you we are all very proud of what you did."

"I didn't do anything," I say.

"On the contrary, you put into practice several very powerful messages."

I nod again.

"You showed all of us what one person can do by getting involved and telling people when you see something that is wrong. You also demonstrated what has come to be known as Girl Power. I prefer to call it people power, meaning young women, like yourself, speaking up, taking action and changing things for the better. Believe me, with two young daughters, I hear a lot about that. And not least, you reminded us all what courage in the face of danger looks like."

I start to say that I was scared, but I remember what Olie said, "no fear, no courage required," so I don't say anything.

"These are difficult times," he continues, "and we can all use a reminder of what the goodness of humanity looks like." We talk for a few more minutes, and then he hangs up.

I look at Uncle Teddy. "It was really him," I say. "He just wanted to check in to see how I was doing. He asked a lot of questions. And guess what? His daughters asked him to call. They were concerned about me. He had a meeting to go to, but he invited me to Washington."

Uncle Teddy nods and smiles.

"Bring your family, he said. I'd like to meet you, and your dad."

I glance at Loren who is blowing up a rubber-glove balloon.

"He said he'd show us around the White House. Maybe arrange for me to meet his daughters. How cool is that? I wish I'd talked to his daughters."

That evening, while everyone is having dinner in the hospital cafeteria, a knock on the door wakes me. "Can a stranger make a visit?" a deep gentle voice comes from outside. My hand shifts under my chin and my shoulder screams for relief as I roll over. I notice the sweet aroma of pipe smoke and know who is outside.

"Yeah, sure, come on in," I say.

A crinkly face appears around the door. The old wrinkled hat turns in his hands, "I've come to pay my respects to our Local Hero," he says with a twinkle in his eye. I pull the sheets up and adjust the bed so I can sit up. He has a small bag in his hand that he holds out as he approaches. "I brought you a little something."

With Olie, a kind of calm walks into the room. The tobacco odor mixed with the flower scent makes my head spin. I remember how frightened I'd been of him. Now I like that he wants to visit.

"For me? Thank you," I say and take the white paper bundle. Small bumps and ridges move under my fingers. I open the top and peer in. Brightly colored beads in a long strand sit on a bed of blue-black feathers.

Eager for me to understand, he says, "It's a hair wrap." He turns his head and points to his pony tail. I stare for a moment then take the strand between my fingers and pull out the beautiful gift. "You can weave it into a braid, or wrap it around like mine," he continues, but his voice almost disappears as a joy rises up in my being.

"Oh gosh, thank you so much," I choke out.

"Scá'a'," he adds, "the crow, he contributed a few feathers."

The iridescent plume rests across my palm and I recall the crow on the deck. I smile at the feeling of peace and safety they give me. I look into Olie's face. "My animal spirit guide, the crow," he says. "He guided Ahanu to you."

My eyebrows push together and he continues.

"It's hard to understand that sometimes nature and animals guide us, if we listen," he says.

My thumb strokes the smooth strands of the feathers, "I'm grateful and I do understand." I pause two beats. "What about Zach?"

Olie shifts his weight to one leg, "Yes, about Ahanu, he did some terrible things." Olie crushes the rim of his hat between his large fingers. "He wants to make amends. Ahanu came after you and helped capture the fishermen, but he knows that's not enough."

I remain silent.

"He asked if he could visit you?"

I remember Zach's smile as he walked off the beach, how he protected me against Freddy, but he also hurt, maybe killed, seals. And he worked with men who tried to kill me. The warmth and safety the gift had brought disappears and a cold shudder crosses my chest. "I don't want to see him," I say, "not now."

"Of course."

"What happened to him?" I ask.

"Ahanu's been arrested along with the fishermen. The Captain and his men are in jail pending charges and a trial. The police impounded their boat. Ahanu was held overnight, and released to my custody until a hearing and possible trial."

"What about Freddy?" I ask, his name almost making me sick.

"Freddy," Olie hesitates, "Freddy has disappeared."

I jerk up. "Disappeared? You don't know where he is?" A memory of the beach ... "I get you bitch," he screamed. "But what if he comes back?" I ask.

Olie closes his eyes, "I expect Freddy ran a long way from here, and after the beating his father gave him, I don't think he will return." His palm rests gently on my head, "You are family now Little One. We will protect you."

Family. As good as that sounds, it doesn't touch the dread that rests in my belly.

"Is the crow my spirit guide too?" I ask as I stroke the feathers and hope for protection.

His warm smile lights the room. "That is not for me to say, but I suspect your spirit guide might come from the sea."

I laugh out loud, "Yes, I think you might be right."

As the images of an Orca leaping out of the water, and a sea lion winking at me, flash in my mind, the door swings open and a parade of people march in. Uncle Teddy, with Liz and Loren, lead Lieutenant Gretchen Hanson, Doctor Kristy Singh, and Simone Dubois, who each carry a plant of some sort. Loren has the rubber gloves and surgical mask on and sits in a strategically placed chair where I can't reach him. Uncle Teddy stands at the end of the bed; Liz, Simone, Gretchen and Kristy surrounding him like bookends. Sun lights their faces and I burst out laughing as he stands there beaming a smile as big as the moon. His phrase, you're welcome ANY TIME, comes to mind.

"Look who I've brought," Uncle Teddy says, his arms extending, as far as he is able, around all four women. Laughter erupts and a general commotion of well wishes begins. Somewhere in the next hour I drift off, Simone's sweet Creole voice the last thing I remember, "Honey, you come visit soon--real soon."

Chapter Sixty-Three

The nurse insists I sit in a wheel chair to leave the hospital. Uncle Teddy pushes while Loren and Liz carry their glove-balloons.

At home, I sleep most of the afternoon and through the night. The next morning, I lie in bed feeling like I've just woken from a bad dream. I move my arm and a streak of pain reminds me the dream is real. Sliding my legs off the bed to sit up, my knees and feet needle and my head aches. A sweet perfume surrounds me. I take a breath and fill with a faintly familiar scent. The roses from my hospital room are standing at attention around the floor, but that isn't the source. On the dresser is a huge bouquet of white Jasmine--like Mom's incense. Hanging from the vase is a gold ribbon, with a white envelope. On it is a round blue and gold seal. It reads, "President of the United States"

Totally sweet!

I sit for a few moments, slowly scoot off the bed to standing, and pause while my muscles scream. Even my fingers hurt. Holding on to the bed, I reach for my robe, inch it on and straight-legged, hobble out the door. I take one step at a time up the stairs and into the kitchen which is exploding with morning sunlight. "I'm coming," I say, wincing and covering my eyes. Uncle Teddy sits at the counter alone, glancing through a pile of papers in a huge wicker basket.

"Hey Kiddo. How are you doing?"

"What's it like when a truck hits you?" I ask.

He laughs. "Probably better than you feel, from the looks of you."

"Thanks," I say. "Am I that bad."

"Are you kidding? You're beautiful. The most beautiful sight I can imagine this morning."

"Thanks," I say again. This time with sincerity. The kitchen smells of bacon and toast. I look around. "Where's Loren?"

"He went with Liz to get some blueberries for pancakes. Okay?"

"Sure," I say, as he pushes the basket toward me.

"Letters and email for you. They came in overnight," he says.

He's opened about twenty envelopes. I hold one in my hand, trying to decide if I want to open it or not. I glance at the opened letters. They are mostly from people I don't know, some news people, and a few with foreign country names. The words begin to blur, so I push the letters aside. Uncle Teddy pours me an orange juice. He sits down next to me and rests his hand on my shoulder. I totally swallow the Ouch!

"I heard from your dad yesterday," he says. "He's in Portland, at a shelter."

My stomach drops about three floors. "Is he okay?"

"Well, physically he seems fine. He asked me to give you his love, and say he's sorry he can't be here."

A deep-freeze sweeps through me as I distract myself by leafing through more mail.

"The good thing is he's reached out," Uncle Teddy says. "He's realized he needs help, but I'm not sure he's ready."

I'd learned about drugs and addictions in school, so I understand a little about what he is saying. "If he doesn't want help, we can't help him. Right?" I say.

"Yes, normally, but he made contact, and I know where he is now, so we have a good start."

We sit for a while, not saying anything. I'm pushed on all sides about Dad: He's a hero, he's an ass, he lives on the streets, he has PTSD. Worst of all, I feel bad, like I am responsible. He's never been there for me, I keep telling myself, but it doesn't help. He's got all the good excuses, and all I'm left with is guilt.

"I don't like him very much." I finally say, my chin on my chest.

"I understand, Kiddo. I don't blame you," Uncle Teddy says. "It's not for you to fix. This isn't your fault, and you've got enough going on in your life. I love him though, and I'm going to try and help him."

As Uncle Teddy talks, his words filter through me, like sunlight filters through your hand when you hold it up to a window, diffused in a million ways, so all you see is brightness. Slowly the word Love comes into focus, landing like a butterfly somewhere in my consciousness, and instantly it becomes clear--Mom loved him. It doesn't matter how I feel or what I think of him, Mom loved him and she loved me. The thought is so startling my head snaps up, like a marionette picked up on a string. "I'll help," I blurt out. "I mean, I would like to help, so tell me what I can do."

Uncle Teddy stares at me. His eyes get all pooly, he sniffles and wipes his nose with a napkin. "You're something, Kiddo. Really something."

Heat rises in my cheeks.

"Don't worry, I'll keep you posted. I'll let you know what we can do," he says. "For right now, you take care of yourself. We need to make sure you heal completely from your trauma."

"What trauma?" I say, throwing my arms in the air like an Olympic champion and hopping off the stool. The lightning bolts shoot through arms, legs, feet, shoulders, everywhere. I wince, "Okay," I add. "A few more days and I'll be good as new. For now, I'll just lie down, watch some TV."

"Good idea," Uncle Teddy confirms. "By the way, school starts in a few weeks. When you're ready, we'll make an appointment to meet the school principal and get you enrolled."

School, I think. OMG, I'd forgotten all about school. "Can I get a Presidential pardon?"

I sleep most of the day and through the night. Midmorning, the next day, Uncle Teddy knocks, "Got a minute?" he says.

"Sure, come on in."

He pushes the door open and the end of a white dresser pokes through. Drawers appear with painted flowers around white pull knobs. Sunlight streams in and brightens the blossoms, each different of course; Mom never painted two the same.

"Oh my gosh," I squeal. "How did you get the dresser?"

"Before your dad moved out, I did a little scavenging myself. I thought you might like to have this," he says with a grin.

"You are so totally awesome," is all I can say. I hesitate and raise an eyebrow. "Yes," he says, "I brought Loren's too."

He rests on the dresser. "I want to talk with you about something." He looks around my room, like someone might be listening. "I want to talk about how we are here, as a family."

His voice gets lower, like he is trying to think and talk at the same time.

"How do you like living here?"

My head bobs up, "I thought you already knew. I love being here."

He pauses, "How are you doing ... without your Mom I mean?"

I clench my hands, "I'm fine." My words hit the floor like an anchor. "Well, not fine. I miss her a lot, but I'm okay."

Red and yellow petals catch my attention from flowers around the pull knobs. "Actually, I miss her a lot." Without thinking, I continue, "Sometimes I even feel ... angry." I speak like I knew this before, but I didn't. Until those words slipped out, I was not aware of how angry I really am at her.

"In the hospital, I wanted her." I say. "She should have been with me." The heat of shame rises up my neck. Uncle Teddy steps closer and I push into him. "She should be here," I say. "It's not fair. She should be here." And then as if from a child, I hear myself, "I want my mommy."

The words tumble out with sobs and chokes and tears; I can't stop. I empty a box of tissues, fill the room with a kind of heartbreak I'd never experienced and finally push my face in a pillow until I can hardly breathe.

Grief fills the room like incense, mixing with my shame, and becomes silence. I keep my face in the pillow until Uncle Teddy says, "Me too."

Our eyes meet and he gives me a twisted smile. His hand reaches out, not quite touching me, "I'm angry too, like it was her fault or something. How silly is that?"

I cough out a laugh, "Yeah, silly."

We both take deep breaths, like we've just finished a marathon. "I still love her," I add.

"Oh Kiddo, I understand, believe me," he says.

My face is all scrunched and twisted. "Will the pain go away?" I ask.

"I don't know, but it will change with time--not the love, but maybe the pain."

I love that Uncle Teddy doesn't try to make things okay when they're not. He treats me like an adult when we talk. He doesn't get distracted or look away. He focuses on me.

"It's easier being here with you," I add. "Thanks for having us."

He smiles. "You're welcome. Actually, I don't have much of a choice. You're the only family I have, and I love you way too much to not have you here. Besides, who would I chase around the islands?"

We both giggle and the mood shifts as I sink into Uncle Teddy's arms and his love. "Good point," I say, hugging him.

He adds, out of the blue, "I got an inquiry about a job and I'm wondering if you might like to go with me. Actually, you've been requested."

Eyes narrowing, I say, "What? By who?"

"Your new BFF, the President."

"You're kidding. The President is asking me to go on a job with you?"

"Yup. You're a VIP these days. Anyway, the trip is in about two weeks, so if you want to go, you can."

"Yeah, sure. I'm in. Where are we going?"

"Can't tell you, but I'll let you know as soon as I can. Pack some warm clothes and your hiking boots. Do you have hiking boots?"

"Yeah. No. I mean I don't have boots, but I have warm clothes. Where are we going?"

"Can't say. Top secret. Need to know basis and all that."

"Need to know," I yell as he walks out the door, laughing. "I need to know everything."

Chapter Sixty-Four

Sunlight fills my bedroom and spreads warmth like butter on fresh bread. I sit still for a while and let the cozy feeling sink in. Hands pushed against the headboard, I stretch and roll out of bed, every muscle protesting. I am totally a mess, but it feels good to get up. Loose shorts and top slip on easily, without too much pain. I shuffle to the back door. The garden is ripe with dew, bees just beginning to collect pollen. Seagulls squawk and boat masts tip in the breeze. A crow flies up and rests near the top of a tall fir tree. I wave.

The morning air is damp and fresh. I lean against the door frame and soak in the coolness from the threshold resting under my toes. I wiggle my right foot and a small spider inspecting my big toe scurries away. I think about the old house in Portland, Mom's empty room and Dad sitting like a rag doll with his head on his arm. It seems like a thousand years ago that I stepped out that door.

Two weeks and everything has changed. Well, not everything. Birds still sing, bees buzz, and life moves both over and under the ocean. But the world isn't like I hoped. I want Mom back and I want Dad to be like Uncle Teddy. I never thought I'd say it, but I even want Loren to never ever leave me.

Mom had a little card she put in front of her incense. It read something like: Focus on what you can change, and let go of what you can't. I never knew what that meant, but I'm beginning to understand. There are millions of things I can't change. But, like Simone said, I can change myself to be whatever I want, and that change has already begun.

My back straightens and I smile at the trees, the water, insects, birds, and all the life surrounding me. It's so beautiful. I'm reminded of what the President said, "We all need to be reminded of the goodness of humanity." And he's right. In spite of the bad guys, there is a lot of goodness in our world.

"I don't know what will happen next," I say to the Universe, "but I believe I can handle whatever you send my way."

I touch the locket strung around my neck, push loose strands of hair behind my ear, take a deep breath, and step over the threshold.

Letters from Sammy

Dear Reader,

Thank you for reading my story. I know some of it was kind of sad, and other parts were scary (for me), but I want you to know I'm okay. I'm at Uncle Teddy's (my) house now. I'm recovering quickly. I'll start high-school this year, like some of you, and I'm kind of scared about that. But I get to go on an adventure with Uncle Teddy soon. He won't tell me what it is, but I'm sure it will be exciting. The President has asked me to come, so I may get to meet him, and maybe his daughters. I'll be sure to write about it. Be well, and believe in yourself.

Love,

Sammy

Dear Dad,

We haven't spoken for a few weeks, but I thought I should write and tell you that I'm okay. Uncle Teddy is taking real good care of Loren and me, and I've met some really nice people up here at Loon Song Harbor. I just wanted you to know, we are doing fine.

Uncle Teddy told me you're having a difficult time. I guess you moved out of the house and are living in a new place. He also told me about your PTSD. I'm sorry you are sick. I know you have talked with Uncle Teddy, but I want to help too. I don't know what I can do, but I hope you will tell me if you think of something.

I miss Mom terribly. I know you do too. Loren misses her and you a lot too. Please come and visit us when you feel better. We have lots of room for you.

Well, that is about all for now. Oh, I'm feeling really good after my kidnapping. I got a call from the President. His daughters were worried about me. That was so cool.

Love,

Sammy

PS: You can write to me or txt me or phone if you want.

Zach Ahanu Smith

Dear Zach (Ahanu),

I am writing to you to tell you that it's okay, I am fine. Liz told me that it was you who warned Olie about Freddy, and the fisherman. You saved my life. It was terrible what those fisherman had you and Freddy do to those seals, and that was bad. But you changed your mind and did something very brave.

I heard that you were arrested, but they let you go while you wait for your trial. I also heard that Freddy ran away. He's a total coward. Your Aunt Liz told me that instead of jail, they are asking if you can work with Simone Dubois doing community service helping her with Harbor Seal preservation. That sounds very exciting and something I would like to do. If that works out, maybe I can help this winter.

Anyway, Zach, thank you for helping save me. I hope someday we can be friends.

Sincerely,

Sammy Carlisle

Lt. Gretchen Hanson,

Dear Gretchen,

Thank you for helping save my life and for sending me flowers. They are in my bedroom and smell very nice. Uncle Teddy told me how you captured the fishermen on the island. I can imagine how you Laura Crofted them. They really deserved it. It was so cool how the sea lion found me. I think he might have pushed me up on the island when I was underwater. I am so happy he had that purple tag.

I am doing fine now, so I hope I will see you again when you are in Loon Song Harbor. As Uncle Teddy says, "You are welcome ANY TIME."

Thank you.

Sincerely,

Sammy Carlisle

PS: The President called me and I think Uncle Teddy and I will be going to deliver something to him.

Simone Dubois

University of Washington Marine Research Center

Dear Simone,

Thank you for the flowers you sent me in the hospital. They are in my bedroom and look beautiful. I am feeling much better and I'm happy that the kidnapping thing is all over. Thank you for showing me your office and for inviting me to visit. I would like that very much.

I heard that Zach Smith may do volunteer (sort of volunteer) work with you. You already know Zach because you are Liz's BFF, but I wanted to say that Zach is a very nice person. I think he just got involved with some very bad people. I don't know if it is okay, but I would like to volunteer to work with you some time when he is working. Then we could talk about what we learn.

Thank you again for sending me the flowers and you don't have to write back. Just txt.

Sincerely,

Sammy Carlisle

Dr. Kristy Singh, ACSI

Animal Crime Scene Investigation (ACSI)

Dear Dr Singh,

Thank you for the beautiful flowers. They are in my bedroom and smell very nice. Since leaving the hospital I've been doing fine and feel much better. I haven't seen the sea lion with the purple tag since the kidnapping. I don't suppose I'll ever see her again. I think about her a lot. She is a smart sea lion.

Your work looking at animals that are kidnapped, abused, or carried into the United States illegally sounds very interesting. I do not like looking at dead animals, but I know the autopsies you perform save the lives of many other animals. It is very important work. Someday I would like to visit Animal Crime Scene Investigation.

Thank you again and I hope to visit soon.

Sincerely,

Samantha (Sammy) Carlisle

PS: Loren wants to know, "Do you really not carry a gun?"

The President of the United States of America

Dear Mr. President,

Thank you for sending me flowers. They were jasmine, my mom's favorite flower. She died about a month ago, so they were perfect. The kidnappers were arrested and I guess they are going to be punished for what they did. I feel bad for my friend Zach, who helped them. He changed his mind and did the right thing by turning them in. If you can help him I'd appreciate it. He's a nice person.

Thank you for inviting us to the White House. Uncle Teddy says we can do that over the winter. I also want to thank your daughters for asking you to call me. That was really nice. Please tell them that I want to visit you and meet them really soon. Maybe we can be friends or something.

My Uncle Teddy told me you asked him to do something for you, and bring me along. I'm very excited about that, but would really like to know what it is. Uncle Teddy says it is on a Need to Know basis, but you can tell me if you like.

Thank you again.

Sincerely,

Samantha Carlisle

Lizina Kuzminski-Smith

Dear Liz,

Even though I see you almost every day, I am writing to you because I am writing to everyone else and it seemed right that I write to you too. I mainly just want you to know how much I love you and thank you for being my friend. I love Loren and all, but you are like my sister and I don't know what I would do without you. Thank you for giving me a job, and for helping me with, well, girl things, and for being around with Uncle Teddy. He is cool and all, but he doesn't always get me like you do.

He said we were going on another trip soon. Some top secret mission. Maybe you can go? I'll ask if you like.

I probably won't mail this. I'll just hand it to you and go sit on the porch with Olie while you read it. Thank you. Lots of hugs and kisses.

Love,

Sammy

John Hania Olie Smith

Dear Olie,

I want to thank you for the beautiful hair wrap, and for what you did with finding out about Freddy and helping save my life. I am sorry Zach was involved, but he told the truth and that was important. He helped save my life too. It is funny, I was kind of scared of you when I got here at Loon Song Harbor. Now I really like coming to the store with you on the porch. I look forward to seeing you and your Scá'a (crow).

I can't write to Scá'a, so please tell him that I'm very grateful for his help with leading Ahanu to me on the island. And, thank him for his contribution of feathers to the hair wrap you gave me. They're beautiful. I hope they grow back.

See you soon.

Your friend,

Sammy

If you enjoyed Sea Whisperer

please give us a review on Amazon.com

and Goodreads.com. Just search for Sea Whisperer.

For more information on

Empath Series, do to www.empathteen.com

While there, register for the Sammy newsletter,

and tell us your favorite scene from Sea Whisperer.

visit:

www.empathteen.com

Acknowledgements

L ike all authors, my book required many eyes to complete. Each paragraph and chapter required the constant and often laborious reading by my wife and primary contributor, Janet. Without her feedback and constant encouragement, Sammy would not exist in print. I also want to thank my primary editor, Vera Haddan, whose gentle advice and invaluable guidance eased me over rough spots and eliminated obstacles. To those who read my manuscripts and offered feedback, I am grateful and humbled by their positive response.

All images used in this book were licensed or used by permission of the owner.

Reference to Katniss (Hunger Games) copyright Susan Collins, publisher Scholastic Press. Reference to Nancy Drew (Girl Detective) by Carolyn Keene, copyright Simon & Schuster.

Author

When not traveling, Nickolai Vasilieff can be found bent over his computer in a cabin, on the bank of the Necanicum River, in Northwest Oregon, USA.

Nick is a Navy veteran, private pilot, and writer, who has traveled to over forty countries, including a one-year, around the world trip, living out of a backpack. The San Juan Express stories were partly inspired by those trips and summer vacations in the San Juan Islands with his two children. The stories he made up during those trips eventually evolved into the *Sammy and the San Juan Express* series.

"Young Adult novels are of particular interest to me, where the imagination of youth is combined with an insatiable appetite for knowledge and adventure, and where confidence is fragile yet boundless. Creating challenges through which characters grow in mind and spirit is a constant objective, along with spinning a good tale, of course."

A Conversation with the Author

Q — What was your inspiration for this story?

NV: *The idea of Sammy and the San Juan Express came out of several vacations I took with my two children on a small boat in the San Juan Islands. They were between six and twelve years old at that time, and during the evenings I'd make up stories to keep them occupied. Later, as an adult, my daughter, Nikole, encouraged me to write them down. The result is the San Juan Express series.*

Q — So you plan to write more novels?

NV: *Yes. The second book is almost complete with more in the works.*

Q — Did you base this story on you or your children's experience?

NV: *No. This story is completely fiction. If there are elements of reality or truth, they are in the emotions that the characters experience, and hopefully the reader experiences.*

Q — This story begins with heartbreak, the loss of Sammy's mother. Why begin with such a sad incident?

NV: *Sammy's story is really about her courage and finding her own inner strength. I originally planned on starting with her simply visiting Uncle Teddy, but as the story developed it became apparent that she had suffered a great tragedy. I can't imagine a greater tragedy for a young woman than the death of her mother.*

Q — So, is Sammy based on a real person?

NV: *No. This story is complete fiction. Sammy is a composite of the hundreds of children I've known. My granddaughter, my nieces, and the children I've met in my travels around the world.*

Q — The story moves very quickly, only about two weeks. Was your approach to writing this novel to outline a story arc and then fill in with details?

NV: *To a certain degree. I began with a very rough first draft, then revised extensively as I began my rewrites. The original draft turned out to be more about character development, than story line. The story began to write itself as I identified who and what the characters were. Sammy, of course, being the driving force behind the others.*

Q — It sounds like you're saying the story wrote itself?

NV: *Yes, to a certain degree. I don't know what other authors mean by that, but for me, all stories come from the author's imagination. When I say the story wrote itself, I mean that one scene will dictate the necessity of another scene, one action will dictate another action, and so on.*

Q — So the story flowed for you?

NV: *Laughter — No, I can't say it flowed. This novel took years to write, rewrite, edit, and finalize. What flowed was certain scenes during the writing. I especially enjoyed some of the scenes with dialogue. They often seemed to write themselves.*

Q — Can you give me an example of such a scene?

NV: *There are several but one is the confrontation with Freddy and Zach on the beach. Sammy's dialogue with Freddy was exciting to write. It flowed easily and as I recall, required little rewrite. Another is the scene when Sammy meets Olie on the porch. I especially enjoy Olie.*

Q — Sammy seems to swing from courageous to frightened throughout the story. Since she had special insight, why doesn't she know what is safe and what isn't?

NV: *Sammy's insight is what I've called empathic sensitivity. In a sense, it is a metaphor for the intuition we all have. That ability to feel when something isn't right, or safe. The problem is that most of us don't trust our intuition, so we keep searching. Sammy's empathic sensitivity is an extreme form of intuition. She feels what animals feel, and so she knows what is happening to them. In the beginning, she is aware of her special sensitivity, but doesn't trust it. As the story develops she is challenged to trust her feelings and eventually trust in herself. Her swings between courage and fear are the natural questions we all ask ourselves when faced with difficult decisions.*

Q — In the end, is Sammy's trust in herself really what her special sensitivity is all about?

NV: *In a way, yes. I've given Sammy a special power, her ability to feel animal's emotions. I don't think most of us have that capability. What I think most people have, especially young people, is greater knowingness than we are aware of or acknowledge. We want to think about everything, but sometimes we just know something, without thinking. That's Sammy's special power. The ability to not think and just know. To do that, she had to trust in herself.*

Q — Do you think that is possible for a fourteen-year-old.

NV: *Absolutely. Trust is what we're born with. It's what we lose as we get older. My hope is that Sammy will inspire all of us to regain that trust.*

Q — Did you retain that trust?

NV — Laughter: *I'm getting there. Maybe after a few more Sammy stories.*

Book Club Questions

1. How did you experience Sammy and the San Juan Express? Were you engaged immediately, or did it take you a while to get into it? How did you feel reading it— amused, sad, disturbed, confused, bored ...?

2. Does Sammy and the San Juan Express remind you of other novels? Is so, which ones?

3. What makes Sammy and the San Juan Express unique?

4. Although Sammy was aware of her "special sensitivity," she learns the true strength of this empathic gift through her compassion for animals and adversity. Does Sammy's experience compare to an experience or awakening in your life?

5. Uncle Teddy is kind, compassionate, wise, and dashing. Is he too good to be true, or do you see Uncle Teddy's character as a metaphor for something more universal? What does Uncle Teddy represent to you?

6. The death of Sammy's mother is devastating, yet somehow Sammy manages to live a lifetime of experience in just two weeks. Do you feel rebounding from a devastating loss is easier for children or teenagers? Why or why not? Do you feel Sammy responded appropriately in her situation? How might you react under similar circumstances?

7. Sammy's empathic sensitivity allows her to feel what animals (and humans, to a lesser degree) feel. Some have called this a light fantasy, others call it too fantastic to believe, and others call it real. How do you respond

to Sammy's empathic sensitivity, and have you ever experienced something similar?

8. In this story Sammy is surrounded by women who represent different aspects of her mother. Sammy begins to rebuild her family. Is Sammy doing this intentionally, or is this the Universe rising up to take care of her? Do you believe this happens in real life? Have you experienced anything like this?

9. Sammy's story is one of self discovery, coming of age, and survival. In the end, she steps across a threshold into a new life. Do you see this as inspirational, or does this kind of transformation seem overly optimistic and unrealistic? Is the ending satisfying? If so, why? If not, why not...and how would you change it?

10. Has reading Sammy and the San Juan Express changed you—broadened your perspective? Have you learned something new or been exposed to different ideas about people or a certain part of the world?

Resources

Learn more about Sammy's friends from these online wildlife resources.

US Fish and Wildlife Service. Forensics Laboratory. Ashland, Oregon. (Known as ACSI in Sammy and the San Juan Express)

http://www.fws.gov/lab/index.php

"The U.S. Fish & Wildlife Service Forensics Laboratory is the only lab in the world dedicated to crimes against wildlife.

Our crime laboratory is very much like a 'typical' police lab, except the victim is an animal.

We examine, identify, and compare evidence using a wide range of scientific procedures and instruments, in the attempt to link suspect, victim, and crime scene with physical evidence."

The Center for Whale Research. Friday Harbor, Washington

http://www.whaleresearch.com/#!orca-store/c1i6k

"For four decades, the Center for Whale Research (CWR) has conducted an annual photo-identification study of the Southern Resident Killer Whale population that frequents the inland waters of Washington State and lower British Columbia. Since their initiation, these studies have provided unprecedented baseline information on population dynamics and demography, social structure, and individual life histories."

The Marine Mammal Center—Steller Sea Lions

http://www.marinemammalcenter.org/

Steller Sea Lions

"Steller or northern sea lions are sometimes confused with California sea lions, but are much larger and lighter in color. Males may grow to 11 feet (3.25 m) in length and weigh almost 2,500 pounds (1120 kg). Females are much smaller and may grow to nine feet (2.9 m) in length and weigh 1,000 pounds (350 kg). Steller sea lions are light tan to reddish brown in color. They have a blunt face and a boxy, bear-like head. Adult males do not have a visible sagittal crest (the bump on the top of their heads) as is seen in adult male California sea lions. Adult male Stellers have a bulky build and a very thick neck with longer fur that resembles a lion's mane, hence the name "sea lion.""

Pacific Harbor Seal

"Pacific harbor seals have spotted coats in a variety of shades from white or silver-gray to black or dark brown. They reach five to six feet (1.7-1.9 m) in length and weigh up to 300 pounds (140 kg). Males are slightly larger than females. They are true or crawling seals, having no external ear flaps. True seals have small flippers and must move on land by flopping along on their bellies. In San Francisco Bay, many harbor seals are fully or partially reddish in color. This may be caused by an accumulation of trace elements such as iron or selenium in the ocean or a change in the hair follicle."

The Seadoc Society—People and Science Healing the Sea

http://www.seadocsociety.org/

"The SeaDoc Society works to protect the health of marine wildlife and their ecosystems through science and education."

American Cetacean Society—Education, conservation, and research from the world's first cetacean protection organization.

http://acsonline.org/fact-sheets/gray-whale/

Definition of Cetacean: A mammal (such as a whale, dolphin, or porpoise) that lives in the ocean.

Gray Whale

"The only member of the family Eschrichtiidae, the gray whale is a mysticete, or baleen whale. It is a "coastal" whale that migrates along the North American Pacific Coast between arctic seas and the lagoons of Baja California, Mexico. Frequently visible from shore, gray whales provide a unique opportunity for land and boat observation, and commercial whale watching has become a major industry along its migration route. Visitors to the calving and breeding lagoons sometimes encounter the phenomenon of the "friendlies"; gray whales that closely approach small boats and allow themselves to be touched by humans."

OSU Marine Mammal Institute

http://mmi.oregonstate.edu/whale-telemetry-group

"Whale Telemetry Group (WTG)

"The Marine Mammal Institute's Whale Tel
(WTG) has pioneered the development of sat
monitored radio tags to study the movements, critical habitats, and dive characteristics of free-ranging whales and dolphins around the world. Since the first deployment of a satellite tag on a humpback whale off Newfoundland, Canada, in 1986, the WTG has tagged a total of 462 whales from 11 different species. This work has led to the discovery of previously unknown migration routes and seasonal distribution (wintering and summering areas), as well as descriptions of diving behavior."

North Pacific Universities Marine Mammal Research Consortium

http://www.marinemammal.org/research/killer-whale-research/

Top predators (animals at the top of the food chain) play an important role in structuring terrestrial and marine ecosystems. Killer whales (*Orcinus orca*) are a top predator in the North Pacific ecosystem. However, their ecological role, particularly with respect to their impact on marine mammal populations, is not fully understood.

CPSIA information can be obtained
at www.ICGtesting.com
Printed in the USA
LVHW011019020520
654893LV00001B/190